"Did You Drop from Heaven?"

He asked in delirium. "You look like the angel in my Sunday School book."

He closed his eyes and lovely Jess Ramsay's heart almost stopped. It wasn't every day a handsome Major parachuted onto the lawns of Karrisbrooke, Aunt Ellen's great plantation.

Major Vance Trent recovered completely, but Jess never did. For almost immediately he left her for another girl.

Staunchly, Jess went on, pursued by a married man, parrying the attentions of a handsome fortune hunter—all to gain knowledge of a plot against the war effort.

Little did she know that Vance Trent was working toward the same end; they would meet again one velvet midnight to embrace in the heart of danger . . .

Bantam Books by Emilie Loring
Ask your bookseller for the books you have missed

EMILIE LORING
RAINBOW AT DUSK

*This low-priced Bantam Book
has been completely reset in a type face
designed for easy reading, and was printed
from new plates. It contains the complete
text of the original hard-cover edition.*
NOT ONE WORD HAS BEEN OMITTED.

RAINBOW AT DUSK

*A Bantam Book | published by arrangement with
Little, Brown and Company, Inc.*

PRINTING HISTORY

Little, Brown edition published September 1942
2nd printing .. November 1942   3rd printing .... June 1943
Grosset & Dunlap edition published October 1942
2nd printing .... July 1946
Bantam edition | September 1966
2nd printing .. December 1966   5th printing .... April 1968
3rd printing .... May 1967   6th printing .. November 1968
4th printing .. September 1967   7th printing .... May 1969
8th printing .... November 1969
New Bantam edition | March 1971
2nd printing .. November 1971   3rd printing .... April 1979

ISBN 0-553-12948-1

Published simultaneously in the United States and Canada

PRINTED IN THE UNITED STATES OF AMERICA

The names of all characters in this novel, all episodes are fictitious. Use of a name which is the same as that of any living person is coincidental.

RAINBOW AT DUSK

"You're tellin' me. You've forgotten that Claire and I are invited. I don't see why we are always counted in on Korolenko's bashes. It's evident that both my wife and I are puteen-in-the-backdoor to pits killen."

...wn between the gardens, came the fragrance of ...e annuals and perennials in full bloom. From the ...ie-covered red brick house above them darted the ...ent chime of a clock's bell telling the hour.

1

From the parterres on the three terraces, parted in the center by a grass path, broken by steps, which ran down between the gardens, came the fragrance of late annuals and perennials in full bloom. From the vine-covered red brick house above them drifted the faint chime of a clock's bell telling the hour.

The girl seated on a bench near the riverbank counted. Five. At the exact instant of the last stroke she heard the diminishing drone of a plane, saw the whitish spot against the sky now turning a soft, dusky violet above the pink afterglow. A parachute. Completely filled. Must have come from the Camp, twenty miles away, where soldiers from all parts of the country had assembled for war games. It was nearer now and whiter, hovering above the river. If it came down in the swift treacherous current it might mean death for the dark, dangling puppet beneath it, in his heavy harness.

She sprang up. The Airedale terrier who had been dozing at her feet came to life with a sharp bark and stood looking up at her, his soul in his eyes, his short tail waving in uncertainty. She held her breath as she watched; waved her hands as if by the action she could conjure the drifting thing toward her. It was halfway across the water. It was dropping. The boat! She might be in time to help him. She raced toward the old plantation wharf, her eyes on the sky, the dog at her heels. If only she could reach the man before he was dragged under.

"We must. Lucky, we *must!*" The terrier, as if understanding her appeal, barked again and increased his pace. A little gust of wind lifted the chute and sent it whirling toward her. The paratrooper was pulling at the shrouds. Thank heaven it was coming in. It was over the lawn now. She stopped to watch it.

Suddenly the white cloud shot up, then, as if exasperated by its own vacillation, dropped with incredible speed, dragged the man clinging to it, collapsed and spread over him.

She held the tugging dog tight by his collar while she watched the chute undulate like a white silk wave on a white silk ocean. Suppose instead of being safe and secure at Karrisbrooke, Aunt Ellen's North Carolina home, in this month of September 1941, she were in England? She wouldn't be standing stiff as a robot wondering whether friend or foe would crawl from under, she would be making tracks for the house and a gun.

At last! The bulging and commotion had produced a head in a green helmet. The afterglow turned blue denim overalls to purple. Flat on his back the man loosened the chest and crotch belts of his harness. He was inching backward out of it. He moved slowly. Had he been hurt when he landed? He was standing. Straight. Lean. Taller than Phil Maury, taller than Barry Collins, and they were tall enough. He was down in a crumpled heap.

She ran the distance between them and dropped to her knees beside him. Lucky growled deep in his throat as he pressed close against her. The man sat up and pulled off his helmet. His hair was dark, his eyes seemed enormous in his lean, blood-withdrawn face. He looked up from the ankle he was clutching with a white-knuckled hand. Three deep furrows across his forehead smoothed out when he smiled. His glance was direct and keen.

"Hello!" he greeted. "Did you two drop from a plane? No, I'll bet it was heaven. The angel in my first Sunday School book had red-gold hair, not feather-cut though, and a white dress like yours. Not quite like yours. Hers had flowing sleeves and yours hasn't any that count, and she wasn't wearing pearls or a whopping green jade ring. You are here, aren't you? I'm not just seeing you?"

Even though it was evident that his foot was hurting unbearably his voice had a clear distinctness, with a decisive undertone, unlike the soft slurring Southern utterance she had been hearing for months.

"We're real. We arrived neither by plane nor from heaven. Lucky, my dog, and I live here at Karrisbrooke—for the present. What happened to your foot?"

"Felt infernally like a break when I stood up a minute ago and I'll swear I heard a bone snap when I landed. Better though than if I had come down in that." He indicated the river turned to a fluid sea of glinting amethysts and rubies by the afterglow. "It would have been a tough fight to make the shore in this harness. Boy, from above, it looked wide and swift."

"It is. I saw the chute dallying over the water as if considering a plunge and with all my power willed it this way."

"And it came. That clinches the angel theory." His smile ended in a wry twist of a mouth which, she had decided the first instant she saw it, had been in the habit of giving orders which the owner of said mouth would make sure were carried out. He drew a chute knife from his pocket.

"I'd better get this shoe off pronto. My ankle is swelling and sending red-hot daggers jabbing at my leg."

"Let me do it. Lie down, Lucky."

The dog dropped to the lawn and tucked his nose between his hairy forepaws while he kept his bright eyes on the man. The girl carefully slit the seam of the leg of his overall and turned it back before she cautiously cut the lacing of the heavy army field-shoe.

"Hold tight, I'll ease it off. There! We won't have to do that again. *That's* behind us."

His brows stood out like little black wings above eyes brilliant with pain, his small mustache like a heavy black line against the whiteness of his face glistening with faint sweat. His smile was slightly twisted.

"You're not by any chance doubling as dentist's

assistant and angel, are you? I've heard a line like that before."

"No. I had two years' Red Cross training and served as Nurses' Aide in a hospital before I came South." She gently slit his sock, drew it off and ran her fingers over his ankle.

"This should be taken care of. I'm afraid it's a fracture."

"I'm darn sure it is. Every time I move I feel the bone grate. It acted up like this once before in a football game. Something wrong with the picture when a training officer in a parachute battalion makes an angle landing and breaks an ankle. If you'll phone the Camp I'll stay put until the ambulance comes. I'm Vance Trent, Van to my friends in case you care, Major in the Parachute Battalion. They'll send for me—"

"In time, but you shouldn't lie here waiting with night coming on, soldier. It's a clean break now, we won't risk complications. It might be hours before they arrive. I'll run to the house for splints and bandages. I'm in the Motor Corps, and the ambulance Aunt Ellen gave us is in the garage. Sam, the butler, and Pink, his wife, Aunt Ellen's maid, will bring the stretcher and carry you to the house. Sam's one of the family. His father was born a slave boy in the same year Aunt Ellen made her entrance into the world. They'll move you carefully. Have you a flask?"

"In my kit—Angel."

"The name is Jessamine, Jess to my friends, in case you care. At the time I was born the little yellow flowers of star jessamine were rioting over the piazza trellis here at Karrisbrooke, Mother's family home. She's a romantic and Southern. Do you get the connection? Drink this."

He took the flask-cup she had filled to the brim and drained it.

"Good L—Lord that brandy's po—tent." He choked. "I don't drink and it got me by the throat. I gulped it to steady the world which started to go around when I moved my foot. All right now."

"Lie down." She drew a fold of the chute over him.

"Here are your cigarettes and lighter. Promise not to move till I get back?"

"At least I can promise not to run away."

"Lucky, stay and keep him company. I won't be a minute."

"Walk not run—" She was off before he could finish the sentence. The dog followed the racing figure with his eyes, drew a long sigh and laid his nose on the man's left arm.

He lay flat looking up at a faint, solitary star. She had said Karrisbrooke, his head had been clear enough then, if now it felt like a thick wad of absorbent cotton full of red-hot splinters of disconnected thoughts. Must be the effect of shock, pain and brandy. *Karrisbrooke.* Where had he heard the name before? The General. This morning. Only this morning? Seemed as if it had been years ago. He had said:—

"Major Trent, there is an extensive and flourishing tobacco plantation twenty miles from here, Karrisbrooke. The owner also operates cotton mills which are filling defense orders. The two plants have become objects of interest to the higher-ups. You have been detailed to drop in and—get acquainted. The fact that you were an efficiency engineer before you joined the Aviation will account for your interest in seeing the mill wheels go round without rousing suspicion that you are there to detect any irregularities of which the owner is unaware."

In answer he had laughed and suggested:—

"Why not give that 'drop-in' a dramatic touch, sir? I'll bail out over the place if you say the word."

"Perfect, Major, perfect, and if . . ." The next words of the sentence skittered off like a drove of frightened sheep. Curious that he didn't remember. He remembered the plane, remembered that he and the pilot had figured out air currents—the pilot had miscalculated distance and it had looked like the river for a few minutes. Then he had seen the girl. He hadn't told her that she had appeared supernatural as she stood with the light behind her making her hair gleam like a halo. The effect had been so startling that it had taken his mind from landing, he had forgotten to favor his right foot as was his habit.

"Here I am! Don't try to sit up." She dropped to her knees beside him, laid splints and a bag on the grass, before she carefully removed the chute which had covered him. She gently ran her fingers over his ankle. "I'm sorry," she said in answer to his involuntary flinch.

"You needn't be. Your touch is like velvet. I knew it would be when I saw your rosy nails. Crimson nails make a hand look cruel and a woman's hand should be tender—like yours. Boy, I'm prattling. Don't mind me. Go to it."

He laid his right arm across his eyes. The dog, as if understanding, laid his cold nose on the clenched left hand.

"Ready. Talk. Talk like a house afire. Tell me about yourself, this place."

"It won't be an exciting story. I was a simple college graduate until I enlisted for defense work. I was pulled out of that three months ago and ordered—that's a figure of speech—here. Mother felt that one of us should be with her Aunt Ellen Marshall, who is eighty-two. She couldn't leave my stepfather, who is ill.

"It's a joke that Aunt Ellen needs my companionship; she doesn't *need* anyone. She would take over the arrangement of my mental and emotional schedule if I didn't fight for the right to life, liberty and the pursuit of happiness. That phrase isn't original in case you're interested.

"Hold tight. It won't last but a minute. Okay!" The word was more a sob than an exclamation. She stole a look at his grim mouth. He was biting his lips. He hadn't fainted.

"Where was I in the story of my life? Oh yes, I love every inch of this place, even if Aunt Ellen's dictatorship sometimes gets on my nerves. It's a genuine antique: outbuildings, stables, smokehouse, wellhouse, offices and slave quarters; there's a two-story ballroom and, believe it or not, a smugglers' passage to the river. There!" She drew a long, unsteady breath. "The worst is behind us."

"Don't stop *talking*. Go on."

"You should see the aforementioned Aunt Ellen at a tobacco auction, watching like a lynx, listening to the bids, sometimes withdrawing her tobacco if she doesn't like the prices, putting her wonder-boy superintendent, Barry Collins, in his place if she doesn't like his advice. He's terribly goodlooking. Romantic type. Greek-god profile. Red hair, with a where-have-you-been-all-my-life light in his gray-green eyes. He's drenched with the old charm, a 'Barry' would be. Kisses a woman's hand when he meets her. I was embarrassed to tears the first time it happened to me. . . . I know that hurt—I'm being as careful as possible." His flinch had sent a sympathetic vibration along her nerves.

"Aunt Ellen raises the bright tobacco, if you understand what that means. She's part owner and whole-time boss of mills that are pouring out cotton drill for defense. She's the matriarch of the tribe of Marshall. Mother and I lived with her from the time my father died when I was two until I was fifteen. I remember the night she was dressed in white satin to attend the Governor's dinner. She wore a diamond tiara. I thought of her then and forever after as Her Majesty, the Queen."

She worked with hands which were skillful and sure. From time to time she glanced at the grim, blue line of his lips and his clean-cut chin which was all she could see of his face.

"It's done. I wish you could have seen Lucky's eyes as they watched every move of my fingers." She filled the flask-cup again, and slipped her hand under his head to raise it.

"You're a hero, soldier. You didn't pass out even under my boring case history. Drink this."

He sat up, pushed away her supporting arm, took the cup from her hand and drained it eagerly.

"That—helps—steady—the—world." He choked between the words. "Okay now. Sit down, quick, Angel.

You're wobbly, I shouldn't have let you do it. Come here."

She shook her head and moved away from his outflung arm.

"I wanted to and I'm not wobbly. I'm out of practice, that's all. If for a minute, when I finished, the ground seemed to be on the heave, I'm all right now. *Lie down, please.* You must keep quiet till they bring the stretcher."

He lay flat again, it was easier to think things through that way. Funny how the face of the General kept bobbing up. He had said something in closing which at the time had seemed mighty queer. He had said—curious how thoughts trailed off to nothing.

"Here he is, Sam." The girl's eager voice penetrated the haze. He could hear even if his eyelids appeared to have leaden weights attached. "Lucky, *don't* lick his face. He doesn't move. Sam! *Sam!* He—he isn't dead, is he?"

A deep Negroid voice said very near:—

"Lordy, no, M's Jess. How much brandy d'yo' say yo' give him?"

"That flask-cup *full*, twice, he looked so ghastly."

"Dis one? Lordy, lordy, 'tain't no wonder he don' move, Ah reckon he done passed out, sho' nuff." A prolonged sniff and a rich chuckle. "Dat's pow'ful stuff, dat is. Pink, yo' lift his laigs when Ah hist his shoulders onto de stretcher. Lucky M's Ellen giv' de Red Cross dat am'lance, M's Jess."

The voices cut through the stupor induced by brandy and pain. He opened heavy eyes and looked up into two dusky faces, one topped by a white turban. He felt arms under him, then a shoot of agony up his leg mercifully sent him drifting off. After a century or two a woman's voice, vital, firm, penetrated the void.

"Who told you to put him in Master Todd's room, Sam?"

"'Twas M's Jess, M's Ellen, she said how it'd be quicker to get him here 'cause 'twas on de groun' floor. She saw him drop from de sky an' w'en she foun' his laig was bust, she came runnin' fer Pink an' me."

"Where is she now?"

"She a-telephonin' to de Camp. The soldier, he daidn't want to be brung to dis house, sho' nuff. On de way, he kep' mutterin', 'I shouldn't a let yo' do it, Angel'—Ah reckon he thought hisself dead and gone to heaven—an' then he'd go mutterin' some more. But, M's Jess—she lak' yo', M's Ellen, folks jes' got to do as she say—she wouldn't leave him layin' there. She said, 'Yo' never cain tell what'll happen when a bone's bust. Fever may set in.'"

Though he kept his eyes securely closed Trent knew when someone came to his side and looked down at him.

"About thirty, isn't he, Sam? Just the age of the young master when he—he—took that last jump." A door opened. "Jessamine, did you phone the Camp?"

"Yes, Aunt Ellen. They are sending a surgeon and ambulance at once."

There was a lilt in the voice which made you feel, even if you were woozy, that the world was a darn fine place where something swell might pop up at any minute.

"We'll need the surgeon, but no ambulance. I'm keeping your soldier here."

It was at that instant that memory cleared and bright red letters jiggled into place as he had seen them on a screen, jiggled into words and broadcast the General's laugh, the General's voice saying:—

"And if you could manage to break a leg in landing it would be all to the good, Major."

II

From the wheel-chaise on the piazza at Karrisbrooke, Vance Trent looked across the myrtle-edged brick walks of the garden. The October woods were a patch of brilliant color against a purple hill beyond

the river, which was as deeply blue as the cloudless
sky above it. The afternoon air was fragrant with the
scent of heliotrope, petunias and lavender, pungent
with the odor of box hedges. The tennis court was
hidden by a row of tall poplars that swayed in the
soft autumn breeze. It was out of sight but not out of
sound, for every few minutes a voice with a lilt drifted toward him calling the score.

"Forty-thirty. Game *and* set." Jess triumphant. "No
more, Phil. Come to the garden-piazza. Time for tea
or what you take in place of the cup that cheers."

"An' how are you today, Major?" The deep voice
switched Trent's attention from tennis court to the
long window which opened on the vine-shaded piazza.

The man who had spoken approached and shook
hands before he dropped into a capacious white
wicker chair with a rosy chintz cushion. "He's terribly
good-looking ... Greek-god profile," Jessamine
Ramsay had said in describing Barry Collins. It was
easy to understand what she meant by, "He's drenched
with the old charm." He had manner, plus. His
immaculate cotton riding clothes fitted as if his tall,
lean figure had been poured into them. His head
would be noticeable anywhere: broad in the smooth
mahogany red-haired crown, tapering to a sharply
pointed chin, strongly marked by a clean-cut mouth
and nose in a once fair skin, now weather-cured to
ruddiness, and lighted by deeply set, brilliant gray-
green eyes under curiously black interrogative brows.
Must be in the early thirties.

"Thanks, I'm in great shape, Mr. Collins. This is the
first time I've been allowed out of my room and the
outlook here seems like heaven. When you're in ace
physical condition you can take a broken bone, a
small one at that, in your stride. I'll be on crutches
tomorrow. High time. It's three weeks since I dropped
from the sky."

"Then you'll be getting back to Camp soon, Major?"

It wasn't what Collins said but the way he said it
that set Trent's imagination tingling. Was the superin-

tendent anxious to get him off the place? Sounded like it. Why?

"I hope so. I'll be glad to trade this green brocade lounge robe for my uniform. The Camp surgeon is coming this evening to check up. I'll have to obey orders, but I hope he says, 'Go.' I don't see how the ankle can act up in this cast. I've intruded on Karrisbrooke hospitality long enough. I've begged and demanded to be taken to the Camp hospital, but Doctor MacDonald just rubbed his chin and shook his head and here I am still quartered on Miss Ellen—I'm beginning to think for the duration."

"And is this such a bad place in which to be quartered, Vance Trent?" Ellen Marshall demanded as she crossed the piazza toward him.

Collins sprang to his feet and drew forward a chair with impressive deference. Trent instinctively tried to rise, then sank back in the wheel-chaise as his hostess laid a restraining hand on his shoulder. As he smiled response to her peppery greeting, he felt the same disbelief he had felt each time he had seen her. It was incredible that she was eighty-two years old. Her abundant hair, short, smartly cut and waved, was as silvery gray as her modish frock and slim shoes. The skin of her still beautiful face was creamy except for a delicate pink at the cheekbones. There were lines at the corners of her keen blue eyes, plenty of them, and a rather grim set to her mouth—must be the fighting cut of her jaw which kept the chin from sagging. She was straight, tall and thin with no suggestion of scragginess.

"Young man, when you're through staring at me perhaps you'll explain what you meant by that word, 'intruded.' Have you been made to feel like an intruder? Collins, are you responsible for this?"

"I am not, Miss Ellen." The superintendent's indignant denial deepened his already ruddy color, "I feel we are honored by having an officer of the United States here. I am out one hundred per cent to help in every way possible those foreign countries which are fighting for existence. Because I was forced at an early age to get out and take it, to size up competitors, to fight to the finish for what I wanted without yelling for help, doesn't mean that I would be inhospitable to a man whose life had been softer."

It sounded like an appeal to his employer for sympathy because of an underprivileged youth. Had he worked that line to obtain his present position?

"There, there, Collins, martyrs are obsolete." The bite in Ellen Marshall's voice lighted little sparks in her superintendent's eyes. "I agree with all you say about helping other countries, but first a steady, unwavering tide of determination to restore law and order at home and *freedom* for each citizen to work where, when and how he pleases, is what this country needs most. Millions of man-days lost and nothing being done about it!

"You'll have to hand it to North Carolina, Vance; not a strike has occurred affecting essential defense materials in this state. This has been a record year of industrial production. I've crowed enough about that. It's only fair to show another side of the picture. During a short period federal agents raided moonshine stills and captured one hundred and fifty gallons of spirits and 8545 gallons of mash. I have the figures right, haven't I, Collins?"

"As your figures are always correct, I'll accept them. I'm not posted on moonshiners' activities, Miss Ellen." There was a trace of resentment in the superintendent's voice.

"I presume not. Sorry you've been made to feel like an intruder, Major. That's a reflection on our Carolina hospitality."

"Please understand, Miss Ellen, I have not been made to feel like an intruder by anyone—" Trent swallowed "except by Philip Maury" in the nick of time. "I've been made so royally welcome it will be a wrench to leave. Do sit down or I'll have to get on my feet, ankle or no ankle."

She seated herself in the deep chair Barry Collins again pushed forward, ignored the cushion he solicitously placed at her back and sat straight and stiff. She drew ivory needles and a mass of khaki wool from the purple satin bag on her arm and began to knit on a partially completed sweater; the diamonds in the rings on her fingers sent out iridescent sparks with every movement of her patrician hands.

"Know why I was staring, Miss Ellen? What I was thinking 'I don't believe it' about? I'll give you two guesses."

"Humpl You can't switch me from cross-examination with that devastating grin, Vance. I know what you don't believe, that I'm eighty-two. Between you and me I don't believe it myself. I'm as full of zest and ambition as I was at forty. Must be a mistake in the birth record. Jessamine, my dear, you shouldn't play tennis with the thermometer at ninety, though that is normal temperature for North Carolina at this time of year. You're not used to the heat. How's your wife today, Philip?"

It was evident from his frown, quickly suppressed, that the question annoyed the tall brown-haired man who had followed the girl in the short white tennis frock to the porch. She was in turn followed by the terrier with a ball in his mouth, who after an instant of indecision carefully deposited it at the feet of Ellen Marshall, who shook her head at him.

"Claire's feelin' fine today, M's Ellen." Maury's soft drawl made the clipped *g's* more noticeable. His heavy-lidded, brown eyes were in character with his voice as were the indolent motions of his body. "Said she might run over for tea this afternoon. She's just pinin' to see your interestin' invalid, marm. Keep that wet ball off my white slacks, you cur!" He kicked at the terrier, who backed away to the accompaniment of a menacing growl. "How you gettin' on, Major?"

"Fine, thanks. Who won—Miss Ramsay?" Trent caught back "Angel" just in time.

"I—and was I good!" She dropped to a low chair beside the wheel-chaise and retied the silvery blue ribbon which held back her red-gold hair. "Lucky, stop whining and teasing Aunt Ellen to throw that ball. Lie down." The terrier dropped with a discouraged grunt and tucked his nose between his paws.

"Good at everything aren't you, Miss Jess?" Barry Collins leaned forward, his gray-green eyes were warm with admiration, a hint of passion pricked through the lightness of his voice. "You've got the class in nutrition you started in the old school house for the colored women going fine and I've just heard that 'twas you who did an A 1 First Aid job on the Major's ankle."

"She did." Trent spoke before the girl could answer; he resented the proprietary note in the superintendent's voice. Was the man in love with her? "The Camp surgeon reports that she did a professional piece of work. I have a sneaking suspicion he'll try to snitch her for his staff of nurses. Think you'd like it, Miss Jess?"

"I'd love it, but I suspect that I will be of more use in Civilian Defense, tending the fires of patriotism on the Home Front—improving domestic conditions—serving in the Motor Corps or as telephone operator, and teaching First Aid, if war really comes. I like the warmth which glows through me when I know I've helped a person over a hard spot." She laughed. "Perhaps it isn't a glow, perhaps it's just a 'What-a-big-girl-am-I complex.'"

"You won't have to leave Karrisbrooke and go to nursing to accomplish that, Jessamine; I need you here."

"But, Aunt Ellen, I'm not doing anything but driving in the Women's Defense Corps and trying to teach a bunch of women the value of food, to make them realize that there is something to eat beside meat, meal and molasses. There is so much else to be done in the world! Sorry, I didn't mean to mount the soapbox. I could care for something long and iced and tinkling. My throat is bone-dry after that burst of oratory."

"I'll get it, Jess."

"Sam will be here with the teacart in a moment, Philip." Ellen Marshall's voice was as restraining as a clutch on the sleeve of Maury's black and white blazer. "Sit down. Relax. You're red as a beet." Which remark served only to deepen the color of the man's face and set his lips in a resentful line.

It was evident that Miss Ellen was posted at her

guns. Wonder why she has it in for Maury? Trent asked himself, then as he caught the expression of the man's eyes as they rested on the girl, he knew. The guy was in love with her and he had a wife. For the first time since he had looked up at it weeks ago, he saw the face of his hostess shadowed by anxiety. So that was the way it was. A married man was making love to her niece, she knew it and was worried. How about the niece herself? Apparently it wasn't troubling her.

"Oh, here you all are!"

A slender woman followed her voice to the piazza. The mist of pale green veil floating from her white hat made a perfect setting for her honey-color hair, small-boned, unhappy face and blue eyes, shadowed, but not by mascara. Her thin green frock gave an impression of refreshing coolness. Behind her, Sam, his face black as ebony, except for the whites of his eyes and gleaming teeth, pushed a cart laden with decanters and tall glasses which tinkled like icy twigs in a breeze.

"Barry, there must be a strong attraction here to lure you from your office at this time of day," she commented with a hint of jealousy in her voice. "Phil, you here *again*. Gettin' to be a second home for him, isn't it, M's Ellen? I've been just dyin' to see your soldier. There's a rumor that he's the best-lookin' man who's appeared in this part of No'th Car'lina in years—if he is a damyankee. My stars, I didn't know he was out here. Fancy my sayin' all that."

"I can fancy it, Claire." Ellen Marshall's voice was grim. "Major Trent, this is our nearest neighbor, if five miles can be called near: Mrs. Philip Maury of River Farm. Smile your prettiest for the lady in appreciation of that laurel wreath she so *naively* placed on your head."

Trent laughed and patted the arm of the chair Jess had abondoned when the woman had made her entrance from the long window. It was quite evident from Miss Ellen's voice that she liked the wife no better than the husband.

"Prove that you forgive me for not rising, Mrs. Maury, by sitting here."

"You poor boy, of course I will." She settled into the chair beside him in a faint aura of perfume. "I adore fussin' over a man. What can I do for you? I'm not a very useful person, I'm not strong enough."

He noted her swift glance at her husband who was perched on the brick wall of the piazza talking to Jess, who stood with her head tipped back against a vine-covered pillar, her left hand under the right elbow, right hand spread on the left forearm. The large turquoise matrix ring on the third finger accentuated the lovely shape of the sun-browned hand. She was watching a cloud floating against the sapphire sky, Collins in turn was watching her.

"I'm not efficient like the No'thern girls Phil's quite crazy about," Mrs. Maury complained. "Sam, wheel the cart over here while I mix the Major a drink."

"He doesn't drink, Claire." Jess left the wall. "You've brought iced coffee for Major Trent, haven't you, Sam?"

"Sho' nuff, M's Jess, sho' nuff. Hasn't I brought it every afternoon since yo' said he liked it? Here 'tis."

Claire Maury picked up the tall tinkling glass he indicated as Jess reached for it.

"Here you are, Major. Phil, bring over that stand and place it where this poor boy can reach it."

"If you say 'Poor boy' in that tone again, Claire, I shall burst into tears," Ellen Marshall observed dryly. "Jessamine, where are you going?" The girl, who was crossing the piazza, turned.

"As I seem to be somewhat of a fifth wheel, I'm going up to change."

"I don't think you're very polite, Jess, to go off when I'm callin'." Claire Maury's lips pouted like those of a child about to cry. "I don't leave the room when you come to my house an' snitch Phil off to play tennis or golf or contract, just as if you were *still* engaged to him. Course I know he thinks I'm not a very satisfactory wife, I'm not efficient, I'm delicate, I haven't given him children—"

"That will do, Claire." Ellen Marshall spoke in a

tone that it would take a daring person to defy. "In the first place a woman who runs herself down is a fool; if she does it in the presence of her husband she's a colossal fool; in the second, your marriage is a private affair, in the adjustments of which I, for one, am not interested. Jessamine, come here. You can change later."

Trent thought for an instant that the girl would persist in leaving the piazza; color had swept from throat to the edge of her hair at her aunt's dictatorial order—or had it been the reference to her engagement to Maury that had flushed her face with anger? He had had no hint of that before. Through his memory echoed her voice saying: "She would take over the arrangement of my mental and emotional schedule ..." Apparently she didn't intend to fight at the moment. Instead, she laughed.

"Her Majesty has spoken. Phil, stop glowering and pass me those luscious sandwiches." From a low seat beside her aunt she smiled at him as he held out a silver tray.

"M's Ellen—" Trent suspected from the purr in Claire Maury's voice that she was about to unsheath claws and scratch. "Folks at the Hunt Club are just dyin' to know why about four weeks ago you called on the Commandin' General at Camp. Now if you'd been younger—" A suggestive shrug completed the sentence.

Trent caught Collins' sharp look at his employer, noted the slight deepening of color at her cheekbones, the quick clenching of her jeweled fingers on the ivory needles, before she answered:—

"My compliments to the folks at the Hunt Club, Claire. You may be my little messenger and tell them that when I discovered that General Carson was the grandson of an old friend, I called to extend the hospitality of Karrisbrooke and offer the use of our fields to the army. I had heard that the greatest war maneuver this country has ever seen was to be staged partly in this neighborhood. I want to help, if possible."

The General's curious remark when he had approved the parachute jump over Karrisbrooke echoed through Trent's memory—"And if you could manage to break a leg in landing it would be all to the good, Major." Was Ellen Marshall's call at Headquarters in any way connected with that suggestion?

"I could die eating Virginia ham." Jessamine's voice broke the silence which had followed her aunt's admission of the call. "Callie, the cook, is teaching me to shave it in these transparent pink slices. When I return to the No'th I intend to open a tea-shoppe." Her perfect imitation of "No'th" had sent color stealing over Claire's face.

"You'll need a financial manager, Jessie. How about takin' me on?" Philip Maury suggested. There was something about the man's caressing drawl that fired Trent with an almost irresistible urge to rise from the wheel-chaise, ankle or no ankle, and paste him one. He unclenched his hands, drew a cigarette from his case and watched the girl above the flame of the lighter. When she had bent over him the first time he had thought her eyes were black. Since then he had seen them blue-green, the color of the sea with the sun on it; sometimes darkly blue with thought, like the sea when a cloud passes between it and the sun; sometimes purple, and often brilliant with laughter as now, when with head tipped slightly she regarded Maury appraisingly.

"Nope, you're not up my street, Phil—my business street—I mean. You'd be a menace to the staff. My assistants would be tearing each other's hair about you. You can't help making love to a woman any more than you can help dropping your g's. We Northern girls are used to cool, calm, unstampedable men like—like Major Trent, for instance; they would have to learn by the trial-and-error process that your fiery protestations of love meant nothing."

"Phil, you naughty boy, have you been deceiving *poor* little Jessamine *again*, that she's so bitter?"

Trent could see that the angry red stain which crept up the girl's cheeks at Claire Maury's malicious thrust had brought stinging tears. She sprang to her feet and laughed.

"The answer is 'No.' Took it right out of your mouth, didn't I, Phil? This time I'm going. I'm due at the Laceys' for dinner before the dance at the Club for the soldier-boys." She paused at the long window.

"I'll save the supper dance for you as I used to, Phil," she flung over her shoulder before her white figure faded into the dusk of the drawing room.

III

In the large, softly lighted, high-ceilinged room Captain MacDonald, Camp surgeon, with a tired sigh, drew his short, squatty figure to its top height of five feet two and shrugged back his thick shoulders.

"Sorry to disappoint you, Major Trent, but the answer is 'No,' again. You're doing fine where you are. We need the space you would take up in the Camp hospital, these war games pile up casualties, not serious, and just at present there's an epidemic of emergency appendectomies. I've been seeing quite a bit of the old-timers in this part of North Carolina and I'm amazed to find that in spite of the influx of rich Northerners, life is as slow and dignified as it was claimed to be eighty years and more ago. That sort of atmosphere for a while won't do you any harm. Your nerves are taut to the snapping point. Being a parachute instructor is no cinch. Don't see why the devil you're grousing about staying in a slick place like this."

He looked around the room. Sheer white curtains at the long windows which opened on a gallery stirred in a fragrant breeze. His eyes came back and lingered on the man in the armchair, whose foot and leg rested on an old-fashioned footstool.

"This is a set the motion-picture people would give their eyes to duplicate. I did considerable antiquing while in private practice and if I know my onions—

and I do—that desk behind you is a museum piece. I wish the Lord would quarter me in a swell living room, bedroom and bath suite on the ground floor for just one week with a heap of mail to read like that I brought over for you. Methinks it hath a feminine look." He nodded at the pile of unopened letters on a small table beside Trent and sank into a chair. He ran stubby, capable fingers through his rampant, graying red hair.

"My God, I'm so tired it seems sometimes as if I couldn't keep going another minute and when I look at you at ease in that swell brocade lounge robe . . ." A sigh finished the sentence.

"I'm sorry you have this twenty-mile trip added to your other calls, Doctor Mack. It isn't a bad break. I ought to have favored my foot but my attention was diverted as I came down and I made an angle landing. Result: Here I am."

"It wasn't a bad break, but it might have been if the girl hadn't been there to render First Aid. If you had come down in the woods and had tried to hobble on that foot you'd have had a compound fracture and perhaps been a cripple for life. Remember that, when you're straining at the leash to get away."

"You don't understand. I've been waited on and taken care of for three weeks now. It is too much to accept."

"Let your Uncle Sam worry about that. One more crumpled rose-leaf in his bed won't bother him. Unless I miss my guess he won't notice it for the nettles he'll be up against soon. I ought to be on my way but—" He winked a brown eye, small and beady as a squirrel's, and pulled a dark and odorous pipe from his pocket. "It's so peaceful here. Smoking allowed?" he asked in a stentorian whisper.

"Sure. What's on your mind, Sam?"

The butler came forward from the threshold where he had been teetering in uncertainty. He carried a silver tray on which were a decanter and glasses.

"M's Ellen's compliments to the Captain Doctor, Major Trent, an' will he take some wine?"

"Will he? Boy, oh boy," the surgeon assented in a hushed whisper.

"Set down the tray, Sam. Ask Miss Ellen—the ladies—if they won't join us."

"It's only M's Ellen at home, sir. M's Jess, she's out aimin' to dance her pretty gold slippers to raigs, Ah reckon, but Ah'll go ask M's Ellen if she'll come, Major Trent."

"Is 'M's Ellen' the old lady of the Manor?" Mac-Donald asked as the butler left the room.

"When you see her you'll can that word 'old.' You won't think of age in connection with her. She's so alive. Who was it said, 'So many of the living are already dead'?"

"Is the aforementioned 'M's Jess' the gal who did the First Aid stunt on your ankle?"

"Yes. She has a Red Cross Nurses' Aide certificate, is a lieutenant in the Women's Civilian Defense Corps, has a class of colored women whom she is trying to teach to buy food wisely, to understand its nutritive value; and, if Sam is to be believed, is qualifying for the job of manager of this plantation. I don't know about the cotton mills but I wouldn't put it past Miss Ellen to expect her to take them on, also."

"That's a big order for one girl to tackle. Is she the Amazon type? Bossy? Bony? Tall?"

"No. The top of her head comes about to my ear. She's slim and chic and beautiful as a magazine model with the spirit and strength of character of a pioneer woman. From what I have observed she's all-out to help and serve in this crisis at no matter what cost to herself."

"Umm, so she's working on the Civilian Defense front. I take off my hat to her if she realizes the importance of that. Astounding, isn't it, what times like these do to people. They call this the mechanistic age. No machine ever has been invented that will equal the human spirit when it is confident that there are wrongs to be righted and glory to be achieved."

"I didn't realize you were a philosopher as well as a surgeon, Doctor Mac."

"Sure, sure, the two go together. No physician is worth his salt if he doesn't get to know the spirit as well as the body of his patient." He hastily thrust his pipe into his pocket and rose as Ellen Marshall appeared in the doorway with Sam looming behind her like a bodyguard.

"Sorry I have been away each time you came, Doctor MacDonald." She seated herself with a swish of mist-gray taffeta in the chair the butler placed beside the small table and filled a glass with wine. "For you, Doctor. How do you find your patient?"

Standing, the surgeon raised his glass. "Your health, Madam." He sniffed the bouquet, arched his sandy brows. "Ah, Scuppernong in its perfection." He sipped. "Sweet and full-bodied. One doesn't often come across it now.

"The Major is getting on like a house afire, Miss Marshall. Sorry I can't order him off your premises but I think he should stay put for a week—or more. He'll be no use at Camp. If he goes back he won't keep off that foot and keep off it he must."

"Good night, Johnny," a girl's clear voice floated into the open window. "Of course I'm glad you were sent to this Camp." The rumble of a deeper voice. "No. Not tonight. I have a terrifically full day tomorrow, that's why I left the dance early. I'm going to bed. No. *No*. I won't be kissed until I'm sure I love you. I won't make the same mistake twice. Johnny! *No—o!*"

Trent's sound foot came down from the stool, he gripped the arms of the chair to raise himself. Ellen Marshall shook her head.

"Don't try to stand, Vance. Jessamine is all right if her voice did sound panicky. 'Johnny'! Must be the boy from home. Thank heaven, he's come. He may break the spell of—" Trent wondered if she had been about to name Phil Maury. "Open the door for Miss Jessamine, Sam."

The slam of a car door, the grind of gears, then incredibly soon a gay voice asking:—

"What's going on here? Army Chiefs in session?"

"Come in, Jessamine." Ellen Marshall's voice was

that of a general giving a no-appeal order. The golden
gauze of the girl's ballerina skirt floated about her as
she came into the room. "Doctor MacDonald, my
grandniece, Jessamine Ramsay."

"How do you find your patient, Doctor—or should I
say Captain? I would hate to make a social blunder so
early in our acquaintance."

MacDonald grinned in response to the laughing
voice.

"Either is all right with me, Miss Ramsay. Except
that he's on the verge of a nervous breakdown because he's causing so much trouble here, the patient's
doing fine." He glanced at his wrist watch. "Lord, I
must get a move on. I'll be court martialed if the C.O.
hears I've been doing the social act." His bow was
unmistakably a hang-over from dancing-school days.

"Thanks for your hospitality, Miss Marshall. It's
been an oasis of pleasure in a desert of work. Good
night, Miss Ramsay. Major, I left a pair of crutches in
the hall. Go easy for a day or two."

"We'll see that he obeys orders." There was a hint
of or-I'll-know-the-reason-why in Ellen Marshall's
voice. "I'm coming to the door with you. I'll leave you
on guard till I return, Jessamine. Our patient is so
eager to get away he may try to escape via the
gallery. Are the war games keeping you busy, Doctor?"

Her voice faded away in the corridor. Jessamine
slipped out of her white fox jacket and sank into the
depths of a large chair. She rested her head against
the exquisite needlework pink and crimson roses on
its tall back.

"Why are you so anxious to leave Karrisbrooke,
Major? Anyone abusing you?"

"You wouldn't understand my reason, Angel. How
was the dance?"

"So-so. It was given at the Club for some of the
soldiers at the Camp. I'm sure they enjoyed it. All
strangers to me but one. Most of the Tarheels, North
Carolinians to you, in the neighborhood are in the
service and have been sent to Northern camps."

"How come Maury hasn't gone?"

"Phil is over thirty-one. He has a tobacco plantation to manage, a share in the cotton mills, a racing-stable which takes care of any surplus income very nicely and a wife who weeps and shows all the symptoms of a nervous collapse if any mention is made of the service. I believe—Aunt Ellen doesn't—that he would have enlisted long ago if he'd had a wife with even a modicum of patriotism."

"The army may get him yet. As the situation abroad gets more critical there's a lot of talk about raising the age-limit of the draft. At present he cuts coupons for a living, I take it."

"Why that snooty tone? What's the matter with cutting coupons if one has them to cut? What do you do for a living when you're not in the service?"

"Now who's being snooty? Before I enlisted a year ago, I was—and am—an efficiency engineer."

"Only a year in the service and a Major! How did you manage it? Marry the General's daughter?"

"Nothing so spectacular. I've had my own plane since I was twenty-one and have kept up with all developments in air technic with special interest in the parachute as a lifesaver. When I enlisted my training was recognized. When not in U.S. uniform I am the sort of guy who snoops round a business, then tells the mogul who runs it what's wrong that he doesn't get better results in production and income."

"*Business!* What's business?"

"What's *business?* Lady, next to love it makes the world go round."

"I didn't mean it that way, I meant—" she glanced at the pile of letters at his elbow. "Are you married, if not to a general's daughter to someone else?"

"Not yet. I'm in that tricky no man's land between having fallen hard for the girl and proposal."

"You mean you haven't asked her? That your heart-beat hasn't said 'Yes'?"

"Or 'No.' Male menace that I am, there's always a chance of 'Nobody loves you, kind sir,' she said."

"For a man in love you seem mighty cheerful about that possible 'No.'"

"I'm an optimist. Was Maury at the Club to claim that supper dance you promised him?"

She thoughtfully examined the rosy nails on her right hand.

"Yes."

"Like him a lot, don't you?"

"Why not?" Defiant eyes on his, she sat forward in the chair and clasped her hands about her knees. "He has time and the know-how to express appreciation of a girl and—"

"And the boy you left behind you in the No'th hadn't? He was cool, calm, unstampedable like Major Trent, I take it. By the way, how come you know so much about my reaction to feminine lure—Angel?"

She flushed till her face was the tint of a petal in the pink rose on the chairback.

"How come you know so much about that boy in the No'th, Major? He isn't in the No'th now. He's at the Camp, was sent South for war games. He brought me home from the dance. Johnny is in Aviation, a Lieutenant."

"The plot thickens. Let's have the awful truth, quick. Is he the Big Moment in your life?"

"Don't laugh, *please*. I wouldn't ask you if you weren't as good as engaged, but—could you turn your efficiency engineering on a life that's in a mess?"

"Is yours?" His voice was grave enough now.

"In a way. It's maddening. I've always known exactly where I was going and now—sometimes I feel as if I were wandering in a maze and couldn't find my way out."

"In love with Maury? I was knocked in a heap when I heard you had been engaged to him. What cracked it? Capulet and Montague trouble? It's obvious that he's not popular with Her Majesty."

"He—cracked it. I was seventeen when I came to visit Aunt Ellen. Phil and I had played together as children and when I arrived, quite grown-up in my estimation, he made desperate love to me and before I realized it, we were engaged. Mother sent for me in a hurry when she heard the news—doubtless from Aunt Ellen. Then my fiery fiancé went through the cooling-off period, met Claire, and wrote me that our engagement had been a mistake, that he realized that I was too young to decide such an important step as marriage."

"And you came back a few months ago determined to show him, to make him fall for you again. I get the setup."

"You forget he has a wife."

"There have been occasions when that fact has not been a bar to love. Are you engaged to this Johnny person?"

"Not exactly."

"What do you mean, not exactly? You are, or you aren't."

"Don't bite, Major. I'll answer. Since I came here I've made a decision. I'll devote my time, my strength, my intelligence to the limit, to my Government, but I won't marry a man in the service and perhaps not know where he is for months. Whenever an announcer says over the radio, 'Three planes did not return,' my heart breaks for the women whose men are missing. Why invite that agony for myself, when there is probably a man doing great things in defense work whom I might love?"

"Suppose you fall in love with a soldier, a sailor or an aviator, what'll you do about it?"

"I won't allow it to happen."

"That's thumbing your nose at Fate. Watch out! I declared I wouldn't fall in love until after Peace had been declared and see where I landed."

" 'In that tricky no man's land between having fallen hard for a girl and proposal'—end quote? As for me, I've lost my faith in the constancy of men. I believed Phil Maury when he told me he would love me forever. Can you imagine a modern girl of seventeen being so young as to believe that?"

"It could happen—constancy, I mean. Some men have an ideal, wait for her, find her—if they do not always get her."

"You're terribly young, yourself, if you believe that."

"I don't like cynicism in women."

"No? I presume the girl you're steaming up your courage to propose to is a honey, no moods, no temper."

"I wouldn't say that," he answered slowly as if giving the matter serious thought. "She's quite human. How did we get switched from your heart interest to mine? About this Johnny? You'll have to give your efficiency expert all details if you expect real help."

"You still see it as a joke, don't you? Your eyes are laughing at me. John Gordon is the son of my stepfather. From the time I was fifteen Johnny and I were like brother and sister, he called me 'kid.' On his vacations we had great fun together. He was the leader, I was his stooge." She laughed.

"Share the joke with me, Angel."

"I was thinking of Johnny's prep-school years when he took a Correspondence Course in detective work. He was determined to qualify for the FBI and I was his female Watson. We nearly drove Mother into a nervous breakdown by our snooping and suspicions."

"Was he a detective before he enlisted?"

"No. He went into the insurance business and then, suddenly, he realized we were not really brother and sister. Mother and her husband want me to marry him—as I intimated, he got the idea first—they don't know that one reason I consented to come to Aunt Ellen was to get a perspective. I got it. I love Johnny but not enough to break my heart over his safety. He is everything a girl could want, has ideas and a surprising number of ideals considering the fact that he has always had too much money to spend; an excellent business; he's terribly good-looking; but he just hasn't something—"

"That Maury has and Maury isn't in the service. I get you. But as you observed a minute ago, Maury has something more he hasn't, a wife."

"Poor Phil. I no longer ache with humiliation or burn with rage when I remember the casual way in which he brushed me off. I'm sorry for him. Claire is a bore. She everlastingly has something the matter with her. Try getting her started on her symptoms and you'll understand what I mean. Besides, she has claws which gouge. My memory still shows scar tissues from them. She's a vixen under that doll face of hers."

"You're cruel. Claire Maury is a disappointed, frustrated woman married to a heel who is torturing her, ably abetted by your charming self. You're old enough to know that 'hands off' is the only sporting approach to another woman's husband. That rule of conduct is merely roughed-in but perhaps you get the gist of it."

"*Get* it!" She was on her feet, white with anger. "I'll say I do. You've fallen hard for Claire's 'You-poor-boy' line, haven't you? Watch *your* step. The lady has a complex, thinks every man she meets is bowled over by her charm. After this showdown of your intuition—or lack of it—I wouldn't give a lead nickel for your advice." She picked up the white fox jacket.

"If Aunt Ellen comes, tell her I was so bored I couldn't keep awake to wait for her. Good night and—" she nodded toward the letters and added—in a voice mockingly sweet—"good reading, Major Trent. Cheerio. She may have written 'Yes.'"

"I guess that does it," he countered grimly. "Good *night*."

IV

"Hi, there!"

Philip Maury in riding clothes, leaning against one of the great iron gates, hailed Jessamine Ramsay as she approached the entrance to River Farm in her sedan. Behind him a colored boy was leading a saddled horse, whose coat shone like satin, up and down the drive.

"I've been waiting for an hour—more or less—to thumb a ride," Maury announced, as he opened the car door and slipped into the seat beside her. "Take him to the stable, Lem," he called to the boy. As the car purred forward he complained:—

"You don't appear glad to see me and I gave up the races this afternoon that I might be on hand when you came along in case the gas test did you up. Was it bad enough to set your lips in a grim line like M's Ellen's when she's on the warpath? You know that look, as if she'd been appointed by the Almighty to run the world. A bossy woman's the meanest work of God. That's neat. Just popped into my mind. Take care or you'll have a mouth set like hers before you're thirty—only six years leeway, my girl—then watch the lads cross the other side of the street."

Was her fight to maintain a mind of her own setting her mouth like Aunt Ellen's?, Jess asked herself in sudden fright. Phil knew she would hate that, knew that the direful threat would change her mood; what he didn't know was that the moment she saw him leaning lazily against the iron gate memory had broadcast Van Trent's voice:—

"You're cruel. Claire Maury is a disappointed, frustrated woman married to a heel who is torturing her, ably abetted by your charming self." He had said that a week ago. The man was insulting. As if she, Jessamine Ramsay, would help torture anyone. Had she? The question pricked. She had come back to Karrisbrooke with the determination to "show" Phil Maury that she was quite grown-up now, that she could take his flirtations in her stride; but she had not intended to hurt Claire—how could a person who knew her think she would? It was some satisfaction that she had managed not to speak to the Major since.

"Still grim after my horrible warning," Phil Maury hectored. "Perhaps it's the effect of the brown uniform you're wearing—hate women in uniform, I like 'em frilly and feminine and soft in my arms as you used to be—or perhaps they put the convoy through poison gas? Won't you cry out your troubles on your pal's shoulder, Jessie? Haven't we played together va-

cations since I was a man of twelve and you were a
girl of five, and weren't we—"

His wheedling voice cleared her conscience of the
fog of self-condemnation—almost.

"*Don't* call me 'Jessie' and don't ever again refer to
that silly schoolgirl affair between us. You know I
hate them both. Thanks for the kind offer of your
brawny shoulder, but I did my crying at the Camp.
They gave us the works. A two-hour test which included an introduction to chemical warfare, a gas-
mask drill, a visit to a gas chamber and a convoy trip
through tear gas and a smoke screen over roads
inches thick with dust. We took it like heroes. By the
time we came through—without one welsher—we
knew what it was all about. What I saw today of
modern methods of warfare makes me appreciate the
peace and beauty of this gorgeous world. October in
North Carolina! The air is like wine—"

"Lot you know about wine. You never touch anything stronger than fruit punch or ginger ale."

"Know why? I once read that alcohol perforates the
brain till it's full of little holes like a sponge. A sponge
in place of a brain. It's a sobering thought." That
wasn't the real reason but he wouldn't understand the
other. "Aren't the trees spectacular? Crimson, brown,
yellow, see those maples spouting scarlet flames. The
hills with mist like violet maline wound round their
tops look for all the world as if they were wearing
veiled hats. Even from here can't you feel their
brooding stillness?"

"Not interested in scenery or millinery." He slid his
arm across the back of the seat. "I'm interested in
you. You know I'm still crazy about you, don't you?
What are we going to do about it?"

"The first thing, take your arm away, Phil, quick."

"Okay, Aunt Ellen. You're gettin' more like her
every day, Jessie, and she's still a virgin at eighty-two,
perhaps that's why she's so lucky. Everything sure
goes her way."

Jess was grateful for the sulky complaint which
showed that his thoughts had been switched from
herself.

"Lucky! Phooey. I'm tired of hearing of 'the luck of Ellen Marshall,' when it is her head for business management which does the trick. Even in the post-crash era her plantation flourished, she had the intelligence to put back into the soil more than she took out of it. She, herself, studied erosion, land waste, crops. She didn't leave it to others. Her mills operated at a profit," she elaborated to keep him off the subject of herself, "she has system and works at it, which is more than—"

"I do." He completed her sentence. "Why should I delve at the mills? I hate the infernal outfit anyway. As soon as I get a chance I intend to sell my interest. M's Ellen wouldn't listen to me even if I kept my nose to the grindstone—my mistake—it would be wheels there, wouldn't it? You're positively vitriolic today, Jessie. How come? Did you see that Yank boy friend of yours at Camp and have a fight with him?"

"Johnny Gordon? No. He is up to his eyes in war games."

"While we are on the subject of the U.S. Army—how long is the Major figurin' on enjoyin' the hospitality of Karrisbrooke?"

To what was he leading up? His voice was too elaborately casual.

"Doctor MacDonald told Aunt Ellen that Major Trent's superior officers intended to keep him away from Camp until his ankle was sound again. It seems he is a valuable man in his department. One of the best training officers they have in the Parachute Battalion of the service, and a glutton for work." Irrelevantly she remembered her first impression of the Major, that he was a man accustomed to giving orders he would make sure were carried out. Aloud she said:—

"They won't take the chance of his being permanently disabled, and that might happen if he puts too great a strain on his foot. His General and Colonel have both been to Karrisbrooke to see him—Aunt Ellen has adored having them come—she's entertaining them at dinner tonight and will it be an occasion. Sam's been polishing silver for days, Pink has been cleaning diamonds, and Callie is in the seventh heaven bringing up her shock-troops—the maids to you—preparing the dinner."

"You're tellin' me. You've forgotten that Claire and I are invited. I don't know why we are always counted in on Karrisbrooke festivities; it's evident that both my wife and I are poison-at-the-box-office to M's Ellen."

"You're neighbors, old-family, and you know how that counts in the Carolinas. If only you would try to please her, Phil. You know how she feels about racing and betting and—"

"Don't cry about it, Jessie."

"I'm not crying and *don't* call me Jessie."

"Okay, we'll switch to another station. Remember Claire reported that your aunt had called at Camp Headquarters? There was something phony in M's Ellen's reply that she went to offer hospitality to the grandson of an old friend, the use of a part of Karrisbrooke for war games. Hospitality! War games, my eye! That woman makes me think of a female spider, weavin' a web in which she sets out to catch us all."

"Aunt Ellen a spider! You're crazy. A spider is cruel. Have you ever known her to hurt a person?"

"Call her a puppeteer, it's a prettier word. We're all marionettes danglin' from strings which she manipulates to suit her purposes."

"Speak for yourself, foolish. I'm not a puppet. She doesn't dangle me."

"You think she doesn't, but wait and see, Jessie. Have you asked her why she called on the General?"

"*I* ask Aunt Ellen to explain a move in her game of life? Sometimes I think I make a lot of blunders, but—not that one."

"I'll bet Collins is right. He thinks the Major's bein' kept at Karrisbrooke for a purpose—that bailin' out over the lawn was a cooked-up scheme—that the ankle stuff is a smoke screen."

" 'Purpose'! 'Ankle stuff'! If you had turned as faint as I did when I felt that broken bone, you wouldn't talk so glibly about a smoke screen. The world did a cartwheel, so did my stomach. Are you implying that we have a mystery-man at Karrisbrooke? What possible motive could there be for keeping him there? Of course, the Marshall silver and Aunt Ellen's jewels are of fabulous value—but the Government would hardly confiscate those while there was anyone left in the country to tax."

"Go ahead, laugh; but when you wake up one fine mornin' and discover that the great Ellen Marshall is bein' involved in perhaps a national complication it won't seem so funny."

"That's what you think. I don't like Major Trent, in fact I cordially dislike him, but I don't believe he would accept Aunt Ellen's hospitality and double-cross her. I wonder to whom that snappy roadster parked in our drive belongs."

He opened the sedan door and stepped out.

"Scram and freshen up, then come down and we'll find out."

"I hear women's voices on the garden-piazza. Probably your wife has spread the news that our guest is—and I quote—'the best-lookin' man who's appeared in this part of No'th Carolina in years'—end of quote—and some of the females of the species have dropped in to confirm the verdict. I wouldn't face the most charitable of my sex in my present dusty condition. Go in, Phil, like the perfect little gentleman you are, but don't say I've arrived. I'll change and appear later."

So much later that Vance Trent would have gone to his rooms, she told herself. She entered the broad, cool hall, picked up an envelope from the console and tucked it into her coat pocket. The letter from her mother was thick. Had she at last found time to answer her daughter's many questions?

The terrier catapulted down the circular stairway, skidded across the black-and-white marble-tiled floor and jumped on her in frenzied greeting. She rumpled the dog's soft ears.

"Someday you'll knock me down, rushing at me like that, young fella."

"Oh, there you is, M's Jess." Sam's explosive exclamation reverberated from wall to wall, his white linen clothes fairly crackled with eagerness. "M's Ellen, she heard the car an' she wants you should come to the p'azza right away."

"Not so loud, Sam. I can't. I—"

"M's Ellen, she be mighty put out ef yo' don't come quick, Ah reckon, an' yo' know how she am w'en she's put out, M's Jess." His whisper had even more carrying power than his voice. He rolled his eyes upward till only the bluish whites were visible. "Ah's got orders to serve tea and drinks jes' as soon as yo' gets thar. So, yo's go right 'long out thar, chile."

"The iron hand in the velvet glove. I don't mean yours, Sam. You win. Take Lucky to the pantry with you. He's a nuisance when there are eats around. Come on, Phil. Her Majesty wouldn't be so insistent for run-of-the-mill neighbors. It's probably one of her schoolgirl pals of the Carolina aristocracy, suh. It will serve her right for not giving me a chance to change if she feels disgraced by my appearance. She's such a stickler for etiquette. How's this?"

She tipped her brown-visored cap at a rakish angle on her wavy, shining hair, tightened the brown necktie on her khaki shirt, and swished at her tan shoes with the handkerchief she pulled from his coat pocket.

"You're a pain in the neck, Jessie. Your uniform is thick with dust. Your face is burned from wind and sun. Where's your lipstick? Where's your powder?"

"In the car and in my room. I go as I am, or not at all. Come on, and *don't* call me *Jessie*."

Before she stepped from the long window she grinned impishly over her shoulder at Maury behind her. The smile stiffened as she turned and saw the woman seated near Vance Trent who was on the wheel-chaise. No old-schoolgirl-of-the-Carolina-aristocracy about her. She was tall and lithe, with hair—what there was visible below a smart hat—like blue black satin, with challenging dark eyes—a bit too near together—which made one wonder what secrets lay behind them. From head to shoes on her slim feet, she might have come straight from modeling light-mourning at a fashion show.

"You rate this for makin' yourself a scarecrow. Don't run, brazen it out," whispered a voice behind her. She hotly resented Phil Maury's chuckle. How did he know she had been tempted to dash back into the house?

"Come here, Jessamine, and meet Vance's cousin." The voice was Ellen Marshall's at its most dictatorial. "My niece, Jessamine Ramsay, Mrs. Hugh Carter, and our neighbor, Philip Maury."

"Hey!" A girl of perhaps eight darted from behind a column and barely missed colliding with Sam and the tea-cart. She was dark and elfish, if the word could be applied to a child dressed in pale pink from the ribbons on her stiff pigtails to the socks above her white shoes. Her pug nose, quite out of character with the other features, was dusted with freckles.

"Are you *Jess?*" Her voice and face expressed utter, bitter disillusion. "Heck, Uncle Van wrote me you were pretty as a dream walking. You look an awful mess, if you ask me."

"Rebecca!" Mrs. Carter reproved petulantly. Ellen Marshall glared, and Phil Maury chuckled. Vance Trent's face was dark with annoyance.

"Becky, your mind is a dictaphone. You hear or read something and thereafter you can repeat it word for word. Apologize to Miss Ramsay for your rudeness at once."

"But why, Uncle Van?"

"She's right—'Why, Uncle Van?'" Jess echoed. "I realize that I'm not in top form. Aunt Ellen, Phil and I are famishing for our tea. I've just come from a day in Camp. Do sit down, Major, you know you're not supposed to stand. Mrs. Carter, what has brought you to this part of the world? Stupid question—the Major, of course. Phil, a sandwich for a starving gal."

She ignored her aunt's annoyed frown and smiled at Maury when he set tea and a plate of sandwiches on the white wicker stand she had drawn in front of her chair in the hope of hiding her tan shoes, which, with every passing moment, were appearing to her more dusty, bedraggled and huge in contrast to the dainty footgear of the caller.

"I was answering your question as to why we came, Miss Ramsay." Had the chic brunette been explaining? She had been so upset by this whole awkward situation, she hadn't even known the woman was speaking.

"Forgive me. My brain is still a'little gassy from the day's test, Mrs. Carter. Naturally you came if you are the Major's cousin."

"I'm his cousin *only* by marriage."

The positive announcement set Jessamine wondering if the woman had matrimonial designs on her late husband's relative.

"Are you planning to stay long in our neighborhood, Mrs. Carter?"

Ellen Marshall's polite but cool question brought her niece's attention back to the vine-draped piazza and its occupants. It was evident by her voice that Aunt Ellen didn't like the Major's cousin-in-law, either.

"I have taken a bungalow at the Fox and Rabbit Inn for the duration of Van's convalescence. The main house is packed to the roof with relatives of the army men."

"For Pete's sake, Helen, don't speak as if I were an invalid. Except for this confounded foot I'm as fit as I ever was in my life. I can't understand why I'm not allowed to get back on the job. I don't think with my feet. It's maddening to be laid up like this when there is so much to be done."

"I knew you would feel like that, Van darling," Mrs. Carter soothed. "The moment I received your letter telling of your accident, I decided that my most urgent call for defense work was to keep you cheerful and happy. It's only paying my debt to you, Van. He was devotion itself to me during the tragic years of my husband's illness, Miss Marshall. He was my escort everywhere. Hugh felt so safe about me when I was with him. Of course it was a bit of a sacrifice to leave home and my host of friends. I'm social-minded and I don't know a soul here." She glanced swiftly at the table on which cards were spread. "I adore contract. I so hope I'll have a chance to keep up my game."

"Won't you dine with us tonight, Mrs. Carter? We are having friends from the Camp here for cards."

"Miss Marshall, how perfectly divine of you! Of course I'll come."

Jess wondered if this was the woman to whom Vance Trent was getting up courage to propose. He had looked ready to bite during her long explanation. It wouldn't take much courage: if she wanted him she'd do the proposing and get him as easily as she maneuvered that invitation from Aunt Ellen.

"That's why Mummy brought me, so I could help entertain Cousin Van," Becky piped up from a hassock beside the wheel-chaise. She sat with elbows on her knees, chin in her fists, her pink-ribbon-tied pigtails akimbo. "You're crazy about me, aren't you, old lamb pie?"

"With reservations, Becky." He tweaked one of her braids affectionately. "It was noble of you, Helen, to leave the ease and luxury of home to come here, but a useless sacrifice. No one could live at Karrisbrooke and be anything but cheerful and happy. Dear Miss Ellen gives us all courage, keeps us pepped up."

"Thank you, Vance."

To Jessamine's infinite surprise tears glinted in her aunt's bright blue eyes and husked her voice. Was it possible that she *cared* about being liked? She had seemed so invulnerable to the opinions of lesser humans.

"May we join you all, M's Ellen?"

Claire Maury took consent for granted and crossed the piazza followed by Barry Collins. They were in riding clothes. Had they been out together? Phil's face was as dark with anger as a skin as fair as his could be; Claire's eyes blazed defiance as they met her husband's. He would be angrily resentful of this man's attentions to his wife—even though he raced and drank with him.

"Whom do you think we met when we stopped at the Hunt Club?" Claire Maury demanded gaily, after she had responded to the introduction to Mrs. Hugh

Carter and had settled into a chair with her tea.
"That funny little Scotch doctor of yours, Major. He
said he was dinin' at Karrisbrooke tonight and would
give you the once-over. My stars, I hope he doesn't
send you back to that horrid Camp, Jess would miss
you terribly, wouldn't you, Jessamine?"

"Cry my eyes out." Even as she flung the flippant
rejoinder Jess caught the exchange of glances between Collins and Phil. Through her memory echoed
Phil's voice:—

"I'll bet Collins is right. He thinks the Major's bein'
kept at Karrisbrooke for a purpose—that the ankle
stuff is a smoke screen."

What did it mean? For what possible undercover
reason would an officer of the air arm of the service
be kept at Karrisbrooke? Aunt Ellen already had
offered the use of the place. Why was Barry Collins
trying to throw suspicion on Vance Trent, not only on
him but on his superior officers? Perhaps the Major
should be put on guard. Was the warning up to her?

"You look as if all the problems of the Administration had suddenly been dumped on your shoulders,
Miss Jess? Can't I help? I'd give my life to spare you
trouble!"

She had been so engrossed with her thoughts she
hadn't noticed that Collins had seated himself on the
wall close beside her chair. She resented the caressing
break in his low voice, resented the impassioned light
in his eyes. Instinctively she shrank from him.

"I know what you're thinking," he said in a low
voice, "that I'm implying that I love you, at the same
time I'm playing tame-cat to Claire. I can explain, if
you'll only let me."

Jessamine's eyes were attracted to Trent's as by a
magnet. He needn't look so amused just because he
didn't like her. She'd show him. She smiled radiantly
at the man looking down at her.

"It's a date. Don't forget," she declared in a voice
she hoped would carry.

It did, but not in the direction she had intended.

"One after another they succumb to your fatal
charm, don't they, Jess?" Claire Maury's voice was

high and strained. "If you care for your cousin-in-law,
Mrs. Carter, you've come not a minute too soon to
save him—for yourself."

V

Physically rested and mentally refreshed after a
fragrant bubble-bath and icy shower, Jessamine
glanced at the banjo clock above the mantel in her
room with its soft creamy curtains, hangings the green
of the sea in sunlight and bed and dressing table
painted to match. There were cream rugs on the
floor, mirrors with heavy gold frames on the walls
that gave back the picture of a girl snuggled in a
deep chair. She hugged her knees as she stared at her
reflection. Her short, waved hair appeared bronze in
contrast to the flame-color of her satin lounge-coat.

"If I say it who shouldn't, I'm not too hard to look
at, Lucky," she confided to the dog stretched flat on
the floor. "Not the *femme fatale* type like Mrs. Hugh
Carter, but definitely not grubby, right?"

The Airedale opened one sleepy eye in answer
before he rolled over on his side with a long sigh of
utter exhaustion. She laughed.

"Pardon me for boring you, fella. Sometimes it helps
clarify a situation to tell you about it, but don't let me
keep you awake."

She glanced at the clock again. There would be
time to read her mother's letter before she slipped
into her chartreuse-and-silver dinner frock. She hadn't
dined at home since the night Vance Trent had been
so insulting. It wouldn't be difficult to avoid him this
evening, naturally her aunt's military guests would be
entitled to her entire attention.

She drew the closely written pages from the envelope and regarded them unseeingly while her
thoughts flashed back to the hour on the garden-

piazza at teatime. The Major hadn't appeared over-joyed at the advent of the smart woman who had left her home, sweet home, her friends, her contract, to repay his devotion to her. A sick husband and a devoted cousin-in-law. Did it sum up to the same old triangle? Van Trent didn't seem like that sort of person. His eyes were too direct, his mouth too firm for treachery.

Aunt Ellen, by virtue of generations behind her who had had an outsized sense of social supremacy, had been as coolly gracious to the lady Carter as the ice-cubes in the silver tub on the tea wagon. Why had she invited her to dine tonight? Was she preparing to add another marionette to her collection of puppets? Darn Phil Maury for putting that idea into her head. Aunt Ellen adored contract. Mrs. Carter played. Result, an invitation for the evening. Nothing Machi-avellian about that. Phil had been furious with Claire because she had been riding with the superintendent of Karrisbrooke, even as he exchanged significant glances with the man; and all the time she, herself, had been hotly aware that she looked "an awful mess." The party had died on its feet after Claire's shrilled "One after another they succumb to your fatal charm, don't they, Jess?" Forget it, she told herself, or you'll burn up with fury.

She tried to thrust back the memory of those few minutes with Collins but it wouldn't stay put. She didn't like the man, didn't trust him. Why had she encouraged him to explain his flirtation with Claire? To show the apparently amused Major that she didn't care a rap for his opinion, of course. Silly, as if he were really interested in what she did.

The old clock in the corridor intoned the half-hour. If she intended to read her mother's letter before dinner she'd better get at it. It was a long one. She tucked her feet more comfortably under her and rap-idly scanned the first page, which referred to her hus-band's increasing need of care, their delight that Johnny was at Camp near Karrisbrooke—his father had pulled wires to get him there—and that they hoped ...

She skipped those hopes—she knew them by heart—
and turned the page.

I have waited until you had been with Aunt Ellen three
months before going into details as to the reason you were
asked to stay with her [her mother wrote]. It seemed
vitally necessary that one member of the family should divine what currents and undercurrents are undermining the
emotional—and possibly the financial—foundation of Karrisbrooke, if it is being undermined as may be possible, but *I*
believe improbable. Besides being the only person available
you are, after me, the logical heir to the estate, and, what
is even more to the point, you have the brains and intuition to find out if any funny business is going on.

"Funny business! This is going to be good, Lucky,
my lad," she exclaimed, settled deeper into the capacious chair and turned a page.

I shall have to refer to ancient history [the letter went
on]. When your Aunt Ellen was eighteen and a great belle
and beauty, even more lovely than the portrait of her in the
dining room, there came to Karrisbrooke a handsome, self-
made, young Northerner to be overseer. The feeling left by
the War Between the States was growing increasingly bitter. You can imagine your great-grandfather's fury when he
discovered that his elder daughter, Ellen—the very light
of his eyes, whom he was proudly training to share with
her brother the management of the estate—was clandes-
tinely meeting this man, who had the double handicap of
being his overseer, quite out of her class socially—and a
Northerner.

The affair went so fast and so far that the two were on
their way to be married when Ellen's father stopped them
on the Karrisbrooke grounds armed, so legend has it, with
a Simon Legree horsewhip which he applied unsparingly
to young Lochinvar. From all accounts the angry parent
literally dragged the elopers apart. Life was not without
melodrama in the late seventies.

There was the usual nine-days scandal, but before gossip
had died down, the man had given up his position and
vanished. Not until after the death of your great-grandfather did his son Todd, and my mother, his younger

daughter, know what had happened. They found a record of the man's career. He had deserted from the Union Army. They found also an endorsed cheque for ten thousand dollars made out to Barry Collins by their father.

Barry Collins! Aunt Ellen's superintendent must be the son, no, the grandson of that overseer at Karrisbrooke! Little anticipatory shivers pricked through her veins. Had chance flung him into Ellen Marshall's life, or, knowing of his ancestor's romance, had he come counting on turning a woman's memory of a lover to his advantage? Whatever the explanation the present situation offered all the excitement of a movie thriller. She returned eagerly to the letter.

So you see, it wasn't entirely paternal pride that blocked the romance. The lover was weak, as the army desertion and his willingness to be bought off proved, and Ellen's father stood between her and what would have proved a tragic marriage. It was learned that later, abroad, he married a girl of good family and deserted her after a son was born. Barry Collins at Karrisbrooke must be a son of that son, who also married a foreigner.

Time marched on. Ellen took on alone the management of the tobacco plantation and cotton mills when her brother Todd died leaving a son to carry on the Marshall name. You know what happened to him. Killed in a steeplechase. Three months ago Judge William Sutcliffe, the lawyer who inherited the legal care of the Marshall estate from his grandfather and father, came to me in great perturbation. He declared that Aunt Ellen had hinted that she might make Barry Collins her heir. Already she had given him the job of superintendent of the plantation, made him a director in the cotton mills and welcome at her home.

The Judge felt that giving him the two positions was a romantic throw-back so out of character with Ellen Marshall, as he knew her, that he feared she was verging on senility. He admitted that the man was well-educated, had a charm of manner that would coax the birds from the bushes, which, turned full force on an old woman who had loved, wanted to marry and apparently remained faithful to the memory of his grandfather, might influence her against her family if that were his scheme.

The Judge reminded me that the house at Karrisbrooke and her own ample fortune were hers to dispose of as she pleased—Mother's share of the estate came to me when I married—that it would be nothing short of a crime if she left her property outside the family because of a romantic brainstorm.

He suggested that I make a long visit at Karrisbrooke. I couldn't leave my husband and I knew he wouldn't be really welcome. Aunt Ellen gave me a grand wedding and the string of perfect pearls I have passed on to you, when I married Duke Ramsay, the New Englander who was your father, though the fact that I was not marrying a Carolinian was hard for her to bear. He died and I went back to Karrisbrooke with you, only two years old. You were fifteen when I married John Gordon from Massachusetts. Even though she has mellowed a lot toward Northerners I feel that Aunt Ellen has never quite forgiven me for again marrying a "damyankee."

So, I sent you in my place, knowing that with your straight-thinking mind, an inheritance part Ramsay and part Marshall—you are more like Aunt Ellen than I am, Jess—if there were a scheme behind Barry Collins' presence at Karrisbrooke you would find it out. If Aunt Ellen intends to leave the man property doubtless her will to that effect already has been made. A person at eighty-two—even one who is as certain of immortality as Ellen Marshall appears to be—doesn't put off setting her house in order.

I've had a suspicion, since Judge Sutcliffe poured out his doubt and anxiety to me, that this Barry Collins might have the romantic scheme of becoming master, perhaps by chicanery, of the very plantation from which the first Barry Collins had been horsewhipped. It may be a crazy idea, but, before this, families have been known to harbor revenge for generations.

That's the story. That there may be a conspiracy to cheat Aunt Ellen I can easily believe—it may take the form of sabotage at the mills, or speculating with her tobacco —but that it can be successfully put across I can't. At eighty-two or one hundred and two, Ellen Marshall of Karrisbrooke, who has kept one fortune and made another through the keenness of her mind and her uncanny intuition, will be Captain of her mind and soul to the end.

But as Judge Sutcliffe reminded me, I haven't seen her
for a year and he has been in touch with her almost daily.

We have given you time to settle into the life of the
plantation before telling you why you are there. You are
not a spy, remember, you are at Karrisbrooke for the protection of one of the grandest women in the world. I can't
let her be duped and humiliated by a cheap adventurer
if the prevention is in my power. I am sending her my
dearest possession. I'm banking on you, daughter.

                                                MOTHER

P.S. I am sure Aunt Ellen will like Johnny when she knows
him even if he isn't a Carolinian. He is such a dear. You
do agree with me, don't you, honey?

VI

Jess impatiently brushed the postscript of the letter
from her mind, sat motionless as she thought back.
Sometimes she had wondered if her great-aunt gave a
continental that she had come to Karrisbrooke. At
times she would look up and catch a quizzical look in
the keen blue eyes watching her and sometimes she
felt the warm glow of the older woman's affection.
Could a person with Ellen Marshall's experience of
life and humanity be fooled by a man like Barry
Collins whom she, herself, had distrusted the first
moment she saw him? It was the incredible, the im-
possible, that was happening in the world now, wasn't
it? Looked as if life here, which had been a trifle on
the monotonous side, might break into amazing, exciting drama.

Pretty poor judgment on the part of her mother
and Judge Sutcliffe not to have told her before she
came what her job was to be at Karrisbrooke. Three
months wasted. She would be on the watch for undercurrents from this minute on. The letter had made
her hotly anti-Collins where before she had been

tepidly distrustful. He mustn't suspect that. She had been uneasily aware that he admired her; there had been times, when she had snubbed him unmercifully, when the "I'll-bide-my-time" glint in his eyes which had followed had set her heart pounding from an emotion that if not fright was first cousin to it, and this afternoon for the first time she had been stupid enough to encourage him. She had wanted to show Van Trent. What price spite? Was her mother's suspicion correct, that the present superintendent was nursing a deep-laid scheme to acquire possession of Karrisbrooke? Was one part of it the intention to marry the girl who was heir presumptive? That was a shattering thought.

She had a vision of his eyes this afternoon as they met Phil Maury's. He had made Phil suspicious of Vance Trent. Why? That was a cross-current it was up to her to follow which, in turn would necessitate dropping her animosity toward the Major. She would pretend to be friendly. She never could be really. Hadn't he accused her of being cruel to Claire?

"M's Jess! M's Jess! M's Ellen says w'y don' yo's come to de drawin' room?"

Sam's voice. Sam's emphatic knocks startled her back to the present and the Airedale to his feet. Head cocked, tail wagging, he watched the door. She glanced at the clock. Glory be, she was late.

"Yo' hear me, M's Jess? De Gen'ul an' de Cunnel, dey's done came, sho' nuff—yo' should have seen dere go'geous capes, dark blue with light blue linin', showed w'en dey trowed 'em back—mmn! mmn! An' Mr. an' M's Lacey, they's came, an' yo's de only one not down an' M's Ellen she sent—"

"I know, Sam, I'm terribly late. Run along and tell Aunt Ellen I'll be there with bells on in one minute."

She gave a hasty brush at her already shining hair, dropped the lounge-coat in a shimmering heap on the floor and slipped the silver-and-chartreuse frock over her head.

"W'at yo' mean, bells, M's Jess? Dis ain't no Chris'mas party," Sam protested close to the door.

"My mistake. Run along and report or M's Ellen

will come up herself and we neither of us would like that. Yo' know how she is w'en she's put out, Sam."

It was nearer five minutes than one later, that she ran down the circular staircase and crossed the black-and-white marble floor of the hall. The diamond clasp of her pearls had acted up—they were now in her silver bag—to detain her.

The softly lighted drawing room was murmurous with conversation, redolent of roses and the faint bouquet of rare sherry. General Carson and Colonel Slade, six-footers, bronzed of face, slightly grizzled as to hair, both exceptionally handsome, in the blue of full-dress army uniforms, were talking with their hostess, who, gowned in gleaming white satin, stood under the twinkling crystal chandelier. Barry Collins, groomed till he glistened, attired in impeccable evening clothes, hovered near chatting with the Laceys, a couple out of the same mold as the Maurys, except that Estelle glittered in silver sequins and Claire in green and gold. Was she imagining it or had the superintendent of Karrisbrooke assumed a master-of-the-house manner? She quickly averted her eyes as they met his. Their expression set merry-pranks prickling through her veins.

This is a gilt-edged occasion, she thought, as she caught the sparkle of the diamond-and-ruby dog-collar which encircled her aunt's throat. Her Majesty doesn't get that out for the common herd. Mrs. Hugh Carter in a smart and revealing black frock stood in front of the Carrara marble mantel laughing, apparently at a remark of Doctor MacDonald's who resembled a puffed-up penguin in shape if not in coloring. It was evident that Major Trent, in the dress uniform of the Army Aviation, with the silver wings and parachute insignia on his left breast, standing with the aid of a cane, wasn't in tune with that portion of the universe, if the three furrows cut deep across his forehead were to be taken as an indication of his mood.

"Why are you standin' in the doorway, Jess? All you need is to stick your thumb in your mouth to look like the shy kid who came to my birthday parties. What you afraid of?" Phil Maury in white evening clothes offered a glass on a small silver tray.

"Here's your tomato juice. It's been on the table lookin' as lonesome among the glasses of sherry as that dollar bill Collins dropped on the collection plate at Sam's church the one time he went there with us. How'd you dare come late to M's Ellen's dinner?"

"I was reading a letter from Mother and didn't watch the time; I wouldn't be here now if I had waited to fasten my pearls. The catch wouldn't snap."

"Where are they?"

"In my bag. I feel positively undressed without them."

"Hand them over. I'll fasten them for you."

"Not now. Take this glass. I'll report to Aunt Ellen, she is so surrounded she can't see that I'm here."

Barry Collins stepped forward eagerly as she approached.

"You're late, Miss Jess. I was beginning to fear something had happened to you."

"Nothing ever happens to me. I'm not the sort of person who attracts adventure, worse luck."

"You were in on a parachute landing which quartered Major Trent at Karrisbrooke for weeks, though perhaps you don't call that adventure?"

She laughed.

"If I were writing fiction I would describe that last remark as being 'laden with portent.' That isn't my idea of adventure. Sam is speaking to Aunt Ellen. Dinner is served. Better find the lady you are to take in."

"It is Mrs. Lacey. I hoped it would be you. You haven't forgotten, have you, that you said, 'It's a date'? Hope you didn't mind Claire Maury's blow-up. She's edgy these days. I'll arrange with Miss Ellen that we play cards at the same table."

I'll arrange with Miss Ellen that we don't, she told herself. Claire "edgy," that's an understatement if ever there were one.

An inexplicable wave of emotion tightened her throat, stung her eyes when, seated at the table, she glanced about the great mahogany-paneled room softly lighted by wax candles in the immense crystal chandelier and tall yellow tapers in massive silver candelabra on the table, at the rich orange brocade hangings which repeated the color of the satin frock in the portrait above the fireplace. This was the home in which generations of her forebears had lived and died. The gleaming silver, even some of the sparkling crystal, the delicate china, had come down through the years.

My heritage. Is it? Her heart skipped a beat as her mother's written words flashed on the screen of memory.

"He reminded me that the house at Karrisbrooke and her ample fortune were here to dispose of as she pleased."

Would a woman of Ellen Marshall's background and pride in family divert a home like this from its rightful heirs? She glanced at the regal hostess presiding at the head of her table, then at the handsome, suave superintendent who was laughing at a remark of Estelle Lacey's. It wouldn't be the first time a young, fascinating man had fooled an old woman.

She looked at the portrait above the mantel. It was unbelievable that the romance of that young girl could influence the woman of years and experience. The fire below threw a flickering light on the dark curls and set the painted face alive, as if thoughts were changing its expression from grave to gay.

"Why are you gazing at the portrait of Miss Ellen as if attempting to drag her secret thoughts from behind that magnolia-tinted face?" inquired an amused voice beside her.

She turned. Vance Trent, at the opposite end of the table from the hostess, was in the seat which in years past had been occupied by the master of Karrisbrooke. She had been uncomfortably aware of his nearness, had turned her back toward him as she chatted with Colonel Slade, who had taken her in to dinner.

Perhaps he is the favorite, she thought. Perhaps since Van came—Aunt Ellen has shown more affection for him than I've ever seen her show anyone—

Barry Collins hasn't a chance with her and knows it. Perhaps that's why he is making Phil suspicious of the Major, perhaps he scents danger to his plan of marrying me to get the estate. My word, why did I allow that crazy idea to take root in my mind?

"What's wrong—Angel?" The low, disturbed voice recalled her to the present. "What did I say to frighten you?"

"Me? Frightened? What gave you that foolish idea, Major? I had determined not to speak to you after you implied that I was—the word was cruel—then to find myself beside you—naturally I was shocked to speechlessness."

"Not what I would call a lucid explanation but we'll let it pass. There's something important I want to talk over with you. Invite me to drive to the tobacco acution tomorrow morning, will you? I can't use this confounded foot on the brake, yet."

"Van, darling," Mrs. Carter, aglitter with black sequins which were a dramatic foil for her beautiful neck and gardenia-tinted shoulders, spoke across sulky Phil Maury to whom she had been allotted as a dinner partner. "Doctor Mac," she smiled at the man at her other side, "you don't mind if I call you Mac, do you? Formality is so silly in this age." As the Doctor signified by a fatuous grin that he didn't, she went on, "Mac says you won't be permitted to return to Camp for two weeks, that the crowned heads—your superior officers to you—have decided you'll get fit faster here."

"Those crowned heads have another guess coming."

"You've got the situation wrong, Mrs. Carter," Phil Maury cut in smoothly. "It isn't the army, it's M's Ellen who's keepin' him here. Haven't you found out yet that the Major is her white-haired boy?"

"Phil!"

It wasn't the words, it was the sneer in his voice which forced the shocked whisper through Jessamine's lips. For one horrified instant she thought Van Trent would rise and hit him, then he settled down in his chair, the color swept back to his face.

"How did the parachute attack come out today, Colonel?" he asked.

Jess drew a long, ragged breath. The crisis had passed. Colonel Slade's lean, tanned, grave face lighted with enthusiasm.

"Fifty were captured but the one hundred and twenty-seven men flung themselves out of the army transports at twelve hundred feet and cleared their planes in ten minutes, seven minutes faster than last week's jumps."

"Good work. Wish I'd been there."

"Don't talk shop, Van," Mrs. Carter commanded and switched the conversation.

Delectable courses came and went: Callie's partridges broiled in butter; little rolls, feather-light. Wines were served. Conversation became more animated, voices higher, laughter more continuous. Jess was thankful when her aunt rose from the table. Even though one knew that the bulk of the food had been raised on the estate, the sight of so much was sickening when one thought of the rationing in England.

Tables were set for cards in the drawing room. While the hostess was imperiously allotting partners and places, Jess slipped out a long window of the drawing room to the gallery to cool her hot cheeks. Indignation had set them afire when she had glimpsed Claire Maury, arm in Trent's, gazing up into his face while he talked to her. He'd better watch out or she would begin to whisper that he was mad about her. Thank goodness, it was cool outside. She drew the pearls from her bag; they would be safer on.

"Alone at last," Phil Maury exclaimed theatrically behind her.

"My goodness, you startled me. I'm glad of a chance to tell you, Phil, you were disgustingly rude to Major Trent at dinner. He showed his breeding and background by letting it pass."

"Oh, you think that, do you? Goin' off the deep end about the soldier-boy, are you? Better not; to hear her tell it, he's gettin' that way about my wife."

His voice warned her. It would have been wiser if

she had left the subject alone. She shifted conversational gears:—

"Fasten my pearls, will you? How did you manage to escape? I thought the man-eating widow Carter had you in her clutches for the evening." She tipped back her head to smile at him as the clasp snapped.

"With you in the same room, Jess? You *know* better." His rough voice warned her. She tried to slip away. His arms closed round her, his lips pressed hers in a long, hard kiss.

She thought for an instant her brain would burst from fury. Her arms were pinioned as in a vice, she couldn't move them—she still had her feet, hadn't she? She dug a spiked heel into his instep with a force that loosened his arms and freed his voice at the same instant.

"You—you vixen—" He groaned, grabbed his foot in one hand and hopped in agony. "You've cut—"

"What sort of an act are you putting on, Maury?" Trent's amused inquiry came from the window behind them. "Giving a stork imitation? Looks a lot like it, prancing around on one leg like that. Miss Ramsay, your aunt sent me to tell you the game is on." He held back the rose damask hanging. "Coming?"

How long had he been standing there, how much had he seen, Jess asked herself frantically? Aloud she said flippantly:—

"Of course I'm coming. You don't think for a minute I would dare defy Her Majesty for Phil and moonlight—or do you?"

VII

Since awakening at dawn Jess had had a dozen minds about granting Van Trent's request to drive with her this morning. Curiosity turned the scale in his favor.

First, he had said he had something important to talk over with her. What could it be? Second, it seemed as if she couldn't endure the prickling uncertainty as to whether or not he had seen her in Phil Maury's arms on the gallery last night. If he hadn't, no explanation would be necessary. If he had, she must set him right, it would be unbearable to have him think with more reason than before—if he were to believe his eyes—that she hadn't principle and honor enough to keep "hands off" another woman's husband.

From under the brim of her sapphire-blue felt hat she glanced at him as he sat beside her in the yellow station-wagon. Snappy uniform. Perfectly tailored. Gold leaves on his shoulders. Silver wings with a parachute above the left pocket of his blouse. The firmness of his mouth and chin which had impressed her the first time she saw him had been accentuated during these last weeks. His dark, amused eyes met hers as if aware of her scrutiny.

"You're right. I saw you on the gallery last evening," he translated. "That's what you're thinking about, isn't it? I also noticed that Maury limped as if in torture when he followed you into the drawing room. I have observed those wicked heels you affect in the evening—just as I noticed the sensible Oxfords you are wearing with your present beige jersey outfit. I don't know the provocation, but, whatever it was, Maury is old enough to resist temptation. Verdict for you—not guilty."

Her cheeks warmed under his laughing eyes.

"I done you wrong. I didn't know you could be so charitable. I presume you can't understand Phil, that you are the big, strong type, the dragon-slayer who would fight temptation in the shape of a married woman and always win." She resisted the urge to warn, "Beware of Claire." Hadn't Phil said last night, "To hear her tell it he's gettin' that way about my wife"? Even if she didn't like him she would admit that his laugh had what it takes.

"Fight! Not a chance. I run away. That's the only infallible safeguard to keep one out of that sort of tragic mess."

To hear Helen Carter tell it, he hadn't run away from his cousin's wife. The thought flashed through her mind before he added:—

"I suggest you practice running—and don't think for an instant I haven't Maury's number. I had that the first time I saw him."

"He was inexcusably rude to you at dinner. I'm sorry. Don't mind him. He's a typical Southern fire-eater—that doesn't mean that other Carolina gentlemen would necessarily be as unbearable as he was—and he knows Aunt Ellen doesn't like him. I told him what I thought of him last night."

"Hands off my battles, Miss Ramsay. I can take care of them—and how."

His grim announcement ended conversation for a while. They drove along a highway bordered with big oaks and pine trees. An orange bus lumbering ahead stopped to pick up two children dressed in blue-and-white-checked gingham waiting under a sycamore tree. From the little house of split juniper logs behind them drifted the smell of pork and coffee cooking and a woman's voice singing.

As they neared the town the road became crowded with troops, trailers and trucks loaded with hogsheads of tobacco. Tanks churned up dust. A white horse jogged by dragging the big-wheeled cart of a truck farmer. They passed the cast-iron Confederate who year in and year out stood like a sentinel on his monument at the crossroads. A truck laden with cotton bales wrapped in jute, banded with iron strips, lumbered past. Dine and dance places flashed neon signs even so early in the day. Automobiles filled the streets. Blacks and whites pushed and jostled before shop windows.

"Money has come to North Carolina," Jessamine broke the silence. "The population of the state has been doubled by the influx of troops. The enormous increase in the military establishments in this state has given employment to nearly tweny-five thousand workmen, practically all of whom are North Carolinians."

"Pretty proud of this state, aren't you, Angel? I

believe you're rapidly changing from a New Englander to a rabid Tarheeler."

"No—o, I wouldn't say quite that." She took his
teasing seriously. "It's the practical New England half
of me that helps me appreciate what this state has
accomplished. Have you noticed the absence of flam-
boyant advertising billboards on the highways?
They've been ruled out. Never before have I seen this
street so crowded. We're approaching the warehouses. I hope you'll feel repaid for this long trip by
what you see."

"It hasn't seemed long to me, Angel. I don't like the
edge in your voice. You and I must be friends, that's
the important thing I wanted to talk over with you.
Miss Ellen has asked me to make an efficiency survey
of the plantation and mills."

"Her Majesty has called in an expert? You dreamed
it."

"It's true."

"But—you're in the Parachute Battalion. How can
you give time to outside work?"

"I'm not doing much in military affairs now, am I?
I've been ordered to remain at Karrisbrooke two
weeks longer. Soon after that I will be detailed to the
Special Assignments Section. The duties include visiting aircraft factories with War Department officials
on a 'Keep 'Em Flying' campaign."

"Will you like that?"

"If I were allowed a choice I'd take command of
paratroopers in active service, if we get in the war.
But the higher-ups have placed me where they believe I will be most useful and I'll admit the job is
right down my street. Meanwhile, if I can help Miss
Ellen get better results in production and income
from tobacco plantations and mills, I shall be only too
happy to serve her."

"I presume it will mean making yourself familiar
with every nook and cranny of her affairs."

"Only business affairs. Nothing personal."

Nothing personal. The personal problem had been
put up to her to solve. Perhaps in his business survey
Vance Trent would unearth the truth as to the reason

of the presence of Barry Collins at Karrisbrooke—if there were an undercover reason. She must be friendly with him, if only apparently. She might need his help—terribly—sometime, if her crazy suspicion that she was to be used by Collins to acquire the Karrisbrooke estate were not one hundred per cent brainstorm.

"Have you decided to take the job?"

"Then you're not asleep? You've been silent so long, I wondered. It's up to you whether or not I take it."

"To *me!* If you think Aunt Ellen would be influenced by my views as to her need of an efficiency engineer you have another think coming to you."

"That isn't the point. She has nominated you to show me the aforementioned 'nooks and crannies.' You don't like me. Even to help a woman whom I love and respect as I love and respect Miss Ellen—I didn't believe in love at first sight until I came to Karrisbrooke—I won't force a disagreeable task on you. It would mean at least half of your time every day while I am on the job."

"Of all things!" Her eyes, big and darkly violet, lighted with little gold sparks as they met his. "Why should *I* be drafted? Of course I'll do it, but I wonder—" She became intent on steering the car through a bawling herd of black and white cattle. The diversion was a lucky break. She had almost told him that she wondered if the motive underlying Aunt Ellen's plan to have her niece act as cicerone to the efficiency engineer wasn't to spike that same niece's renewed friendship with Phil Maury? She couldn't know that Phil had spiked it himself for keeps, last night.

"You were wondering—" Trent prompted.

"What those cows are doing in the middle of town and if there is anything more stupid in this gorgeous world than a herd of cattle? And it is gorgeous, this portion of it particularly. Golden clouds of forsythia in March. Banks of pastel-colored azaleas in April. Each month has its beauty show. Look at the October backdrop. The woods all bronzy gold, the hills purple and pinkish haze like a maline veil softening it all. Do you realize that there are twenty peaks among those mountains that rise higher into the clouds than our Mt. Washington?"

"Having made that colorful and educational detour suppose we return to the subject of Miss Ellen and her efficiency engineer. Do you approve?"

"Yes, I approve. Selfishly. It will give me something definite to do. I'm beginning to despair of my class in home economics. Those women either can't or won't grasp the importance of knowing how to buy, how to feed their families now that some of them have more money in a month than they had before during their whole lives. Forgive me for unloading my discouragement on you. Is your sudden interest in a tobacco auction the first step in your resumed business career? If so, here we are in the midst of warehouses. Aren't they huge and long and brown? Smell the tobacco? I'll take you to Aunt Ellen's favorite trading post and then park the station-wagon. Wait for me at the steps so I may explain the procedure. If I'm to be your guide, philosopher and friend I intend to make a finished job of it."

As Trent braced against the great door, resting his weight on one foot and the cane, he thought over his conversation with Ellen Marshall. She had said:—

"Collins is not to know that I have engaged you to help me, Vance."

"Won't he think it strange that I am showing such interest in your affairs, Miss Ellen?"

"Not if you are as good an actor as I think you." That was not when she had proposed Jess as his guide. "You are not yet fit to report for air duty. Most natural thing in the world that a man of your intelligence would want to occupy his time learning something of the world into which accident—possibly Fate in the shape of a parachute—had dropped him." There had been a hint of amusement in the last sentence which had set the General's words echoing in his memory.

"And if you could manage to break a leg in landing it would be all to the good, Major." Was there something behind this efficiency survey he wasn't being told?

"We'll see and hear better inside." Jess's voice shattered the mirror of memory.

The auction was on when they entered the warehouse. Buyers and sellers passed up and down between rows of tobacco-filled baskets, feeling, smelling the freshly cured leaves. The shirt-sleeved auctioneer swaggered back and forth, clapped his hands, shouted from the corner of an apparently clamped mouth between mops at his moist red face:—

"Twenty-five, six, six, gimme seven!"

A clerk followed close, watching signals, recording purchases. Sweating farmers, Negroes in ragged, faded-blue overalls, white men in business suits passed back and forth apparently undisturbed by the heat, confusion and tobacco-heavy air. At the end of the barnlike room men sprawled in sleep exhausted by the long preparation for the sale, undisturbed by raucous shouts, ribald laughter or profane anger.

The morning sun slanted in through a crack in the boarded sides of the building, lighted Jessamine's hair till it shone like burnished copper, picked out the glittering whites of a Negro's eyes, silvered the green shirt of the auctioneer and threw into sudden startling relief "a Greek-god profile" with brilliant gray-green eyes under somber, frowning brows.

"Does Collins take all auctions as seriously or is he giving me the meat-ax look because he resents my being here, Angel?" Trent inquired in a low voice.

"Doesn't he know?" she whispered.

"No. Miss Ellen doesn't want anyone wise to my assignment but we three. How are you at keeping things off the record?"

"Number One ace. I maintain a bottomless pit into which I drop all 'promise-you-won't tell' tidbits and clamp down the cover. They never get out. Collins is coming this way."

"That Dictator manner of his will get under my skin if I see him often."

"You'll see him often if you carry out your efficiency engineering plan, Major. He covers the plants and he's good at his job. He bosses everything Aunt Ellen doesn't." For a mad instant she was tempted to tell him of her suspicion that by fair means or foul Barry Collins intended to acquire Karrisbrooke. She dismissed the urge with a mental jibe, "Now you *are* crazy."

"That doesn't include you, does it? The bossing, I mean. I haven't noticed that Miss Ellen has you cowed."

"She wouldn't want me cowed, she isn't like that. My conscience has pricked ever since that first evening when I told you about her. I really adore her. She's a grand person. I hope I'll be just like her. Phil says I will, that I'm growing so opinionated, so like her, that I'll remain unmarried at eighty-two. Awful thought, that no one will like me enough to want to marry me, isn't it?"

She looked at him in startled wonder. She hadn't known he could laugh like that.

"It—is. You said that as if you really believe it. We'll have to see what can be done about it. Doubtless if worse came to worst you *might* marry a soldier. Good morning, Collins."

The superintendent's frown had smoothed out. His voice boomed welcome. Even in the heat he appeared immaculately groomed. His powder-blue shirt with a smashing monogram on the left sleeve was as unwilted as if it had just left the laundry.

"Good morning, Miss Jess. What d'you think of a tobacco auction, Major Trent?"

"They put on a great show. I'm deaf from the noise and dumb with admiration when I watch the auctioneer. It's nothing short of a miracle that he can make sense in this Tower of Babel. I presume he is making good or he'd be out of a job."

"Sure, he's made some big sales. This has been a great year for the planters. Not so much sold but better prices. We've managed to keep the pinhookers out this morning."

"Pinhookers?"

"Speculators to you, Major. They buy, re-sort the tobacco and offer it for sale the next day at a profit of five or ten dollars a hundred pounds. When it happens the growers are fit to tie. They—"

A large, plump, hairy hand came down on his shoulder and cut off his voice. He turned. A man, stout, red-faced, sharp-eyed, flashily clothed in a suit of blatant black-and-white checks was regarding him between half-closed lids. A man forty-five if he was a day.

"How you doing, Barry?" he inquired. He glanced at Jess, ran his tongue across his lips like a cat savoring cream, before his ferret eyes moved on to Trent. "I see the army has invaded the tobacco market," he observed in a smooth voice which just missed the lightness intended. "Introduce me, pal."

For a split second Collins hesitated. The hand on his shoulder tightened.

"Miss Ramsay, Major Trent, Gus Peckett," he said.

Peckett released his shoulder and edged quickly between the girl and the officer.

"Interested in bidding, Miss Ramsay?" he inquired. "I'd be tickled purple to give you points. Who knows, might show you how to make a dollar or two."

She adroitly moved to the other side of Trent and tucked her hand under his arm. She distrusted the storm-signals in his eyes.

"Thanks a million, Mr. Peckett, but I don't need your help. I know all the ropes in an auction. I live here. If we don't start at once, Major, we won't complete our itinerary before lunch. Let's go."

On the way to the station-wagon Trent observed:—

"Collins balked at presenting his friend, didn't he? He's that way about you, isn't he? Watch your step, lady." She opened her lips impetuously. He held up a protesting hand. "Let's not argue about *that*. Who is Peckett?"

If he but knew it she had had no intention of arguing, again she had had that mad urge to confide her suspicion as to the matrimonial plans of Collins.

"I have seen him before in the distance. I've suspected he was a pinhooker. He's always on hand when our tobacco is being sold, but apparently I did him wrong. Collins might stand for many things but not for a speculator. You gave me the scare of my life.

For one hectic moment I thought you intended to hit him."

"I did. Believe it or not, I used to be a peaceful guy; but now, every once in a while I get the urge to beat up someone, like a minute ago. No one can step between you and me and get away with it, especially a man with what is known in the 'Westerns' as a 'slinkin' eye." He answered her quick look with an engaging grin. "Was the fear that I was about to hand him one the reason you seized my arm?"

"It was. You didn't take it for a gesture of affection, I hope."

"No. I took it for what it was, a bit of friendly window-dressing to impress a man whom you dislike even more than you dislike me. By the way, what did you think of the burly Peckett?"

"I didn't like him. The dictionary has a word for a voice like his, oleaginous, 'oily' to you. Something tells me that Collins isn't entirely sold on him, either, he acted as if he were afraid of him."

"You're a mind-reader. Collins is afraid of him. Why? Is the genial 'Gus' a pinhooker sharing spoils with the superintendent of Karrisbrooke, or is he perchance interested in the cotton mills and their defense orders for denim, or some other undercover activity? It's up to you and me to find out which, Angel."

VIII

"We'll just about make the Club for lunch," Jess announced as the station-wagon purred forward.

"Why the Club? I like Callie's Virginia ham with dropped eggs and Hollandaise sauce and hot rolls dripping with butter. Boy, they're great! Why not home, Karrisbrooke to you?"

"Because, with the men away in the service, I feel I

owe a glimpse of the best-lookin' man who's appeared in this part of No'th Car'lina in years' to the neighborhood gals, suh. Perhaps I should warn them that there's a lien on you."

"A lien?"

"Don't be dumb. You know what I mean. Didn't you confide that you were in that tricky no man's land between having fallen hard for a girl and proposal? I presume it's Mrs. Carter who is keeping you dangling? She called you 'darling.' "

"Helen calls everyone 'darling.' It doesn't mean a thing. Now when I call a person 'darling,' the word will carry the pledge of a lifetime of devotion."

"So you think. I've heard something like that before."

"You'll hear it again, someday, Angel, and the lucky man will make you believe it—forever!"

After that, minutes passed in silence. They drove along a back road once used by oxen and mules, too rough and rutted to be popular with a car. They passed the rear gates to a plantation, caught a glimpse of the sparkling blue of a river. Came to a stretch of woods.

"Look at those uniformed men disappearing among the trees. What are they doing? Are they a part of the war games?"

"Yes. Paratroopers. Some of my men. They landed to destroy, theoretically, gasoline, ammunition and ration dumps and to take a crack at communication lines."

"Will they do it?"

"That's what they are there for, to demonstrate that that Air Arm of the service can do an outstanding job in war. I hope they'll pull it off. Do you realize that the largest, most complete military maneuvers ever undertaken in this country are going on here, now? They are using 350,000 soldiers drawn from all over the country."

"I realize that this whole state is alive with troops, construction workers and honky-tonks that trail them, that the powers that be have sent out an SOS for 78,712 dozen eggs for the camps—78,712 *dozen!* This is the time for every patriotic hen to come to the aid of her country. It's a little more than you can bear, to be out of it all, isn't it?"

"There are compensations. What's going on at that stand ahead?"

"A barbecue. Can't you smell roasting pig?"

"I can. See those plank tables among the trees? Have a heart, Angel, don't take me to the Club. Let's eat here."

"The ayes have it. I'd love it."

They watched while a white man, his face blackened by smoke, basted with a peppery sauce the pig roasting over a pit full of red coals. When it was cooked to a turn they ate roast pork and corn pones crisped on a hot griddle, at one of the long tables.

"Those were the corn pones of my dreams. I'm at peace with the world," Trent declared and offered a cigarette case. Smoke?"

"No, thanks. Here comes a gipsy. It's the perfect dramatic finale to our morning."

The woman in garish red and blue held out a dirty hand. Gold hoops in her ears dangled below the stringy black hair which framed her leathery brown face.

"Cross my palm with silver, pretty lady, and I'll tell you a be—eau—tiful fortune."

Trent caught Jessamine's wrist as her fingers went to her coat pocket.

"Don't," he said. "She's a fraud."

"Why not! It's part of the fun." She laid a shiny new half-dollar in the dirty palm. "Okay, gipsy, remember you promised me a good one."

The woman threw a vicious glance at Trent before she began her stereotyped singsong. That finished, she warned theatrically:—

"Beware a dark man"—she rolled big black eyes toward Trent: "he'll make you believe you're the only girl in his life—but there's a woman with yellow hair he wants, she's near—trust the blond man." She glanced up at a plane droning overhead. "Your fate will drop from the sky. You'll be married many, many years, have the same husband all the time and six children." She peered at the girl's palm through half-closed lids, gave a theatrical gasp of fright.

"Lady, lady, take care!" The hoarse warning sent chills coasting down Jessamine's spine. "You and one you love are the victims of a plot. You may lose house and money. Stay away from mountains. Look out for him." She pointed a dirty finger at Trent before she slipped behind a tree and vanished.

"Stop shivering, Angel. You certainly got your money's worth of piffle—plus."

"And your face is a deep red with fury," she countered. "She got you wrong, Major. You're not the dark man in my life—but she was right about the woman you want, only she had the color of the hair wrong. Page Helen Carter. Johnny Gordon is dark, not blond, and he does make me believe—almost—that I'm the only girl in his life. He's a flier, too. If she knew so much why didn't she know that I won't marry a soldier? Come on, let's forget her. We've spent so much time at lunch, we'll have to adjourn this personally conducted tour until tomorrow. I have a date this afternoon."

Again on the highway she concentrated on passing a line of army trucks filled with khaki-clad men.

"The same old penny for your thoughts," Trent offered, when the rumble of wheels had died away. "Still worrying over that hag's rigamarole?"

"No, I didn't take her seriously, but something she said pricks like nettles. Remember her warning, 'You and one you love are the victims of a plot'?"

"I remember that she prophesied also that your fate would drop from the sky. I beg to remind you that I bailed out into your life. Having established that point we'll return to the gipsy's phony warning. Why should it trouble you? It's part of her build-up to get your money."

"It may be, but somehow it clicks with what I've had on my mind. It set me wondering if I should tell you what Mother wrote me about Aunt Ellen and Barry Collins."

"Don't wonder. Spill it. Quick. It may help me advise Miss Ellen."

She reported parts of her mother's letter. When she came to the suspicion that Collins might have the melodramatic plan of becoming master, perhaps by chicanery, of the plantation from which his grandfather had been horse-whipped, he interrupted by a long, low whistle.

"That could account for a lot of things I haven't understood."

"Then you don't think Mother's imagination slipped its leash?"

"I do not, but I agree with her that it is incredible that Ellen Marshall can be fooled by anyone. She isn't by Collins. Sometimes her voice packs a wallop when she speaks to him. If she were fond enough of him to will him a fortune she wouldn't snub him as she does. If there is any idea of his becoming master of Karrisbrooke the bee is in his bonnet, not in hers. Have you told all?"

"Ye—es."

"I don't like your hesitation. Play ball, Angel, if there is anything more I ought to know, tell me."

"There isn't really. It's just something I imagined. It's too silly to repeat."

"Okay, I'm trusting you, but, get this, anything you imagine may be of importance—to me—in my investigation, I mean."

How could I tell him I had a crazy idea that Barry Collins would try to marry me to get Karrisbrooke? I couldn't, so go back in your corner, Conscience, and sit down, she commanded.

He was looking at her as if weighing the truth of her statement. His eyes were the sort one couldn't lie to easily. She said hastily:—

"Aren't we letting our imaginations run away with us? After all, Barry Collins may be simply a man who is tremendously interested in his job and—clothes. You'll have to admit he is a snappy dresser."

"I saw you making big eyes at his sleeve. I make haste to inform you that my shirts are monogrammed."

"So what? You know you're a lot of fun—when not giving advice."

"And you are lovely with that laugh in your eyes and that adorable curve to your mouth."

"Mine! You're so subtle, Major."

"Advising is my job." He picked up the conversation as coolly as if there had been no tingling interlude. "When I see conditions that should be improved I'm supposed to say so and—"

"Keep after your victim till the change is made to your approval. You needn't say it, your mouth shows that."

He stroked his small dark mustache and frowned.

"What's the matter with my mouth?"

"I wouldn't know. It's—it's dictatorish, that's all."

"Charge that up to life. I was an only child. My parents died in an accident when I was ten. I was taken to live with a brother of my mother's, an uncle who had four husky sons older than I. From that day on life was a battle. I don't mean that I was abused, but I had to make those four guys respect me even if I was—"

Had he been about to add, "dependent on their father"? Poor little kid. He mustn't say it.

"Did you have to fight at school too?"

She felt his quick glance at her. Did he suspect how she had finished the sentence in her mind?

"Yes and no. One fought about different things, there and at college. Life is a battle for integrity, to keep the faith, all the way along, isn't it? If it isn't a fight for a living it may be for ideas and ideals. Some are born with them. Some acquire them, but there isn't a person on earth who doesn't have to fight to achieve them."

"Fight, I'll say so. Do you ever sit up straight in bed and say 'Ooch!' when you think of the things you've said and done you wish you hadn't? As for ideals, one of my major ones is never to take a mean crack at anyone, to be the sort of girl upon whom a woman will not be afraid to turn her back when I'm in a group she's leaving. When I remember what I said to you about Claire Maury my face burns. She really has good points. She adores children and she is generous with money."

"Never say 'Ooch!' again about what you tell me, Angel. Use me as a sort of father confessor to whom you may say anything, knowing that it will be understood and held in strict confidence. I'm interested in Claire's husband's racing-stable. Would you call it a going concern?"

She glanced at him quickly.

"Are Phil's affairs included in your efficiency investigation for Aunt Ellen?"

"No can tell—yet. Is that a child ahead trudging toward us? She's wearing pink gingham. I believe it's Becky. It is. What's the youngster doing on this road alone?"

"You're very fond of her, aren't you?"

"Yes. Hugh Carter, her father, was my favorite of the four cousins. When his health failed and he had to cut out evening affairs his wife kept on the social merry-go-round. He asked me to pinch-hit for him at dinners and parties. I did. To feel that I was helping him that way dulled my aching, furious sense of frustration that I was powerless to ease his lingering, painful exit from the world."

His emotion-roughened voice tightened Jessamine's throat. So that's the explanation of his devotion to his cousin's wife, she thought, just as Becky hailed them.

They picked her up. Snuggled in the seat between them she leaned her head against Trent's arm and drew a long, sobbing breath. Her eyelids were swollen and red.

"I'm—I'm so glad you—you found me, ol'—old l-lamb pie."

"Where were you going, Becky?"

"Not going, Cousin Van. I was coming—coming away from Mrs. Maury's."

"The Maurys'. Why were you there?"

" 'Cause she invited me, Miss Jess. I never go unless I'm 'vited. She said she was crazy 'bout children an' would I come to lunch today. Mummy drove me over—she 'vited Claire to a tea she's goin' to have next week—an' left me."

"Why didn't you wait for Mother to come for you?"

"I just couldn't stay another minute, Cousin Van.

We had a dandy lunch, chicken an' whipped potatoes —I had three helpings—and ice cream. After lunch I was on the porch playing with two darling white kittens when I heard a man talking in the room."

"What man?"

"I didn't see him, Cousin Van. I just heard him say, 'You're wastin' your time with Collins, don't you know he means to marry Jess?' An' then Claire said—she asked me to call her Claire, said it made her feel young—'You don't imagine me dumb enough to believe you really think that? I know it's a blind. Why did you break your engagement to her seven years ago to marry me? Because of my money? Now that it looks as if she'd be Ellen Marshall's heir, you're planning to divorce me to marry her yourself. I'll say she's given you plenty of 'couragement.'"

"Becky, before they rolled you off the assembly line they slipped a dictaphone inside your head for good measure. What a memory. Go on. What happened next?"

"I guess she remembered I was there, Cousin Van, for she whispered something, an' the man said very low: 'Why do you have that brat hanging round? It's the second time she's been here.' When I heard that, something hurt here," the child put her hand over her heart. "I couldn't wait for Mummy, I stole down the steps and ran out the drive. I—I didn't want to see anyone. I—I was so 'shamed I'd been where I wasn't wanted an'—an' I'm *not* a brat."

Jessamine's eyes met Trent's above the child's head.

"You're right, life is a battle," she agreed. "You needn't feel ashamed, Becky dear, you were invited and you were wanted by Claire. She loves children. How about coming to Karrisbrooke? We'll phone your mother to pick you up there. Lucky will about wag his tail off when he sees you, because you're kind of young and will play with him. He gets rather bored with me."

"Is it an invitation?"

"The real thing all tied up with pink ribbons."

The child's lovely, young laughter was infectious. Trent and Jessamine smiled in sympathy.

"Then I'll come, Miss Jess. Gee, you're pretty now. I didn't think so the first time I saw you, did you, ol' lamb pie?"

Trent didn't answer. Above her head he was saying:—

"Are you trying to break up that marriage, Angel?"

"I am *not*. It is none of your business, but I don't *want* him. I've gone overboard about someone else— in case you care."

"Johnny Gordon?"

She regarded him with wide, amazed eyes.

"Are you by any chance psychic, Major? Period, not interrogation point. We have with us today, remember—"

"Who've you got with you besides me, Miss Jess?"

"You didn't let me finish my sentence, honey. We have with us today a person who could qualify as top-ranking expert on the Quiz Kid program: Miss Becky Carter."

IX

"Damn that man Hitler!" Johnny Gordon exploded. He sent the motorcycle round a curve with a speed which churned up a fountain of dust, shot the wheels of the sidecar into the air, and sent his passenger's hand to her head in a frenzied clutch.

"Next time you feel called on to cuss the *Fuehrer*, Lieutenant, give me warning and I'll prepare," Jessamine gasped, and readjusted her hat at the angle currently ordained by fashion.

"And just remember, Johnny, that I'm to pour at the tea Mrs. Carter is giving at the Fox and Rabbit this afternoon and go easy on the gas around curves. The first time I met her Becky announced that I was a 'mess.' I hope you'll admit that in this head to heels pastel-pink ensemble—notice the gorgeous gold buttons—I'm a fashion designer's dream come true."

"You're a dream all right, I hope you'll come true for me."

His gruff voice warned her she was on a dangerous airwave. Time to switch to another station.

"Aunt Ellen wasn't any too pleased when I told her you were calling for me, she intended me to arrive in state with her in the Rolls-Royce. She would doubtless have had a nervous breakdown had I told her you were coming on a motorcycle because I was crazy to ride in a sidecar."

"I apologize for the 'damn' and the speed. I got to thinking that if it hadn't been for that sign-painter, paperhanger or what-have-you, I wouldn't have had to step out of the insurance business through which I was blitzkrieging like a ball of fire, that you and I might be married by now and—"

"Not so fast, Johnny. We are not even engaged, remember."

"You're telling me. Nothing but a superman will suit you."

"Why not aim for champagne even if I have to settle for Canada Dry?"

He roared with laughter.

"You're a cute trick, kid. Why am I grouching when I've got you to myself at last?" He frowned down at her. "Gosh, I'd plumb near forgotten in these last weeks that there was such lovely skin, deep dimples, such a saucy nose and violet eyes with little devils in them, in the world."

"I'll return the compliment. You're looking simply grand—harder and leaner; soldiering has done that for you, it's warmed you up a lot too, Johnny. You never used to say such lovely things to me, not that I wanted you to." His eyes warned her that she was playing with explosives. She hurriedly switched to good old Mother Nature.

"Look at those maples spouting like flames above the pines. Smell the wood smoke. I love the world in October, don't you?"

"I get it. You don't want *me* to talk about *us*."

"Better not, Johnny, but don't think from that I don't appreciate the sacrifice you made, when, instead of waiting to be drafted, you volunteered and gave up that precious business."

"Sacrifice, nothing. The first John Gordon arrived with the Massachusetts Bay settlers. I'm the tenth in line. That fact carries a responsibility. The old patriots behind me did their bit, can't let them down. Believing as I do in the great ideals for which this country stands I'm darned glad to be here. Boy, that sounds smug, doesn't it?"

"Nothing in that admission to turn your face a bright and lively crimson, Lieutenant. I have a few ideals myself."

"You're an understanding pal, Jess. While we're on the subject of pals, I hear you've picked three pretty special ones since you came to Karrisbrooke—or they've picked you."

"Only *three!* I must be slipping. What's happened to my technique?"

"Go ahead, laugh. Someday, I *hope,* you'll be eating out your heart for a flapdoodle who doesn't care that you're in the world, if he even knows it; then my remark won't seem so darn funny."

"I'm sorry, Johnny, really I am. I never mean to hurt you." She slipped her hand under his arm and pressed her cheek against his sleeve. The motorcycle swerved crazily.

"Don't do *that.* Your shaky voice and wet-lashed eyes are good, but not good enough to fool me, kid. I get around between war maneuvers. The natives sure are making the army welcome. It'll take me a year of week ends when I get North—or wherever I'm ordered—to write my bread-and-butter letters. To return to our muttons. A little bird whispered that a married guy named Maury to whom you were at one time engaged and disengaged, wants you back and is giving you a rush."

"Must have been a liar-bird who told you that fairy-tale. They're not indigenous to any one locality."

"Hey, is there truth enough in that yarn to make you spittin' mad, Jess? Your eyes shot sparks."

"Certainly *not*. I was wondering to what species this flapdoodle whom you so spitefully wished on me belongs, Johnny." At his indignant glare she disciplined the laughter in her voice. "Youngsters like you shouldn't listen to gossip. Phil Maury has a perfectly good wife."

"So what? A lot of ice that cuts these days."

"Don't be cynical, Lieutenant."

"Okay, let's get on with the line-up. Number Two is that Major who bailed out over Karrisbrooke. I suppose he isn't nuts about you?"

She drew a long, theatrical sigh.

"Alas, my boy, he already had a heartbeat before this phantom of delight first gleamed upon his sight. W. Wordsworth's line, not mine."

"You're trying to be funny and I'm in dead earnest. I want to know what I'm up against in the way of competition."

"Haven't you met Major Trent? You two are in the same arm of the service."

"You're forgetting that he bailed out over Karrisbrooke soon after the arrival of the Parachute Battalion for the war games. I've heard enough about him though—he's a super-popular guy with officers and men—to fear you may fall for him now that you're living in the same house."

"You needn't. Believe it or not, you're not up against competition in that quarter. I don't like Vance Trent."

"Is *that* so! Methinks the lady doth protest too hotly."

"Now you're trying to be humorous. He's crazy about a girl, told me so, himself."

"Oh, yeah? When does he have time to see her? You and he have been touring the country in his roadster this last week, haven't you?"

"You *have* been getting round, Lieutenant. You and the Movietone Newsreel sure cover the world. Just between you and me, the Major and I have been on business for Her Majesty, which has resulted in—grip the wheel hard, Johnny, this is going to be good—having that penthouse on the roof of the administration mill turned over to me for an office. I'm a career girl! I'm the great Ellen Marshall's confidential secretary. Washington grabbed the woman she'd had for years. I'm earning a salary."

"What d'ye know about that, kid! At last you have a chance to use the business course you dug into at college as if you expected only that would stand between you and the Big, Bad Wolf at the door. Who knows, perhaps that detective Correspondence Course the folks at home laughed their heads off about will boost me into the Intelligence branch of the service. That's an idea. Like the Marines I'd see the world and take you with me. How about it?"

His engaging grin, the wheedle in his voice, warned her.

"Nothing doing. I've signed up for a job with Aunt Ellen. I never break a contract. I'm interested in the saga you were relating of the men in my life, Johnny. You've named only two. Who's Number Three?"

"Barry Collins. Smart guy. Tell you now, I don't like him. He's the get-even type."

She regarded him in startled surprise. His conclusion fitted in so perfectly with her mother's suspicion of the motives of Collins.

"If you're really interested to know," Gordon went on, "he's my idea of a flapdoodle. I got his number the first time we met. The first time, mind you. A psychologist might explain it, I can't. Someday when he bends to kiss a woman's hand I'll let my atavistic demon loose and give him a kick where he'll feel it most. I can't understand how your aunt can have him hanging round. Don't suppose he has some kind of hold over her, do you?"

"Hold on Ellen Marshall? You've been seeing too many movies."

"I'll hand it to your laugh—it has everything music has, but I don't like it when I'm the subject."

"Howdy, Miss Ramsay. Hi-ya, Johnny!"

Jess turned to look after the ramshackle topless roadster from which a girl's hail had come, then up at Johnny Gordon, whose face had turned brick red.

"Where in the world did you meet Goldie Mellor? She's a switchboard operator at the mill, that's why she knew me. She appears to be extremely well acquainted with you." She realized at once as she saw the set of Johnny's lips that her comment hadn't helped matters.

"That's just her way. If she were to meet the King of England, she'd yell, 'Hi-ya, George!' Anything the matter with Goldie Mellor that I shouldn't meet her because she's a telephone operator? Never knew you to be snooty before."

"I'm not snooty. Her job has nothing to do with my question. She's in my First Aid class and a natural in the work. She doesn't seem your kind, that's all. I've never seen her when she wasn't chewing gum. I've never heard a word against her name. I was surprised that you had met her," and stunned that she should call you "Johnny," she added to herself.

"You meet all kinds of people when you're so'jering. She may be cheap but she's a square-shooter and mighty good company. Here we are."

He turned into a drive beside which swung a brilliantly colored sign depicting a red fox in pursuit of a white rabbit with shrill-pink ears.

As she waited on the porch while he parked the motorcycle she visualized his face when Goldie Mellor had hailed him. It had been a guilty color. Where had he met her? He had said she was "mighty good company." He must have been out with her somewhere. Why worry? He was a man grown and, as he had reminded her, he "got around between war maneuvers."

She resolutely switched her train of thought. Curious that he should feel as Judge Sutcliffe, her mother, she and Van Trent felt about Collins. He usually took people at their face value, never probing beneath the surface for the real person.

From where she stood she could see the distant camp, rows of dark barracks, pacing sentries, midget-size, the gorgeous Red, White and Blue of the United States Ensign floating against a turquoise sky tinted faintly pink from the glow of the slanting sun. Even with that teeming camp in sight the world about her seemed at peace this perfect late October afternoon.

The notes of a bugle tightened her throat. The orchestra inside broke into "God Bless America." Voices joined in the chorus. Suddenly it was as if she saw swift and terrible thunderheads of war surging up from the glowing horizon. For an instant terror stopped her breath.

"What's happened to you, Jess?" Johnny Gordon's hand on her shoulder administered a slight shake. "Snap out of it. You look like a snow-girl in a trance."

"I'm all right, Johnny. Just for a minute I was terrified by the thought of what war would mean to those men in the Camp and to their families."

"Sherman had the right word for it. Forget it. Have I time for a smoke before we make our entrance?" He drew a cigarette case from his pocket. "Remember this? I carry it in the pocket over my heart."

She had given him the khaki-colored case when he had enlisted. Across one corner was a band of air force blue edged with gold service braid, under that a pair of silver wings.

"I couldn't forget it, Johnny, my heart was blocking my tight throat when I bought it for you and thought of where you were going."

"Hey, don't go wet-lashed on me. I can't stand it. Smile for the gentleman, quick! That's better. Come in and don't let me down. Remember I haven't met the old girl who is giving the party."

"Old girl. Better not let the dashing Widow Carter hear you say that, Lieutenant," she warned gaily, glad of any thought that would restore her emotional balance.

In the hall he stopped before a long mirror.

"Darned fine figger of a man you're going out with, Jess. Hope you realize your luck." He grinned and winked at the reflection of a dark-haired, dark-eyed lieutenant in impeccable olive drab, a silver bar on his shoulder, wings above his heart and adjusted his already perfectly adjusted black tie. "What's so funny about that to give you the giggles, kid?"

"I don't like to talk about myself, but—" Her laughing eyes met his in the mirror. "Something tells me that my pastel-pink suit-frock, topped with the last word in an out-size matching hat, also has what it takes, or hasn't it?"

"It has. Lady, take a bow. You're a little bit of all right." He cleared his voice of gruffness. "Come on. Lead me to her."

The hostess, dressed in white which accentuated the richness of her brunette coloring, was receiving in a ballroom bordered with scarlet leather banquettes. Jessamine presented her escort. Mrs. Carter detained them long enough to say:—

"Thanks for helping out, Miss Ramsay. Ready for you at the tea table," then passed them along with the speed of a practised White House hand-shaker.

The tearoom was quite empty for the moment except for the honey-color blonde behind an urn at one end of the lavishly laden refreshment table.

"At last, Jess. I thought you were never comin'," Claire Maury reproached. "Do present that handsome boy with you. My stars, they are cert'nly catchin' the officers young and terribly good-lookin'."

Jessamine named them to each other. Johnny Gordon rose to the bait.

"You're something to write home about yourself," he answered with such sincerity that Jess's startled eyes flew to the woman over whose hand he was bending with an air of devotion.

"He *means* it," she told herself. Why be surprised? Claire was attractive today. There was a tinge of pink under her usually too pale skin, her eyes were aquamarine blue, her vivid lips curved up instead of down. She was dressed from hat to shoes in white, the only spots of color being the green of an enormous diamond-set emerald in a clip at the V-neck of her frock and in a massive matching bracelet. The same gems were repeated in the elaborate gold frame of her white bag. To a person meeting her for the first time, she might seem a little bit of heaven. Suppose Johnny should be taken in by it? Suppose—

She'd better stop worrying about Johnny Gordon. First it had been Goldie Mellor, now Claire Maury.

Because of his family background, money and personal charm, he had been the quarry of mothers with daughters and daughters without mothers since his college freshman days. He knew his way around.

The room was filling. From where she sat she could see Barry Collins in the ballroom. He appeared to know everyone present. Women smiled when he bent his red head over their hand. The men responded stiffly to his greeting. Evidently he had majored in feminine psychology. Too suave. Too smooth. Someday he would be bound to skid.

"Why that pleased smirk?" demanded a voice. "How about a cup of coffee for me?"

Her startled eyes returned from the study of her aunt's superintendent to meet the amused regard of her aunt's efficiency engineer in the uniform of the Aviation, who was holding out a cup and saucer.

"Your mistake, I was smiling, not smirking, Major Trent. As to the why, not a chance of stumping this expert this time; here's the answer: 'A light heart lives long'—the late Mister Shakespeare speaking."

"Is the Lieutenant with whom you arrived responsible for the light heart? Is he the man about whom you've 'gone overboard'? I hope the guy realizes his luck."

Without waiting for her answer he carried the filled cup to the other end of the table. Jess's conscience smarted. She had let him believe she loved Johnny in an attempt to convince him that she didn't love Phil. Why get hot about it? She wasn't sure yet that she wouldn't marry Johnny Gordon, after the war was over, was she?

"Greetings, Claire," she heard the Major say.

"Vance Trent in person. Lieutenant," she smiled with seductive friendliness up into Johnny Gordon's eyes, her softly slurred voice was at its most Southern, "I'm starvin' for one of those luscious pink cakes at Miss Ramsay's end of the table. Get one for me, will you?"

"They'll have to walk over my dead body to stop me."

Johnny paused beside Jess to ask:—

"What's her name?" By a movement of his head he indicated the woman at the other end of the table. "I didn't get it."

"Maury, Mrs. Philip—Claire to you from present indications."

"Gosh, Jess, you're not jealous, are you?"

"Jealous! Me? Don't be foolish." She hastened to dash the hope in his voice and eyes. "Just sorry for her. A married woman who flirts with a boy like you is pretty pathetic."

"*Boy!* I'm twenty-six! Two years older than you, and you giving *me* advice. Watch your own step, gal, watch out that you don't give the arch eye to a married man once too often. What's the name of the Major to whom she's giving the glad hand? She was so pleased to see him she didn't present me."

"Trent. Number Two on my stag-line, according to you."

"So that's the irresistible Trent. Darn good-looking. Eagle-eye type. I like the way he ups his head as if challenging, 'Come on, World, I can take it.' I can see why he slays the gals. Your aunt's phony superintendent approaches. Here's where I make my getaway." He snatched up a plate of pink cakes and returned to the other end of the table.

"Coffee, please." Barry Collins bent over her. "How about meeting me in the garden when you get through here, Miss Jess? I still have that explanation to make to which you agreed to listen, remember?"

Fingers on the spigot of the coffee urn, eyes on the cup she was holding under it, she tried to think of an excuse for not meeting him.

An ebony-faced bell-boy, in gold-braided scarlet the exact shade of the leather banquettes in the ballroom, touched Collins' sleeve and held out a note.

"For you, suh."

"Who sent it, Joe?"

"My name ain't Joe, suh, it's George Washin'ton Lewis. A fat, red-faced man in the lounge pointed you out an' said I was to giv' it to you." He rolled eyes that looked like nothing so much as chocolate drops

superimposed on jumbo white peppermints, before he
prodded:—

"He's powerful anxious to see you, I reckon, suh."

Collins took the note and broke the seal just as Van
Trent joined them. He read the words on the card he
drew out, handed the boy a coin.

"Tell him I'll be with him in a minute, G. Washington Lewis. I'll be back to keep that date in the
garden, Miss Jess." He nodded to Trent before he
hurried away.

Her eyes followed him, came back to Van Trent,
who softly stroked his dark mustache while he gazed
thoughtfully at Johnny Gordon's back. As if he felt
the magnetism of the Major's eyes, the Lieutenant
turned, said something to Claire Maury and without a
backward glance left the room. In an offhand, leisure-
ly manner, Trent followed.

Quite unaware that the coffee in the cup she had
been filling was running over, Jess sank back in her
chair in stunned amazement. She recalled Johnny's
answer when she had asked him if he had met Major
Trent:—

"You're forgetting that he bailed out over Karrisbrooke soon after arrival of the Parachute Battalion
for the war games."

Only a few moments ago he had asked the name of
the Major to whom Claire was giving the glad hand.
She had assumed they had not met. Perhaps they
hadn't, perhaps it was her not too reliable imagination
which had suggested that they had exchanged a wireless message. Had the hurried departure of Barry Collins after reading the note anything to do with the
exit of the two officers? The bell-boy had said "a fat,
red-faced man in the lounge" had sent it.

A vision of a fat, red-faced man at the tobacco
auction placing his hairy hand on Collins' shoulder,
the echo of an oily voice saying "Introduce me, pal,"
stopped her breath for a minute. Gus Peckett had
sent that note and Collins hadn't dared ignore the
summons. Why? Were Van Trent and Johnny Gordon
also interested in the answer to that question?

X

At a small desk near the window in the conference room at the mill Jessamine Ramsay looked up from the stenographic notes she had been making. Her vivid lips twitched in a smile.

Aunt Ellen reminds me of a flying fortress protected by a ring of fighting planes, she thought, as she regarded the erect figure in gray tweeds topped by a modish black hat on silvery hair, seated at one end of the oval mahogany table.

Between her and Philip Maury, lounging in a big chair opposite, sat the five superintendents of the mills. She appraised their faces. Strong. Thoughtful. They belonged to men who had ideas and were not afraid to express and fight for them if necessary. Barry Collins sat in at the conference as a director. As she furtively observed him memory reproduced his expression when he had opened the note at the tea at the Inn last week. Before he left the room in answer to the summons from "a fat, red-faced man in the lounge," he had reminded: "I'll be back to keep that date in the garden, Miss Jess."

He hadn't returned. Evidently Gus Peckett, who fitted George Washin'ton Lewis' description to a T, had put on the thumbscrews to keep him. She hadn't seen him since until this morning, and the sight of him now brought back her wonder as to the reason of the departure of Johnny Gordon and Van Trent immediately after his. Had it been merely coincidental or had they been ... ? In response to her aunt's imperative rap on the table with a silver-banded gavel she picked up her pencil.

"There is one more report to be made. Have defense precautions been taken in all the mills, Mr. Darcy?" Ellen Marshall inquired.

A tall, lean, Lincolnesque man rose. He looked like an animated antebellum daguerreotype as he thrust one hand inside his ancient frock coat and rested the finger tips of the other on the polished table.

"Yes, marm. All windows, doors, every skylight has its black curtain. Pails of sand and shovels, electric torches have been placed at strategic points. Sternos for heating, cases of canned and condensed food have been stored in each building in case workers should be trapped within their walls." He smiled a wintry smile at the girl by the window. "Those last precautions were suggested by your niece, Miss Ellen, and I reckon someday they'll prove to be mighty useful, though I hope and pray they won't be needed."

The superintendents smiled at Jessamine and applauded. Barry's hand-clapping, like the name of Abou Ben Adhem, led all the rest. At his end of the table Philip Maury glowered.

"These defense precautions are a lot of hooey. They're costing money, needed for other things," he protested petulantly. "Why persist in thinking in terms of bombs, M's Ellen? We'll not be pulled into this war. The United States is too powerful. No country will dare attack us."

"The United States is powerful, Philip. It is also smug with a complacent sense of superiority which is terrifying when one thinks of the vastness of the problem it may be called upon to solve, in the flash of a gun.

"The precautions have been taken, the money has been spent," Ellen Marshall continued in her firm, vital voice. "With a mammoth artillery post, a huge antiaircraft establishment, a shipbuilding enterprise and a marine base destined to be the largest and most complete in the world, this state will be a bright and shining mark for the enemy if war comes. We must protect our part of it. You seem to have forgotten, Philip, that by indifference like yours, citizens can paralyze preparations for the country's safety; that by wholehearted co-operation like that of our superintendents, they can make it a vital, protective power." She rapped with the gavel.

"Meeting adjourned. Mr. Darcy, wait please. Jessamine, I shall be occupied here for an hour. Type your notes. We will drive home together."

Later, with her report ready for inspection, Jessamine stepped from the penthouse which opened on the broad, flat roof, crossed to the rail and looked down at the river flowing by as soundlessly and smoothly as Time, its dangerous undercurrent imperceptible. Three of the mill motorboats tied to a pier rocked gently on its surface. She drew a long breath. Gorgeous air though it vibrated with the hum of machinery. Not even a hint of frost in it.

Her brows drew together in a thoughtful frown as she glanced at the covered, bright new galvanized iron bins which contained sand that had been placed a few feet apart, along the edge of the roof. Was Phil right? Were such precautions unnecessary? The country was not at war. It did seem incredible that any nation in its right mind would attack the United States. Right mind! There were mad nations on the loose, weren't there?

"Hi, Jessie."

Phil Maury hailed her from the top of the stairs which opened by a trap door on the roof. She had taken the precaution to lock the door that opened on the stairs to the penthouse office. He leaned folded arms on the rail.

"What do you think about all this defense hooey?" he demanded aggressively.

"That it is not hooey and that the person who protests against such preparation isn't in his right mind."

"Meanin' me?"

"Meaning you. I don't understand your attitude, Phil."

"M's Ellen's spendin' a lot of money on it; some of it is mine, remember."

"There'll be a lot more spent if even one bomb strikes this building. It will go up in flames."

"In flames." He gazed thoughtfully at the river. "In *flames*. So it would. So it would. I wonder if the insurance would be paid if fire came from bombs?"

He straightened and thrust his hands into the pockets of his coat. "What's the use lettin' ole goblin war get us? It isn't comin'. How about drivin' home with me, Jessie?"

"Thanks a lot but Aunt Ellen asked me to wait for her."

"Ordered, you mean. Haven't you a mind of your own?" He tucked back a curl of her hair and laid his hand on her shoulder. "Haven't you, honey-chile?" he repeated caressingly.

She shook off his hold. For the split second before she laughed she could hear her heart thumping. The roof looked frighteningly big and empty—the river seemed terribly far below for a dive.

"I have, Phil, and in case you've forgotten I have heels too."

His face flushed.

"Sorry, I got you wrong the other night, Jessie. Once you liked to have me kiss you. When you leaned back against me I took it as an invitation and—accepted it. What man wouldn't?"

"You know that wasn't an invitation, Phil Maury," she refuted passionately. "You know—"

"Oh, Miss Jess!"

Barry Collins' red head appeared above the open trap door. "Miss Ellen sent me to tell you she was waiting for you in the car," he called as he stepped to the roof.

"Thanks. I'll join her immediately." Her departure took on the nature of a rout. Never had she been quite so glad to reach the haven of her so-called office, never had she clicked the key in the door behind her with such a sense of satisfaction. For the first time since she had met Collins she had been unqualifiedly glad to see him. Had Her Majesty known that Phil had come to the roof and sent her superintendent to the rescue? It wouldn't be surprising. Ellen Marshall had eyes not only in front and back of her head but on the sides as well. The dictionary had a word for it. "Omnispective, able to see all things, beholding everything."

On her way out of the mill she stopped at the door

of the telephone room on the ground floor and nodded to the dark-eyed, dark-haired girl at the switchboard.

"Good morning, Lucy. Still like your job?"

The operator removed one earphone and squinted through shell-rimmed spectacles that gave her the expression of a ruminative owl.

"Crazy about it. I'll never stop being grateful to you for teaching me how to do it, Miss Ramsay."

"I only passed along what I learned last winter at a defense class. Any time you need help I'll take over."

"Thank you. I aim to take you up on that, someday when Goldie Mellor, the girl who relieves me, doesn't come. You know Goldie, don't you?"

"Yes. She's in one of my classes." She thought of the girl's, "Hi-ya, Johnny," and felt a prickling of uneasiness. Where had he met her?

"Too many soldiers in her life," Lucy was explaining, not unkindly. "Gee, how they fall for her! She's a pushover for romantic stuff and it isn't always the doughboys either. I worry about her a lot. She isn't any too safe. She's a snappy operator, except in her voice. 'Marshall Cotton Mills,' that's Goldie's style." The exaggerated drawl was a masterpiece of imitation. She hurriedly replaced the earphone as a red light showed on the switchboard. "Marshall Cotton Mills," she answered crisply.

In the late afternoon Jess entered her aunt's sitting room. It was lighted by the smoldering red logs in the large fireplace and the flames under the Georgian silver hot-water kettle on the tea-tray and fragrant with the scent of roses. The walls were lined with books Ellen Marshall had read and prints she had picked up in London. The thick-pile rugs on the floor had been bought in China. Signed photographs of celebrities from all over the world; silver boxes from India and yellow roses in a green glass Lalique bowl were on a table. Chairs and couch were upholstered in beige with an occasional sharp dash of flamingo or emerald-green brocade; the three colors were brought together in the chintz hangings now drawn across the long windows.

Ellen Marshall was the picture of composure and serenity as she sat knitting a navy-blue sweater between the table with its silver and delicate china tea appointments and the fire whose light turned the pale gray of her satin frock to rose.

She hadn't always been so serene, the girl thought, as she prepared tea for herself. She had lived through shock and heartbreak, through war and peace, and visited all the countries in the world and had acquired cool, unstampedable courage. Suppose she, herself, were to lay her cards on the table and ask advice? She had been cockily independent up to date, but Phil Maury was becoming too big a problem to handle alone. Someday he would catch her unaware, renew his despicable love-making; Claire would walk in on them. Then what?

The question brought her abruptly to her feet. She set her cup and saucer on a small table and walked to the window, pulled back the long hangings, looked out.

"The gorgeous afterglow is going down, slowly, steadily, like a mound of melting pink ice-cream," she said, drew the curtains, returned to poke the fire, changed the angle of a silver-framed photograph on the mantel.

"You're restless, Jessamine. I'm beginning to like your pajama costumes." The surprising approval brought her facing her aunt as forcibly as a hand on her shoulder. "I thought them shocking at first, but I have to admit that those sleek black slipper-satin trousers and the white crepe blouse, which might suitably be part of a fencer's costume in an eighteenth-century drama, are extremely attractive. Perhaps it is because you wear them with a touch of gallantry. I'll confess I'm slightly envious. I detest fashions for the so-called older woman—they are so apt to be old-ladyish—size-sixteen styles appeal to me." She laughed her rare laugh, her blue eyes twinkled. "But, I still have, sufficient self-discipline not to buy them."

Aunt Ellen was in a relaxed, jovial mood. Was this the psychical moment to ask advice about Phil?

"Why not have a pajama costume like mine, Aunt

Ellen? You're slim enough and young enough. If you doubt that last, page Van Trent. He'll tell you. He is your ardent admirer."

"Vance Trent regards me with the eyes of affection, but I suspect that his admiration wouldn't stand up under the shock of seeing me striding round in trousers no matter how smart; so I'll remain true to mist-gray chiffon, satin, taffeta, and tweed costumes, Jessamine. Now that we are on the subject of admirers, Philip Maury followed you to your penthouse office today, didn't he?"

"He did, worse luck. He has me completely baffled."

The girl dropped into a low chair and crossed her arms on the back to face the fire. Flames cast rosy patterns on her white blouse, set sparks in her thoughtful eyes.

"I came here more to talk about him than for tea, Aunt Ellen. Phil is developing into a pest. He insists that he is crazy about me, that I love him. I wonder now why I ever became engaged to him. I presume propinquity and youth is the answer."

"You were young for your years and Philip has been an accomplished philanderer since, and doubtless during, prep-school days. After you became engaged to him I didn't draw a long breath until you were back with your mother."

"I'll say I was young for my years. I was too unsophisticated to be afraid of him then. Now that I know more of the world and its ways, he terrifies me."

"Don't blame yourself too much for believing in him, Jessamine. He was, and is, past-master in the art of flirtation. His loves are as quick as mushroom growth and as rootless."

"When he wrote me he was convinced our engagement was a mistake I was furious for a while and, I thought, heartbroken. I emerged from the experience more quickly than I had expected, which fact restored my self-respect. Aunt Ellen, you must have had heaps of experience turning down men who were too conceited to realize that you didn't find them irresistible. What shall I do to make Phil understand that I detest him?"

Ellen Marshall dropped the mass of knitted navy wool into her lap and regarded her niece over the tops of pale shell-rimmed spectacles.

"There have been times, Jessamine, when you appeared to enjoy the company of this 'pest,' " she reminded dryly. "For a while I was very, very anxious. I tried to think up a way to make you realize where you were drifting."

"I'm sorry. I admit that during the month after I came to Karrisbrooke I had a silly urge to prove to Claire and to Phil that I wasn't too unattractive, she was so maddeningly smug. I'm ashamed of myself. I've grown up considerably since then. It's a pity that a mirror hasn't been invented that would reflect one's inner self, show the business one's mind or spirit is about—or is it? I'd hate to face what I'm thinking of that couple this minute. Even if I wanted to re-love Phil—I don't, I *do not*—the fact that he has a wife would hold me back. I have some principle, I hope."

"The anchor called principle has been known to drag in a hard blow of love—or passion. Philip Maury has a wife, and a tricky and unscrupulous one. She resents his previous engagement. Don't forget that, Jessamine."

"I haven't forgotten her for a minute, she wouldn't let me if I wanted to. It's a mess. As he is our neighbor it would look queer if we never invited him here, refused to admit him if he came. The county would buzz like bees preparing to swarm from the hive." She frowned at the fire. "Of course I can go home, but I'd hate like the dickens to be driven away from this place I love by a selfish, unscrupulous man whose intelligence is so coated with conceit that he won't believe I mean what I say."

"Do you love Karrisbrooke, Jessamine?"

"I adore every inch if it, Aunt Ellen. As a boy, Phil was selfish. Now that he's a man his bump of fairness is a dent. He had fine people behind him, why hasn't he more—more—call it character for want of a better word?"

"First, he has had too little to do. Not that there haven't been ways he could have relieved me of care at the mills. There has been plenty of worth-while work in this country that needed doing, but he couldn't see it that way; even now, he won't co-operate to the extent of approving defense preparations. Second, his marriage was unfortunate. With his temperament I wonder he has lived with Claire as long as he has. I can understand your attraction for him. You have found yourself, have developed an inner confidence, a soul, and a gay courage that will carry you through inevitable periods of strain and heartbreak. He has sufficient character left to recognize and admire that."

Jessamine blinked suddenly wet lashes and swallowed the lump in her throat.

"Thank you, Aunt Ellen."

"Thirdly," Ellen Marshall went on as if there had been no emotional interruption, "Phil has thrown everything he has into that racing-stable and lost it. I wonder sometimes why the financier who was Claire's guardian until she married doesn't check up on her property to make sure her husband hasn't helped himself to some of it."

"You can't mean that Phil would use hers? That he hasn't any money?"

"I should have excepted the income from his half-ownership in the cotton mills. He still has that. He would have disposed of his share for cash—cash is what he wants—long ago if he'd had his way, but in his will Maury Senior made my consent obligatory before his son can sell his holdings. I won't permit him to throw those on the junk-heap; I had too high a regard for his grandfather and father to allow their descendant to become a pauper or dependent on a wife. Few men can stand that last test without becoming either supine or bitter. Claire wouldn't make his life's walk easy under those conditions. I don't know why I should care. A stretch of rough going would do him good, but, much as I would like to buy him out and get rid of his annoying interference, I have a sense of responsibility as to his welfare."

She tapped the tips of the long, jeweled fingers of her right hand on the chair-arm before she added:—

"Have you thought that the flame of Philip Maury's ardor for you, Jessamine, may have been rekindled by his expectancy that you will be my sole heir now that young Todd has left us? Karrisbrooke and River Farm lands joined by marriage would make an impressive estate. I felt that aim was partly behind his first proposal—though you were very attractive. He should be reminded that counting on an inheritance is as futile as counting chickens before they've hatched."

The amused cynicism of her voice flashed certain words on the screen of Jessamine's memory.

"If Aunt Ellen intends to leave the man property doubtless her will to that effect already has been made," her mother had written. Had it? Would Barry Collins—

"M's Ellen." Sam spoke from the doorway. "Major Trent, he phoned he wouldn't be here for dinner. 'Portant business keepin' him, Ah reckon."

"You're breathless, Sam. The Major hasn't met with an accident, has he?"

"No, marm. M's Ellen, don't yo' go bein' scared 'bout him. That Major he kin take care of hisself." The butler indicated by a toothy grin and rolling eyes the absurdity of the question. "Ah reckon he jes' dinin' wid the widow lady, cause he phoned from de Inn." The tea equipment rattled as he picked up the laden tray. "Sho' nuff, Ah almos' forget to tell you, M's Jess, dat Lieut'nant frien' of yo's is waitin' in de library fo' yo'."

Jessamine, who had been curiously observing the shakiness of Sam's usually steady hands, his poorly repressed excitement, sprang to her feet.

"Johnny here? Excuse me, will you, Aunt Ellen?"

"Jessamine." Ellen Marshall's voice stopped her on the threshold. "Why not marry this Johnny? That would settle the problem of our philandering neighbor very nicely."

Marry Johnny! Jess remembered the postscript in her mother's letter, remembered her very words, "I am sure Aunt Ellen will like Johnny." Were the two women conspiring to bring about the marriage? It had been difficult enough to combat the wishes of her mother, but if Ellen Marshall joined with her—

"We're all marionettes danglin' from strings which she manipulates," Phil had said.

"If you don't watch your step you'll be Mrs. John Gordon, Junior, before you know it," Jess warned Jess as she crossed the hall.

XI

As she started down the circular stairway Jessamine saw Johnny Gordon slip into the library. Curious. Sam had said he was waiting for her there. Not like him to be wandering around a strange house. Now that she thought of it, he hadn't been inside Karrisbrooke before. The few times he had been on leave and had come to take her out she had met him at the front steps to save his precious time. He wasn't an inquisitive person, but there had been something furtive in the way he had gum-shoed into the room, as if afraid of being seen in the hall.

She entered the many-windowed, lamp-lighted library with its huge fireplace at one end, a piano, a deep-seated sofa and a variety of old-blue and raspberry brocaded chairs of inviting shapes. He was looking up at the portrait of the first North Carolina Marshall hung above the carved mahogany mantel, painted in the manner of Van Dyck's portrait of Robert Rich, the Earl of Warwick.

"Great stuff, isn't it?" he approved over his shoulder. "I'll bet that old fella ruled his plantation with an iron hand." He turned.

"Hey, Grandmamma! What big eyes you've got!"

"My eyes are big with surprise at seeing you. Stop chuckling, Johnny, and tell me how you managed to get away from Camp at this time of day. You haven't gone AWOL, have you?"

"I have not. I've been on an errand for G.H.Q. Having a few extra minutes, decided I'd take a look-see to make sure you were safe and okay."

She curbed the impulse to ask why he had been prowling in the hall when Sam had shown him into the library. Silly to be suspicious of Johnny Gordon. It was natural for him to want to see the interior of one of the few genuine plantation homes which had been preserved, wasn't it?

"Why shouldn't I be okay, Johnny?" she asked gaily. "Your hectic imagination hadn't pictured me as kidnaped, had it? No young Lochinvar will ride out of the West to fling me across his saddle, worse luck."

" 'Worse luck'? That's you. Boy, I bet you'd eat up that sort of adventure, you've never known what fear is. Cool and tough would be your line in a crisis. Sit on that sofa. All set? I want to talk to you. You're a knock-out in that white-and-black rig against the pale blue brocade."

He drew up a straight-back chair done in faded raspberry and faced her.

"Where was I when sidetracked by your smart get-up? I have it. I—"

"Is this a preview of a court-martial, Lieutenant? You've gone serious as a Judge Advocate. With what crime is the trembling prisoner charged?"

"Cut out the merry quips, Jess. I am serious and my reason for coming wasn't entirely to make sure you were safe. Half an hour ago I met Collins and his man Friday—Peckett to you—headed this way, and I shot along to be sure they weren't en route to annoy you."

"Annoy *me!* Why should they? There are several places on this road to which they might be going, the Maury stables beyond here for instance. Are you by any chance collecting material for a movie, Lieutenant?"

"Go ahead, giggle. All right with me, only remember, 'He laughs best who laughs last.' "

"Your voice gives me the shivers. Not pinch-hitting for the lady Cassandra, are you, Johnny?"

"I'm not prophesying, I'm just telling you. Have you ever encouraged Barry Collins to believe you will marry him?"

"Marry him! *Never!* Didn't I tell you the other day I didn't like him?"

"Don't be so explosive. Remember the old adage, 'Walls have ears.' Here's a choice tidbit of news. Your aunt's superintendent thinks he has the aforementioned marriage all sewed up; in short, he has been sufficiently sure of it to borrow money on the prospect from Peckett."

"Johnny! My imagination wasn't so screwy after all."

She told him that her mother's letter had occasioned her own suspicion that Collins might plan to marry her as a means of acquiring Karrisbrooke.

"But I never thought of myself as being put up as collateral."

"Knowing my own reactions to your sweetness and light I wouldn't swear that money is his only reason, Jess, but we won't go into that at present."

"How did you find out? I don't mean about so-called reactions," she corrected hurriedly as his eyes deepened with a look that, figuratively speaking, sent her scurrying to the other side of the street. "I mean the matrimonial scheme of Collins and his man Friday? Has Johnny the Boy Detective emerged from his Rip Van Winkle sleep?"

"Can't go into that. Don't ask questions about any cockeyed move I may make, or repeat to anyone what I have told you this afternoon. Promise?"

Had exploring the lower floor of this house been part of a "cockeyed move"?

"I promise."

She sternly disciplined the urge to inquire if he had answered a wireless from Van Trent's eyes when he had so suddenly left the tearoom at the Inn the afternoon Collins had received the note. No. He had asked her not to question him and she had promised.

"Thanks for the vote of confidence, Jess. There's another thing you can do to help. Keep an eye on that ex-fiancé of yours. He's scraping the bottom of his bank account to meet racing losses. I have a hunch he's up to his ears in the marry-the-boss's-niece scheme."

"Phil Maury! Planning my marriage to Barry Collins! You're crazy. He's been pestering me to—"

"Skip it. Remember anything you say may be used against you."

It was an effort, but she responded to his boyish grin with a laugh.

"Thanks, Johnny, I'll remember."

She rose and slipped her hand under his arm as he stood before her.

"Must you go? If your C.O. can spare you, stay and dine with Aunt Ellen and me, Lieutenant. We'll be alone. We'd love to have you."

"No can do. There may be something to your funny crack about my importance to my Commanding Officer, who knows? War games tonight. If you see a lot of eerie blue lights moving in the woods and along the road you'll know that night blackout troop movements are on." He paused on the threshold. "Speaking of superior officers, is Major Trent still hanging-out here?"

"He is." In spite of her conviction that the two men had met before Mrs. Carter's tea, her voice was as casual as his as she added: "His rooms are there." She indicated a door at the end of the long, broad hall. "They were my cousin Todd's and are the last word in convenience and comfort. Like to see them?"

"Why should I want to see them?"

She would have sworn that a flash of suspicion brightened his dark eyes as they met hers.

"Why snap at the lady, Lieutenant? You've appeared so interested in the Major I thought you might like to see his bailiwick even if you don't know him. I forgot, you did meet him at the Carter tea, didn't you, while you and he were hovering round Claire Maury?"

"You got me wrong. I wasn't hovering. Honey-color blondes are not my dish. Come on to the door and speed the parting guest, will you?"

She went as far as his motorcycle, parked in the

drive. He waited for a plane roaring overhead to pass before he asked:—

"Stepping out tonight?"

"No, thank goodness. I haven't had an evening at home for weeks. I've planned a treat for myself. Reading in bed."

"Is that so?" A quick frown stenciled two deep lines between his brows. He swung up into the seat. Before he started the engine he leaned toward her.

"Don't burn the midnight oil too long, kid. It's bad medicine. Good night."

She puzzled over the frown and "bad medicine" as she leaned back against the white, paneled front door after she had closed it. There had been a hint of melodrama in Johnny's voice, in fact now that she looked back on it, his entire call had smacked of the theater. Was it just his natural bent to dramatize life or did he really know that Collins and Peckett had that incredible scheme up their sleeves? Was there a possibility that he and Van Trent were working together? Had he come to Karrisbrooke to tell the Major what he had told her?

Her eyes traveled to the door near the end of the hall and lingered. Something in the way Johnny Gordon had glanced at it had given her the impression that he knew that door, that he might have entered it before tonight. Sam would know.

She started for the dining room where the butler was busy about the table. Stopped. No. She had promised Johnny that she wouldn't ask questions about any "cockeyed move" he might make. Cross-questioning Sam would be breaking her word.

Hours later, luxuriously braced up in bed with a light above her head perfectly adjusted for reading, with the current best-seller open in her hand, she couldn't concentrate on the story. The actions and reactions of the flesh-and-blood persons in her own real world gave the fictional characters, which in contrast lacked the color and dimension of living people, fierce competition for her attention.

She closed the book. Why try to read when her mind was seething with questions to which she wanted an answer? She thought of Johnny's certainty that Barry Collins was counting on marriage to her to get him out of debt to Peckett. It might be possible, even probable; though her theory that he intended to become master of Karrisbrooke because of a fanatical desire to avenge the whipping his grandfather had received there seemed more logical.

Perhaps Phil Maury's pursuit of her had been merely a blind in case the truth of Collins' scheme ever leaked out. Perhaps he had planned that if he were accused of having had a hand in it, he could come to her and say:—

"You don't believe that, Jess. You know I fell in love with you all over again when you returned to Karrisbrooke, have wanted to marry you as soon as I could get a divorce."

No. Phil Maury's love-making would be entirely by the underground route, he wouldn't come out into the open with a declaration like that no matter of what he was suspected or accused.

Better stop thinking of the mix-up or she'd never get to sleep. Perhaps if she walked about the room she'd stop the merry-go-round of thought. Exercise might prove more effective than counting the proverbial sheep.

She pulled on a green satin lounge-coat, thrust bare feet into gold mules, crossed to the window. In other countries men and women on roofs were watching for bombs, while she could look up at the stars and think only of the majestic beauty of the heavens, of the brilliance of Jupiter which, at the moment, was outshining Mars and Saturn. How long would the sense of security last?

She counted the strokes of the old clock on the stair landing. Twelve. Was Van Trent home? Had the "widow lady" at the Inn kept him away from dinner? Sam had been excited when he had relayed the Major's message. His usually steady hands had been shaky when he removed the tea-tray. Add that to Johnny Gordon's call this afternoon and what did you have? A mystery. It didn't need much gray matter to decide that. He had said he had called just to take a look at her to be sure she was "safe and okay."

· "Safe." It was the word the telephone operator at the mill had used when speaking of her assistant, Goldie Mellor. The girl who "wasn't any too safe," who had too many soldiers in her life, "and it isn't always the doughboys either." . . . Lucy had packed the last part of that sentence with meaning, as if questions would be welcome. Suppose she had inquired who the men were who menaced the girl's safety? What answer would she have received? Would Johnny have been named? Hideous thought. She would stake her life on the certainty that no woman would be endangered by him.

Could she help the drawling Goldie steer clear of rocks? She liked her—admired her quick comprehension of First Aid work. She was a born leader and would make a fine teacher. Silly to think she might advise her. More likely that the girl could give her points on the dangerous rocks and reefs in present-day living. She had had an uneasy feeling, when Lucy Long had confided her doubts as to her assistant's safety, that she might find Barry Collins mixed up in it. A suspicion wholly without ground, because she never had known him to evince the slightest interest in the women workers at the mill. Had she another mystery to face there?

"I don't like mysteries except in fiction," she told herself. "I wish—"

Her eyes focused on the tall box hedge of the tennis court. She drew her hand across them and looked again. Were two figures stealing along in its shadow or had that word "mystery" conjured them in her imagination? They were real. That was the path to—

She swallowed the word, dashed to the enormous wardrobe and collected navy slacks and a dark green pullover. Her satin housecoat fell in a gleaming emerald mass at her feet.

"Those men are moving too furtively not to be up to mischief. They're slinking," she said under her breath as she hurriedly wriggled, zipped and pulled herself into the clothing. Johnny had said that Collins

and Peckett were headed this way. That was hours
ago, idiot. "Perhaps they had waited—or those two
may be going—my word, *that's* an idea."

She slipped into a tweed topcoat and strapped on
an electric wrist-light before she stole stealthily down
the circular stairway to the softly lighted hall. The
house was eerily still. At Trent's door she stopped—
listened. If he answered her knock she would know
he was not one of the persons stealing along the
shrub-border as she had suspected. Okay, so far; better think up an explanation of her presence here at
this hour if he opened the door.

She tapped lightly. Held her breath to listen. Had a
window inside been softly closed or had she imagined
the faint creak? Perhaps Van had entered that way.
She pressed her ear against the door. No sound within. If he were there he would have answered the
second tap.

She gently turned the knob, cautiously entered the
room. Dark as a blackout. The silence sent prickly
chills coasting along her veins. No sound in the bedroom either. She flashed her light from object to
object: A chair overturned. A rug rolled up as if
something had been dragged over it. The desk . . .

"My wor—" She swallowed the rest of the startled
exclamation. The creak of a closing window had not
been imagined. Someone had been in this room who
didn't belong here.

Teeth set sharply in her lips to steady them, she
tiptoed toward the bedroom. The door was open. No
one there. Where was Van? Had he been dragged
across the floor and out the window one side of which
was swinging open?

She turned quickly, her foot struck something and
sent it sliding across the rug. She followed it with the
light from her flash. Walked toward it and looked
down. At her feet lay a khaki cigarette case with a
band of air-force blue, bordered with gold braid
across one corner—and in the center a pair of silver
wings.

"Advising is my job," He picked up the o

XII

General Carson tilted back in the swivel-chair behind his desk at Camp Headquarters. A ray of late afternoon sunlight slanted through a window and set the two silver stars on his right shoulder glistening. He fitted the tips of his long fingers together and spoke to the officer seated opposite.

"You were ordered to drop in on Karrisbrooke for a purpose, Major Trent." He was surprisingly boyish when he grinned. "I didn't expect you to take my suggestion seriously, that it would be all to the good if you broke a leg—but the fracture of your ankle saved me a lot of trouble."

"I wish I could feel that it had saved Miss Marshall trouble, General. For the first three weeks that household had me pretty much on its mind."

"It was her idea to have you come."

"Miss *Ellen's?*"

"You're as surprised as I was when she came here to make the request. My grandfather was one of her beaux, if family legend is to be believed. I was glad as well as curious to see her. I had heard she was a great beauty. It isn't hard to believe that. She came ostensibly to extend the hospitality of her home, and to offer the use of her plantation for war games. Her real object was to confide her suspicion that a troublemaker is at work in her cotton mills and among her field hands. She asked my help in locating the master mind."

"Light is beginning to break, General. I've put in a lot of thought on that order of yours, wondering why the higher-ups were interested in that plantation."

"Haven't been specific before because we wanted you to get your own impressions. It is cruel that an old woman who is working for her country should be

menaced by treachery. As her mills are pouring out
stuff for defense I agreed to go all out to help her.
Also, if there is a subversive element in the neighborhood, it might menace the Camp. So, you see, I am
doubly bound to follow up her request.

"She and I arranged that if I were to send an
aviation officer, mentally equipped to observe any
irregularities on her plantation or in her mills, a
bachelor, of good family—she bore down hard on
those requirements—to her with a letter of introduction there would be no suspicion that he had come for
a purpose and she would make him so welcome that
he would regard the place as a second home." He
chuckled. "Bailing out over Karrisbrooke was your
brilliant scheme. With your combined sense of drama
you two ought to be writing movies for Hollywood."

"Then that's what she meant when she said:—

" 'Only natural that a man of your intelligence
would want to occupy his time learning something of
the world into which accident—possibly Fate in the
guise of a parachute—had dropped him.' "

"Sounds like her. She's a grand person. I could use
her on my staff. She would be the answer to the
voter's prayer in Congress. The report you have made
confirms me in my belief that I picked the right man
when I selected a one-time efficiency engineer for the
job. The discovery you have reported may bear directly on the information I'm after. If it doesn't affect
Miss Marshall's plantations or mills, drop it. We'll let
the civil authorities handle it. It is not for us. Only we
three know why you have been kept at Karrisbrooke
instead of being hospitalized. If deviltry is going on
among Ellen Marshall's employees, it's your job to
uncover it."

"Sherlock Holmes stuff never has been much in my
line, General, but I'll do my best."

"Remember that the slightest irregularity in a man's
conduct, or a woman's for that matter these hectic
days, will bear following up. That's all. Carry on,
Major."

When the General spoke you knew right off why he
had risen from shavetail to his present high office. He

had the dignity and knowledge required for his rank, he had also a quality not so often found in the seats of the military mighty, an understanding heart; the sympathetic reference to Ellen Marshall had shown that.

Late that evening as Vance Trent sat in a deep chair on the gallery outside his room at Karrisbrooke, he went over, word by word, the conversation with General Carson. It was incredible that Ellen Marshall would appeal to anyone for help to combat trouble among the mill and field hands. She was such a despotic—if just—employer. It didn't make sense. Perhaps it didn't, but for what other reason would she have wanted an aviation officer—"bachelor, of good family"—to drop in at Karrisbrooke? Perhaps time would tell if she didn't.

He glanced at the illuminated dial of his watch. Quarter before twelve. Almost zero hour. Time he and Sam were on the move. It was a beautiful night with a slight touch of frost in the fragrant air. Across the heavens, stars were wheeling and twinkling. Blue lights were flashing on the highway where the troops were practising blackout movements. For weeks now army had maneuvered against army in a 10,-000-square-mile tract. Infantry had chased enemy infantry across fields and through woods. Antiaircraft had theoretically spat at planes; paratroopers had dropped to blow up bridges theoretically. Before long the cease-firing command would be given, the war games would be over, troops would be withdrawn and the Carolinas would relax to normal.

Orders to proceed to the Special Assignments Section ought to be forthcoming soon. It was a blow to leave the boys he had trained, he had hoped to be ordered to active service with them, but a man's preferences didn't count these days, he served where he could help most, and there was no question that help in production was a crying need. If war really came he might be given the command of paratroops. Meanwhile, until definite instructions as to his transfer arrived he was to remain at Karrisbrooke. He had been told there was a job to be done there. He had long ago suspected who was the "troublemaker." He was all set tonight to make his first try at uncovering him.

Was it only three weeks since he had met Gus Peckett at the tobacco warehouse? This minute, as clearly as if flashed on a screen, he could see the guy drawing his tongue across his lips as if anticipating a savory morsel. Jess had declared she was sure he wasn't a pinhooker, that Barry Collins wouldn't stand for that no matter how much he was afraid of a man.

Collins was afraid of Peckett. The fact had been evident the moment that plump hand had been laid on the superintendent's shoulder. His fear had been revealed by the wince in his gray-green eyes, by his hesitancy in performing the introduction to Jess when it had been demanded, by his expression at the tea last week when he opened the note and departed in a hurry. Add all that to the suspicion of Jess and of her mother, that Collins was laying his plans to become master of Karrisbrooke, and you had something worth watching. Yet, even in the present melodramatic age, the scheme seemed too melodramatic to believe.

"Ready, suh," the cautious announcement came from the room behind him. He had needed help. Sure of the butler's loyalty, he had confided part of his plan to him.

"Coast clear, Sam?"

"Sho' nuff, suh. Them soldiers done stop fightin', Ah reckon. No more blue lights. All the folks in the house is in their beds. M's Jess, she's home t'night too, fo' a wonder. Pink's akeepin' watch that Callie or none of the maids don't come wanderin' roun' to git in our way, an' Ah see lights down by de ole wharf."

"Okay. I'll sit here a few minutes longer. We'd better leave by the window. We might be heard passing through the hall."

"Yes, suh. Is yo' sho' yo' foot kin stan' it? There's rough walkin' ahead, Ah reckon."

"I can take it. Have everything ready so we can get a move on quickly."

He waited for a few seconds, rose and tossed the cigarette stub over the railing. For the benefit of a possible eavesdropper, he stretched his arms above his head, took a long breath of the crisp box-scented air, and yawned prodigiously. That accomplished he looked and listened.

Sam was right. The blue flashlights had ceased. The young moon had retired early. The stars were mere pricks of gold behind the thin clouds now stealing across the sky. The blackout was complete. The soldiers of both armies were bedded down in the woods. From all visible signs, the world was asleep.

He entered the lighted room. Sam closed the long windows and drew the rose-spattered chintz hangings across them as he had drawn them every night for weeks. His heavy-veined hands weren't quite steady, his black face glistened with sweat, the pupils of his eyes seemed enormous in their white setting. He wore a shabby khaki sweater, blue denim slacks and knee-high rubber boots.

"Anyone call this afternoon, Sam?"

"Dat Lieut'nant frien' ob M's Jess done come here at teatime, Major. Ah showed him in the lib'ary to wait while Ah tells M's Jess he's here, but he didn't stay put, no suh. Ah see him awalkin' through the hall as though he was alookin' for a place to hide, he sure did, Major. 'Twas the second time Ah caught him prowlin'. Yo' sho' he's honest, suh?"

"Sure. Sure." Why the dickens had Johnny Gordon been prowling round here?

"Did Miss Jess see the Lieutenant, Sam?"

"Yes, suh, an' Ah reckon from somethin' he say to me he mighty anxious to see her. Yo' got on dem clothes and galoshes Ah brung yo', Major Trent?"

"Yes. The black pull-on and pants you borrowed for me, Sam, fit me like the paper on the wall. If we should meet any moths in our safari they'll beat it when they get a sniff of naphtha-balls. Where'd you get the clothes or shouldn't I ask?" Trent thrust an electric torch and a tear-gas grenade into the pockets of his flying coat before he put it on.

"They belonged to young Marse Todd, suh. M's Ellen, she done give mos' of his things away, but she kep' a few. Ah reckoned as how you wus workin' to help her this night she'd be willin' fer you's to have his cloes to do it in, sho' nuff, but you'd said 'hush-hush,' so ob course Ah couldn't ask her. We better git goin', suh." He picked up a huge horsewhip.

"Where did you snitch that implement of torture, Sam? Gives me the heebie-jeebies just to look at it."

"This ain't no im-plement, suh. This am a whip." He took a tighter hold of the heavy handle and snapped the long, cruel lash till it curled and writhed on the rug like a sinister black snake. "Ah foun' it in the ol' stable when Ah was huntin' for dese boots Ah'm wearin' an' Ah reckoned as how it might come in kinder useful-like so long's yo' wasn't takin' a gun."

"No guns in this party. Go on, Sam."

He followed the butler's cautious lead out the long window, close around the house, along a path in the shadow of a tall box hedge, past the offices and stables.

"This a way, suh." Sam slipped into the old smoke-house, paused to listen before he flashed a dim light on a flight of stairs. Trent followed him down, across what seemed to be a cellar, to a heavy door with an iron bar.

"The do' to the Smugglers' Passage. It done lead to the ol' plantation wharf at de ribber, where we's agoin', suh."

The hushed Negro voice, the glitter of enormous eyes in the faint light, the man's tense excitement, the weird surroundings, started the prickles at the roots of Trent's hair.

"Sam, speak. Don't whisper."

"'Tain't safe, suh. W'en we gits the odder side ob this do' we mustn't even whisper. 'Twould echo lak a ghost amoanin', sho' nuff. Our feets won't mak' no sounds in these rubber boots, Ah reckon. Yo' close de do' soft behin' yo' after yo' comes tru'. Ready? Ah's aimin' to go first."

He lifted the iron bar. The door swung open on its rusty hinges soundlessly. Sam must have been busy with an oilcan, Trent decided, as he closed it "soft" behind them.

As he stood in a complete blackout and smelled the

dank, damp air, for one breathless instant he wondered if Sam were a traitor, if he had brought him here to trap him and prevent him from following the clue he was sure he had unearthed. Common sense routed suspicion. It was for the protection of Miss Ellen they had embarked on the expedition and the Lord didn't make humans more loyal than this colored servant.

The eerie stillness beat against his ears as he followed close at the heels of the shadowy form ahead. It gave a curious sense of unreality, as if Time had stopped.

Something brushed against his left foot. He swallowed a startled exclamation. Rats? A small, cold tremor of fear struck at the pit of his stomach. It was the same sensation he had experienced the first time he bailed out from a plane. It had lasted till the chute streamed out above him and completely filled. He had laughed exultantly then, he remembered. Now, even though the tremor had ceased, he felt no urge to laugh.

Step by cautious step. Hours? The hands on the dial of his wrist watch showed that only five minutes had passed since they had entered the passage. Faint light on another door. Sam's figure a silhouette against it. A faint creak. A key turning. A blast of fresh air. The distant unearthly hoot of a hunter owl. The lap of water. A door closing softly. The Smugglers' Passage was behind them. The old wharf fifty feet downriver.

Trent crept up steps of placed rocks and crouched below the top one. With his eyes just above the level of the ground he could see the mountains looming shadowy and shapeless beyond the dark sheen of the water; the hulk of a forty-foot motorboat at the wharf; figures of men moving back and forth against the dim light unloading casks. The breeze brought the sound of a voice, always the same voice, apparently directing the workers.

One good look at the boss and the rest of his investigation would either be a cinch or he would have to admit that his suspicion was all wet. There was perhaps thirty feet of open space between him and the heavy clumps of bushes that bordered the river. Cross that, work his way toward the wharf and he would be near enough to see and hear.

He pressed the arm of the butler who huddled beside him. Sam's eyes, gleaming like black-and-white glassies in the dim light, met his. He motioned to himself and then toward the boat. The grizzled head shook a violent negative. He whispered close to the man's ear:—

"If I don't find out who's bossing the job we might as well have kept out of this, Sam. The breeze is coming this way. They can't hear me. I'll worm my way to the bushes, then I'll crawl through them. Take my watch." He unclasped the leather strap. "If I'm not back here in half an hour, return to the house and tell ..." Who the dickens was there to tell? Except for Johnny Gordon he was playing a lone hand, and the Lieutenant couldn't be reached at this time of night or morning at Camp. Someone should know—Jess. She wouldn't be panicked.

"If I'm not back in half an hour, hurry to the house, find Miss Jess, if you have to wake her up, tell her what happened, and tell her to phone General Carson and tell him where I am. Do that *only* if I don't come back, understand?"

"Yes, suh. Ah's understand. Ah'll do jes as yo' say, but—Ah reckon yo' shouldn't go, Major Trent. Ef anything should happen to yo', M's Ellen she tak' on somep'n terrible at me fo' lettin' yo' do it, sho' nuff."

"Nothing will happen. Stay at the foot of these steps. Have the passage door wide open, and the key on the inside ready to lock it. I may come back on the run, but don't call. Don't whisper. Take my coat. It's too bulky to crawl in. Cheerio, Sam. Watch my smoke."

"Yo' jest about gone crazy, Ah reckon, Major. You'll be ketched, sho' nuff." Sam's direful prophecy followed him as he wriggled snakewise across the open space. Thirty feet? He'd bet it was nearer thirty miles to the nearest bush. At last. He'd made it without being seen.

Now to crawl through the undergrowth. More like a jungle. Lucky the breeze was in his favor. On and on. Slowly. Cautiously. Each time he brushed a twig it snapped like a cannon cracker in action. At last—near enough to see that the faces of the men who were unloading the boat were black. They were rolling casks toward the shadow of a cypress tree from which came the directing voice. Unless he got a good look at the owner of that voice his suspicions wouldn't be worth a copper cent.

He crawled nearer. Held his breath at each snap of a twig. Gently parted a bush and looked through. Swore softly under his breath.

The boss was colored. That fact completely washed up his certainty that Peckett would be masterminding the job he had been tipped-off to get a line on tonight, and that behind the slippery Gus, so far behind he would be but a shadow, he would find Collins. Instead he had turned up a bunch of Negroes running whatever illegal enterprise this was. With the elimination of Peckett and Collins went the threat to Miss Ellen's business. As the General had said, this was a matter for the civil authorities to handle, not the army.

Time to back out, with not a minute to lose. Too late. The boss was coming toward him in a hurry. Had a sound in the bushes roused suspicion that a snooper was near? He crouched motionless. Held his breath. The man was near enough now for him to see—

Boy, oh boy!—to see a "slinkin' eye," a red tongue drawn over lips. Peckett! Peckett in blackface!

"Okay, boys. You've got the whisky off; get this stuff on and be quick about it." Peckett's voice.

Vance Trent relaxed. Safe for the present. He strained his eyes to see, almost cracked his eardrums to listen. Now that his eyes had been opened he realized the crew now loading the boat were white men blackened. He sniffed the air.

"Good Lord—gas!" he said under his breath. "Gas, tanks of it. Where is it going?" Undoubtedly whisky was in the casks brought ashore, but why such a quantity of gas going out?

He had the information he had come for and more. Now to make his getaway, quick. He moved backward. Inch by cautious inch, it seemed for miles ... It wasn't so easy as going forward had been. Safe so far ... He peered through the bushes. Must be about opposite the steps to the Smugglers' Passage. He'd remain motionless for a few minutes before he crawled across—Thunderation! Why did that branch have to crack like the report of a pistol? That did it! A voice warned:—

"A snooper! Get him, fellas! There he goes!" Peckett's voice. No oil in it now. The order cut through the air like a whiplash.

Bent double, Trent crashed through the tall bushes. Leaped over short ones. A pack of human hounds in full cry at his heels. Thirty feet of open space to cover between the last bush and the steps. Steps! He mustn't go near those. Too much of a give-away.

A hand grabbed his sweater as he broke from cover. He jerked free and ran. His ankle twisted. He'd forgotten it. Was it going back on him? He shook off another clutch. No matter what happened, he mustn't turn, he must *not* limp. If they suspected who he was, he couldn't follow up what he had discovered tonight. There was nothing about his black trousers and pullover to betray him.

"We got him!"

The exultant shout was so close it made his ears ring. Something flew past his ear. Something that stopped his pursuers and set them gasping, snorting. Something that filled his own eyes with smarting tears. That did it. They couldn't see where he went. He dashed for the steps, tumbled down, leaned against the door Sam had locked behind him.

"Wh-what—ever made y-you think of that tear gas grenade, Sam?" he gasped.

"Ah—Ah aimed to git out wif my whip, an'—an' den M's Jess, she said—"

"Who?" He stared unbelievingly at the girl whose face shone ghostly white in the dim light. "Where did you come from, Angel?"

"I'm r-real," she whispered. "I saw you and Sam

steal out, suspected where you'd gone, and followed. Didn't you say we were partners?"

"In a way, but not this way. I told Sam that if I didn't return, to tell you to phone a message; but I didn't want you here. After this, stop, look, listen before you mix into investigations to which you're not invited." Fear of what might happen to her if it became known she had hurled the gas grenade roughened his low voice.

"That's gratitude—plus. Perhaps I'd better not tell you I heard someone on the gallery outside your room, that I stole down, tapped on your door, and when you didn't answer, went in. Perhaps it will be 'mixing in' to tell you that the window in your bedroom was swinging open—"

"The bedroom window! That's a break! Had the visitor come in the front he would have run into Sam and me sneaking out. Go on. What else did you find?"

"The papers in your desk scattered as if someone had gone through the pigeonholes and drawers in a hurry."

"In my desk? What would anyone want there? Let's get back to the house quick, Angel, and take a look."

"Be keerful w'en yo's go in, don' wake up M's Ellen. She's a pow'ful light sleeper," Sam warned. They nodded comprehension, followed him through the dim passage and up the steps into a star-spangled world.

He entered the dimly lighted hall at Karrisbrooke first, the lash of the great whip trailing behind him. Trent was reminded of the long tail of the devil as he had seen pictures of him, complete with horns and red-hot trident.

They stood together listening. The house was full of little, eerie sounds; a vine tapping at a windowpane, a stairboard creaking, even the old clock on the landing seemed to hush its tick as if holding its breath in expectancy. Sam whispered:—

"Ah's got sandwiches ready, M's Jess, fo'—"

"What's going on here?"

Instinctively Trent flung his arm about Jessamine as

he looked up at the woman in a purple lounge-coat standing in the middle of the stairway. She wasn't looking at him. Her eyes, wide with amazement, were staring at the butler. Emotion working below the surface crumpled the usually firm contour of her face into the tragic droop of old age.

She swayed. Trent started foward. She shook her head, lifted her chin, gripped the banister and drew herself up, straight and tall.

"Where—where did you get that—that *thing* in your hand, Sam?" Her voice—low, hoarse as it was— echoed through the hall.

"This, M's Ellen? This thing am a whip." The butler snapped the long cruel lash in demonstration. "Ah foun' it in de ol' stable."

"It must be—it must be—" Her eyes were burning coals in her white face as she held out her hand.

"Give it to me. I'm glad you found it, Sam. Who knows but that it may *again* prove useful?"

XIII

Days passed. Life at Karrisbrooke had gone on as usual to the accompaniment of world news of fighting, killing, the tragic waste of life and property; proposition after proposition for a basis for settlement of peace in the Pacific between the United States and Japan. Men from the Camps came and went between war games, sometimes officers, sometimes selectees and enlisted men. Ellen Marshall made them welcome. In all the time since, she had never referred to that early morning when she had stared at Sam snapping that cruel lash in the hall. The haggard lines which ravaged her face had betrayed the fact that she recognized it as the whip with which her father had driven away her lover.

Strange that after all these years it should have

been found in the old stable, curious how much longer things lasted than people, Jess thought, as perched
on top of the brick wall of the garden-piazza she
wriggled her dance-weary feet free and dangled the
silver and violet sandals from her toes. Aunt Ellen's
farewell party tonight for the officers scheduled soon
to return to their camps in the North would have
been perfect even if that cocky three-quarters moon
weren't hung in the sky to make it super. There'll be
no lingering in the "no man's land between falling
hard for the girl and proposal" in this light. The men
will drop like divers after a championship-belt and
like it, she told herself.

Warm as spring. So warm that the men guests were
in white dinner jackets. Not much like the last week
of November in New England, her thoughts trooped
on to the accompaniment of the throb and rhythm of
a Viennese waltz that drifted from an open window.

Van Trent would return to Camp tomorrow for
instructions for his new job, he had told her. She had
devoted many half-days to driving him about the
fields, to the tightly chinked tobacco barns, to the
warehouses, even to the cabins of the Negroes. It had
taken every ounce of self-control, if self-control could
be measured by ounces, to keep from asking what he
had discovered at the old wharf; if any of his papers
had been stolen that same night; how and where
Johnny Gordon fitted into the picture, and more than
anything else, if he had heard the incredible story
that Collins had promised Peckett a rake-off when—
not if—he married his employer's niece?

If he wouldn't take her into his confidence she
ought to be too proud to care. She wasn't. She was
unbearably hurt to be shut out. When he left this part
of the country there would be nothing to keep Mrs.
Carter at the Inn. He and she had sat out one dance
after another tonight. Except that his uniform carried
an insignia he might be any civilian in white dinner
clothes.

Would his efficiency recommendations which she
herself had so carefully typed really increase production, Ellen Marshall's income, and, automatically, the

amount of her taxes? Unobtrusively, Barry Collins had attempted to block his investigation at every point possible, but the Major had kept on with the relentlessness of a Juggernaut. She suspected that her aunt's superintendent had been implicated in the wharf episode, but she might as well have tried to elicit information from a stone wall as from Van Trent. He had expertly parried her not too well camouflaged inquiries.

A hand on her shoulder startled her back to the present.

"At last. Victory perches on my banner. The lost is found," Phil Maury declared dramatically. Moonlight turned his white coat to silver, accentuated the sheen of his brown hair, the hard brilliance of his eyes. "In that rhinestone-spattered violet frock you look like a ghost caught in the dew. M's Ellen was just about to get out a search warrant for you. Hidin' from me, honey-chile? You've been avoidin' me lately and I don't like it."

Warned by the caressing note in his voice she hurriedly retrieved her sandals and slipped from the wall to her feet.

"If you call perching here in the full light of that gorgeous moon 'hiding,' then I was. I'll dash in and report to Aunt Ellen before she sends an M.P. after me."

"Oh, no, you don't give me the slip this time." He gripped her shoulders. "I don't like the way you've given me the go-by for the army, sweetness. Do you think I can't see that Trent is making a play for you? Just another poor man trying to marry an heiress. A Major's pay in comparison with what you will inherit one day is mere chicken feed."

"Is my possible inheritance the reason you are *again* trying to make me love you, Phil? You are, aren't you, or am I wrong?"

"Trying to *make* you! I know you love me. I don't blame you for being peeved that I let you down, it was a brainstorm, that's all. If you're afraid of Claire I can take care of that." His arm closed around her shoulders, his feet came down hard on the toes of her sandals, one hand tipped up her chin.

"No chance of spiking me this time, honey—"

"Phil! *Don't* kiss me! *Don't!*"

"Just a minute, Maury." A hand gripped his collar, another hand grabbed the seat of his trousers. A crash indicated that he had landed among the shrubs on the other side of the terrace wall. An arm went round Jess's shoulders, lips pressed hers, just as a voice shrilled:—

"My stars, Barry, this is the third twosome we've interrupted. Must be the moon. Why, it's my husband and—"

Van Trent released the angrily speechless girl and thrust his hands hard into his coat pockets. His eyes blazed in his colorless face. He laughed:—

"Wrong this time, Claire."

"You, *Van!* I've never seen you in white before. I was sure it was Phil. I declare, it's lucky for Jess you spoke when you did. I'm about fed-up with her tryin' to get my husband away from me. I was goin' to shout, 'Come and see—' "

"Be quiet, Claire. I haven't the slightest intention of trying to get your husband. I—"

"Oh, yes you have, Jessamine Ramsay. Barry's noticed it too, haven't you, Barry? You've never forgiven him for throwin' you over for me. My stars, I believe it was Phil kissin' you, that Van's lyin' now, to protect you. I—"

"Don't be silly, Claire. Why shouldn't I want to kiss Jess? Isn't she lovely enough tonight to set a man on fire? I'm neither wood nor stone. Run along, take Collins with you, and for Pete's sake don't break up any *more* twosomes or you'll be poison-at-a-ball forever after."

"Oh, we're going. I'll tell Phil you're just foolin' him while you're carryin' on with Vance Trent, Jessamine Ramsay. I'll tell Helen Carter that you are double-crossin' her, Van dear. Come on, Barry, don't stand there like a dummy. You look as bowled over as if she had been encouragin' you too, and you've told me times enough that she isn't your type."

"Claire! Stop!" Jessamine started after them. A hand caught her shoulder and drew her back into the shadow of the vines.

"Don't spoil it, Angel. That was a close shave for you. Jealousy has upset Claire's mental balance temporarily. In another moment she would have sown the seeds of a grim little scandal it would take you many moons to live down."

The eyes that flashed to his burned with anger behind tears.

"I'm so mad I could cry. *Now* do you think she's merely a disappointed, frustrated woman tortured by her husband and me? *Now,* will you admit that Claire Maury is a vixen?"

"Take it easy, Angel. Remember the conversation Becky overheard and reported? Claire believes that Maury is planning to divorce her and marry you and—you can't get away from the fact that you were once engaged to him."

"Is that silly affair to be held against me all my life? I was young, I came here and met again the boy with whom I played as a child. There's something about a Southern moon and youth and this place and— If you weren't as unimpressionable as that—that brick wall, you'd understand it."

"I understand, all right. I'm not quite the robot you describe, but though I still think you are a lot to blame for what has happened I couldn't let Claire's accusations pass even if that kiss I so gallantly bestowed is likely to wreck my hopes of heaven on earth."

"I'm *not* to blame. I am *not!* Dodging Phil Maury since that evening on the gallery has become a nightmare, like running hard and not getting anywhere; running was your suggestion, remember? If you'd made your theatrical entrance a second sooner you would have heard him accuse me of avoiding him."

"I heard him or I shouldn't have made my 'theatrical' entrance. I heard also your frightened, 'Don't.' That's why I dropped him over the wall. I was standing in the shadow of the vines thinking how exquisite you were in the moonlight—there's romance for you—

and when you struggled in his arms it was my cue for interference. We'd better get out of this quick. After Maury brushes himself off he's likely to come back to settle his score with me and I don't want a row on Miss Ellen's piazza. Where's your Lieutenant tonight?"

"If you mean Johnny Gordon, he's on M.P. duty and he isn't my Lieutenant."

"My mistake. As he isn't here to look after you I will. Come inside. Shall we dance?"

"You shouldn't with that foot. You hurt it the night at the old wharf. You'll never get it strong if—"

"Stop talking and come."

They joined in the Conga, snaked the length of the long white-and-gold ballroom with its domed ceiling abloom with rosy cupids and its gilt-railed balcony where the musicians, eyes sparkling, white teeth gleaming in their black faces, rattled the gourds, thumped the drums, fiddled and crooned; past the great fireplace set in Carrara marble. The lime-green draperies at the French windows repeated the color of the satin coat of the ruddy-faced, peruked Marshall in the gilt-framed portrait above the mantel. One-two-three-kick, one-two-three-kick. Back down the room.

"You're a marvelous dancer," she conceded as they stopped at the door to the hall.

"You're not bad, yourself. I want to talk to you. Come to the library. Quick, before someone asks you to dance. Miss Ellen said it was not open to guests."

"Aren't you a guest?" she countered in an attempt to escape being alone with him. Even though he had come valiantly to her rescue he had admitted that he still considered her to blame for the second impassioned tableau with Phil he had interrupted.

"Tonight I'm still family. Come."

He closed the door softly behind them as they entered the library, fragrant with the scent of yellow roses. Perched on the corner of the large flat desk he lighted a cigarette. Jessamine came so close that her violet frock brushed his knee.

"You're still burning with anger, at Phil—perhaps at me, aren't you? Your eyes are on fire and your face is white. As a fighter you're a natural. I'll wager your family coat of arms has two doubled fists rampant." She cloaked the unsteadiness of her voice with an attempt at gaiety.

"I'm glad you can laugh about it. I can't. Do you realize that your eyes are only a shade darker than that dress you're wearing?"

"Stop evading. You still think I like to have Phil kiss me, don't you?"

"Trust you to get telepathic impressions."

"That means you do think so. I *don't*. I loathe it."

His shrug expressed amused unbelief.

"Then why permit it the second time—my mistake, it may be the third or thirteenth."

"It was not the thirteenth—you *know* it. He is so strong—he caught me and held down my feet with his. I—I couldn't spike him with my heel. I don't for the life of me know why I'm explaining to you. Why do I care if you think I enjoy being kissed like—like that?"

He caught her hands and drew her an infinitesimal degree closer.

"Listen to me—Angel. Even a heel like Maury doesn't kiss a girl as he kissed you unless he has had some encouragement. I haven't forgotten your eyes and smile that afternoon on the garden piazza when you said, 'I'll save the supper dance for you as *usual*, Phil.' You knew you were playing with dynamite. If a girl to whom I'd once been engaged looked and smiled at me like that, I'd kiss her till she was breathless—supposing, of course, I still loved her. Watch your step in future. I can't keep on indefinitely knocking that guy down."

" 'Nobody asked you to, sir, she said.' "

"There are some things a man doesn't have to be asked to do, Angel." He released her hands and slipped from the corner of the desk.

"That wasn't what I brought you here to talk about. Sit in the corner of that huge sofa. Now—" He drew up the straightback chair done in faded raspberry and seated himself facing her.

"I know you've resented my silence about the old

wharf episode but I wouldn't tell you until I had my facts. I have them. Peckett is not interested in the tobacco market—that's a blind. He's doing a little moonshining in the mountains."

"Moonshining. When people are permitted to buy as much whisky as they want anywhere? I don't believe it."

"I *know* it. Remember that Miss Ellen told how Federal agents had raided stills and the amount of stuff they captured? I saw the wily Gus—in black-face—directing the unloading of a boat of it that night. With this part of the state swarming with soldiers he had planned to do a large and lucrative business—*without* a license."

"Did he recognize you?"

"I'm sure he didn't. The tear-gas bomb you hurled blinded the men, they couldn't see where I went. Signs point to the fact that Peckett is uneasy but he doesn't know we've got his number. And he mustn't. Strictly hush-hush again, Angel."

"I understand. Is Barry Collins helping him? You said you knew that Aunt Ellen's superintendent was afraid of Peckett."

"No statement on Collins at present—except that he owes Peckett money."

That confirmed part of Johnny's story of the Collins-Peckett matrimonial deal. If the rest of it were true—

"You're not listening, Angel."

"I am, really I am. Something you said set me to thinking. Go on, please. You were talking about Peckett."

"The genial Gus is also working up antagonism against Miss Ellen among the field hands. There's a potential market for his brew there, too."

"He's wasting his time. The workers adore her. No one can smash their loyalty to her. She's not like some of the new-type employers who have come from the North who do not know where or how their workers live. She knows every one by name, whether they live in unpainted clapboard houses or in chinked log cabins. There are no tumble-down shacks on her estate. Each home has its gardens, its chickens and its high-grade cow. Showing them how to make the most of these products is where I come in, backed to the limit by Aunt Ellen."

"You're a loyal soul, aren't you?"

"I hope so. To me loyalty is one of the most desirable of human traits. You've forgotten to explain about the rifling of your desk that night. Were any of your papers stolen?"

"Yes. The efficiency notes you had typed. Fortunately the carbon copies weren't taken. It stumps me why anyone would be interested enough to steal them, unless it would be to Collins' advantage to block the improvements I suggested and he bribed someone to snitch them. It must have been a person who had a way of knowing I wouldn't be in my room."

For one horrible, disloyal instant she wondered if Johnny had taken those papers. She had told him the Major would not be there for dinner. His cigarette case had been on the floor. Ever since she found it she had striven to confute and annihilate the nagging suspicion, to rout it by bringing up shock troops of reason. Why should he sneak into Van Trent's room? Wasn't she sure he was working *with* him, not against him?

"You heard what I said, Angel?"

"Yes. I was thinking that a lot is happening which stumps the experts. Have you finished your efficiency check-up?"

"I have handed in my report to Miss Ellen. I'm going North for a week. She wants me to return to Karrisbrooke to advise her on changes she is planning. All right with you if I come?"

"Of course. She is so eager to help the Government in every way possible that she has called a conference for tomorrow morning of the four managers who supervise all planting operations. Each has his separate fields for which he's held responsible. She has planned to devote a large area to raising food." She rose. "Now that our business conference is over, we'd better return to the party and please, please keep out of Phil's way if he comes back."

"I will. He can settle with me anywhere away from this place. Not here." He caught her hands and drew her nearer. "Now that I've come across with the result of my sleuthing, how do I stand with you?"

"Okay! Double okay." Her eyes were the purple blue of the sea, sparkling with laughter. "If that is all you have to report to your assistant, Charlie Chan, I'll return to Aunt Ellen's guests."

"It isn't all I have to say, Angel. Quote, 'There's something about a Southern moon and this place,' end quote. I—" His arms closed round her. "You're the very sweetest thing in the world," he whispered and pressed his lips hard on hers.

With all her strength she pushed him away. Her eyes burned unbearably, fury choked her for an instant before she slapped his cheek hard with the palm of her hand.

"It's an old Ramsay custom, Major. Sorry to appear so rough but I really can't allow you to think that I've given *you* encouragement."

His face was colorless except for a brilliant spot of red on his left cheek, his eyes burned down into her heart which was shaking her with its hard thump, thump.

"You can do better than that, I'm sure, if you put your whole mind on it. So can I—I'm referring to my kiss."

"You said when you kissed me before this evening that it was likely to wreck your hope of heaven on earth. Now you boast that you weren't in top form, a minute ago. What will the lovely Helen say when she hears of the second time? And she will, I won't depend on Claire for that."

"Go ahead, spread that kiss over the front page if you like, but—you'll have to admit it was fun while it lasted." He opened the door with exaggerated courtesy.

"After you, Miss Ramsay."

XIV

In her Nurses' Aide uniform with the insignia of a red cross on a white triangle set in a dark blue circle on the left sleeve of her white blouse and the facing of her cap, Jessamine looked over her class in the old schoolhouse. In front of her was a white porcelain table, behind her on the oak wall a large map showed charts of vitamins and calories. A shaft of afternoon sunlight illumined black faces and yellow faces, wrinkled faces and young faces, dull eyes and eager eyes, mouths slack and vacant, firm and smiling.

There was an unusual number of absentees. Had they lost interest? Had she accomplished anything in the hours she had spent demonstrating with spoon and bowl, flour and egg beater—cooking at the range behind her which, except for being larger—and hotter—was identical with the ones in the homes of her pupils? A violently waved hand brought her attention back to her surroundings. She waited for the deep-seated boom of a bomber overhead to diminish before she asked:—

"What is it, Blossom?"

A young girl, brown as to skin, violently yellow and purple as to clothing, eyes rolling like those of a race horse, pointed to a window.

"Look, Miss Jess. Soldiers! Do yo' think they'll shoot!" Her teeth chattered from fright.

She looked. Across the road infantry was attacking infantry. In the background an antitank gun was fighting it out with several truckloads of men in khaki around a pen of turkeys, whose "gobble, gobble" added to the general pandemonium. How could she expect these girls and women to keep their attention on such a colorless subject—to them—as cooking, with war maneuvers going on so near? She couldn't.

"They won't shoot with real bullets, girls. Don't worry. Listen to me for a few minutes and then I'll dismiss the class." Her voice silenced the rustle of preparations for departure. Heads turned toward her reluctantly.

"I want to ask you to look up the members of the class who are absent today and urge them to come. I am trying to teach you to cook food properly that you may keep your families well and efficient, so that your children will grow up sound and strong. Also, I am trying to make you realize that you will be part of a great home army fighting against the only forces which could ever defeat this country, suffering, weakness, hunger and waste. You won't wear uniforms, but—" A wildly waving hand interrupted. She waited for the high-pitched whir of a pursuit plane to fade out, then asked:—

"What is it, Blossom?"

"Why couldn't we-all wear uniforms like yours, Miss Jess, if we's to be part of the army? That pale-blue dress with the full skirt is somep'in we'd all look fine an' dandy in."

"Why couldn't we, Miss Jess?" an excited chorus echoed.

"A uniform with a thing like that on yo' white blouse sleeve?" a single voice shrilled above the throb of a gigantic motor overhead.

Was "uniforms" the only word of all she had said so earnestly that had stuck in their minds? If so, she was wasting her time and strength.

"The insignia on my sleeve means that I passed an eighty-hours' course required by the Red Cross and the office of Civilian Defense. If you are willing to work and earn it perhaps you can have a uniform. No woman should wear one unless she has earned—and I mean earned—the right to wear it. Class dismissed."

"Good-by, Miss Jess. We'll rustle up the folks that didn't come, we sure will. They'll come w'en they knows they'll wear uniforms. Good-by! Good-by! Howdy, Mr. Collins." The entire class piled out the door giggling and chattering.

A pan she was placing in the wall cupboard clat-

tered to the floor as Jess turned in surprise to regard
the man in riding clothes who had to bend his head
as he stood in the doorway. He never had been here
before. Why now? For some absurd reason his
presence set her heart quick-stepping. Could he have
heard of Van Trent's midnight expedition to the old
wharf, of her presence in the Smugglers' Passage that
same night?

"If you've come for a cooking lesson, Mr. Collins,
you are too late. School's out." The lightness of her
voice was nothing short of a triumph considering the
silly tightness of her throat. "Glad you didn't arrive
earlier or you would have seriously interfered with
my Civilian Defense program which has been difficult to carry on with the planes roaring overhead and
war maneuvers across the road. They have been
diverting enough but no one would have paid attention to me after your arrival looking like the male
romantic menace in a motion picture."

"I appeared just in time to hear that request for
uniforms. You are so irresistible in yours I don't wonder those women are clamoring for them. Why isn't it
a corking idea? Why not make them of tomato-red
cotton with a black frying-pan on the sleeve for insignia?"

"It isn't a subject for a joke."

"I'm not joking. To prove I'm serious I'll finance
those uniforms."

"Thanks a lot, but Aunt Ellen wouldn't permit it."
She slipped into a beige tweed topcoat and took a
key from a hook beside the door. "Time to shut up
shop. After you, Mr. Collins." She waited until he
had preceded her to the porch. "I don't wish to spoil
your nice manners but I prefer to do the locking up."

The battling soldiers had departed, but the turkeys
were still working off their excitement by loud and
continuous gobbles. Voices of girls and women singing
as they crossed a field drifted back:—

> "Oh whah yuh go-in', Angel,
>   Wid yo' wings all dipt in gol'?"

Outside the rustic gate Collins slipped the bridle of a saddled horse over his left arm.

"Isn't that Phil Maury's thoroughbred, Pug?" Her surprised question brought a satisfied smirk to his lips.

"It *was* his. It *is* mine."

"Has Phil sold him? I can't believe it. That horse is entered in the March steeplechase."

"He'll be there just the same."

Johnny had said that Phil was scraping the bottom of his bank account to meet racing losses. He must be hard up to sell one of his best jumpers.

The haunting refrain from the field thinned into silence. The bay kept pace with mincing steps as the man and girl walked along the road which would lead, after sundry devious turns, to Karrisbrooke.

"Why this break-neck pace? Practising for a marathon?" Collins demanded. "I came here to talk with you."

"We can talk and walk, can't we?" She glanced at her wrist watch. "I have a date."

"With Maury or the parachute division of the army?"

She stopped.

"By 'parachute division' I presume you refer to Major Trent. Apparently you haven't heard that he has gone North ahead of the troops. Has it occurred to you, Mr. Collins, that the fact that you are superintendent of Miss Marshall's plantation doesn't carry with it the *privilege* of being impertinent to her niece?"

"My mistake, but it was worth that call-down to see your eyes turn to amethysts with red lights in them. Listen. You won't give me a chance to see you alone. The afternoon of Miss Ellen's dinner to the officers I told you I had something important to say to you, you replied, 'It's a date, and you've given me the brush-off since. I came today to tell you I was infernally uncomfortable the night on the garden-piazza when Claire Maury accused you of encouraging her husband to kiss you."

"Why didn't you say something then? Why stand there like a robot while she lied about me?"

"Did she lie? It happens I saw Trent drop Maury over the wall after he had kissed you."

"Phil *did not* kiss me. Having settled that to my satisfaction, at least, stop blocking the road. I'm in a hurry."

He caught her arm in a grip which hurt.

"You're not going until you hear what I have to say. Don't look at me as if I were one of Miss Ellen's field hands. Hasn't she welcomed me as a guest at Karrisbrooke? The superintendent of a plantation the size of hers is on a social level with—call it a Major in the army—besides, though we were poor, my mother's people were as important in her country as your ancestors were in this. Having settled my social status, I now ask you to marry me."

It was out in the open, his first attempt at getting hold of Karrisbrooke through her and at the same time settling his debt to Peckett. Johnny's story of the bargain between the two men still seemed incredible. He was putting on a good act, his face was curiously colorless, his eyes black with earnestness, his voice hoarse. Why not? He had a lot at stake, hadn't he? She shook her head.

"Thanks, but I couldn't."

"Why?"

"It would take too long to answer that question in detail, so I'll mention the most important reason. I don't love you."

"I could change that."

His cocky assurance frightened her, set her to wondering if he could.

"If you are afraid your aunt won't consent, forget it. I can manage her, too. Watch me. You may have noticed at our recent conferences that she listens to my advice. She knows that things will go my way or I'm through. I'm important to her; the plantations, the mills would slump without me."

Would they? She remembered that her mother had written:—

Judge said the man had a charm of manner that could coax the birds from the bushes, which, turned full on an old woman who had loved, wanted to marry and apparently remained faithful to the memory of his grandfather, might influence her against her family.

If his influence was so strong, why had Ellen Marshall when she engaged Van Trent to make the efficiency check-up warned him not to let Collins know he had undertaken the job? Was it possible that the Judge, not the mistress of Karrisbrooke, was the one being fooled?

Perhaps it would be better not to discourage Collins entirely until she could find out if or how he was double-crossing his employer.

Suppose she were to discover facts of a sensational nature that would make the secretive Major Trent open his eyes? Suppose it had been Collins who had stolen papers from his desk? Van had said they were his efficiency notes. The superintendent of the plantation and a director in the cotton mills would have reason enough to want to know what was going on. He had just boasted that things would go his way or he was through. It was a challenge. She'd accept it.

"You're a long time answering a simple question," Collins reminded impatiently.

"Simple! Do you call asking a girl to marry you a simple question? I think it's terrific." She laughed and looked up at him. "And what's even more important, if you can manage Her Majesty you're a bigger man than I think you, Gunga Din. Try it, that's all, just try it."

"Does that mean that if I do win her approval you will—marry me?" His voice was rough with eagerness.

"It means nothing—just nothing, now."

"Think it over. When I am master of Karrisbrooke—"

"Oh, here you are, fella."

Peckett, brick-reddish as to face, pepper-and-saltish as to clothing, stepped from behind an oak tree beside the road. Collins' muttered exclamation was on the profane side. The horse danced, curvetted and rolled enormous brown eyes. His master patted his sleek neck:—

"Quit your fright-act, Pug. You ought to know by this time you can't fool me. Gus, what's the idea trailing me and popping out like a jack-in-the-box? My office is in town."

"Oh, yeah! Who knows that better'n me?" Resentment melted into an ingratiating smile. Peckett ran his tongue over his lips and twirled the soft hat in his hand.

"Sorry to break up the party, Miss Ramsay, but in *my* life I put business before the ladies and I have got something important to tell Barry."

"Don't apologize, Mr. Peckett, the party, as you call it, had already cracked. I won't forget your proposition, Mr. Collins. Good-by, for the present."

She presented each man with a radiant smile and walked on feeling as if their eyes were augers boring into her back. She remembered what Van Trent had said about moonshining, and she remembered that he had been sure Collins was afraid of his pal. Don't hurry, she warned herself; they're watching you. Round and round in her memory whirled Collins' voice with its hint of threat:—

"Think it over. When I am master of Karrisbrooke—"

He had said "when" as if he were sure. Had Aunt Ellen already made a will leaving him the estate? Did he know it? A few moments before he had boasted:—

"Watch me. You may have noticed at our recent conferences that she listens to my advice."

It was unbelievable that the man could have such an influence over hard-headed Ellen Marshall, and yet—he had seemed so sure.

If she had made a will in his favor, Aunt Ellen wasn't safe. He might—he might—be in such a hurry to get the inheritance, to shake off Peckett, that he would—

She didn't finish the terrifying thought, began to run. She must get to Judge Sutcliffe, to someone quick and tell them what Collins had said. If only Van Trent were here.

The road made a sharp turn. Once round that she ran with a frightened sense that it was terribly important to put distance between herself and the two men who might suspect where she was going. She increased her pace. Looked over her shoulder to make sure she was not being followed. Stumbled against something at the side of the road. Pitched forward. Her white cap flew off. She regained her balance and looked down. Her eyes widened in amazed unbelief. Her blood turned to ice. At her feet lay a man in uniform, motionless, rigid.

What had happened to him? A hit-and-run driver? Was she too late to help? The thought sent the blood coursing through her veins again. She pulled off her coat. Knelt beside him. Gently lifted the cap from his face streaked with sickening red. Road and trees went into a dancing-dervish whirl.

"Johnny!" she exclaimed in horror. She tenderly lifted his head into her lap.

"Oh, Johnny! Johnny Gordon!" Her breath came in a harsh sob. "Why did it have to be you?"

Grief tightened her throat. She thought of Johnny and herself when they were younger, of their carefree brother-and-sister companionship, of the many times she had laughed off his attempts to speak of his love for her, and she thought of what the loss of this son would mean to his father. She held his limp hand close in hers, laid her other hand on his hair.

"Johnny, Johnny, dear, come back," she pleaded as if her shaken voice might restore life.

Slowly one of the prostrate soldier's lids opened to disclose a large, twinkling dark eye, closed in a wicked wink. The generous mouth which had been so grim and still spread in a delighted grin.

"You were about to kiss me, weren't you, kid? Go on. I can take it."

XV

The Carolina sky was brilliantly blue where New York's had been gun-metal gray. Trent drew a deep breath. December was already a few days old, yet this was one of those winter days that held a faint scent of spring and flower fragrance.

Great to be back even for a short time, he thought, as he sent his roadster ahead on the long, straight, oak-bordered avenue that led from the highway to the old brick plantation house, with its white-columned façade, now a Hunt Club in which he had guest privileges.

He left his car in a parking space and passed through a superb doorway, through large, high-ceilinged rooms with paneled walls and floors polished to glasslike smoothness, to the porch which commanded a grand view of the river. A lawn swept toward the water in sloping terraces which spread like a gigantic fan. Beyond the garden pool was the "summerhouse," a two-story brick cottage with its iron-lace-framed porch, an antique gem which Ellen Marshall, a director of the Club, had had restored to its original beauty. Except for the dots far to the left which were golf players on greens as smooth as velvet, the place was deserted. Not a sign of life about the house.

The distant midget figures reminded him that he had come to collect his clubs. He might be ordered in a hurry to the new assignment. It would save time if he had them at Karrisbrooke.

A voice stopped him at the door of the locker room. A voice raised above the steady splash of a shower.

"He's hinting he intends to divorce his wife."

"He—is? Now what—d'ye—know about that?" The

sentence had been punctuated by hard-drawn breaths as if the speaker were wielding a gigantic bath towel across wet shoulders.

"Anyone in the locker room?"

Trent imagined the business of looking around, stepped forward to show himself but stopped when a voice answered:—

"Nary a soul. The place is as deserted as the box office after the first-night critics panned my play."

"That guy we were talking about never will try for a divorce," the first voice carried on. "I happen to know he's in dire need of the money he married to keep his racing-stable treading water. Hear he's just sold Pug, that ace jumper of his, to the Karrisbrooke superintendent. There's a guy with his foot on the social ladder. Watch him climb. Climb. Climb."

"He doesn't have to stick to the missus, does he? I'm talking about the horseman, not the superintendent. He's got charm, he has. There are others who have money, or filthy lucre coming up, he can marry. I heard that the twice-mentioned superintendent is up to his neck in that same stable proposition and—I hear—both owners are running neck-and-neck after the same Pot of Gold." The creak of a door. "I intend to speak to the house committee about that flashy guy who hangs round waiting for that same superintendent. He's *persona non grata* here. California here I come! I'm a new man. A hot and cold shower certainly straightens out the cricks in the old joints."

Not the strategic moment to reclaim his clubs, Trent decided, and back-tracked to his car. The men had been careful not to mention names but undoubtedly they had been speaking of Maury and Collins. The "flashy guy" could be none other than Peckett. Was the "Pot of Gold" Jess?

As he sent the roadster ahead he recalled her mother's suspicion that Collins intended by hook or by crook to become master of Karrisbrooke. Perhaps marrying the girl was part of his plan of achieving that. Johnny Gordon had reported the rake-off arrangement between Collins and Peckett if the marriage took place—he wouldn't tell where he had picked up

the incredible yarn—had intimated that Maury was a
party to it. Much as he disliked the owner of River
Farm he couldn't believe that of him. Phil was too
much in love with Jess himself. Where did Peckett fit
into the picture? Had he loaned money to Maury as
well as to Collins?

He thought of what he already knew of the shady
dealings of the two men. Peckett was running a
moonshining still, Collins was trying to undermine the
confidence of the millworkers in Miss Ellen. Did he
hope that by crippling production he could get control? The man's motives were entirely personal and
selfish, there was no undercover plan to hold up
defense work, he was convinced of that. The com-
mentator under the shower had said that Maury was
hinting at a divorce. If he carried out the idea it
might mean that Jess would be involved, Claire
would see that she was. That must not happen.

He was mentally fiercely preparing to go into battle
for her when Sam opened the front door at Karrisbrooke. His face was all eyes and smile in welcome.

"Sho' nuff if 'tain't yo', Major Trent. It sho' is good
to see yo' back in yo' uniform. 'Tain't livin' not to
have a man in this house, Ah reckon. Somep'n not go
right with yo', suh? Yo' sho's look kinder white an'
scared-like."

Was anxiety for Jess so apparent in his face?

"I'm all right, Sam. Flew from New York and
grounded my plane at the army air field just in time
for a demonstration that the plane has not yet been
designed that is absolutely foolproof. A crash always
washes the color from my face."

"Those a'roplanes, they're tricky, yes suh. Ah sho'
wish we could get some of the trash in this country
up in them w'at ain't foolproof, Ah sure do. Leave
that roadster right in the drive an' a boy'll tak' it
roun'. He'll put yo' bags in yo' room, suh."

"It seems like coming home to me, Sam. Where is
Miss Ellen?"

"So warm today she's on de garden-pia'za. Yo're
lady friend from the Inn am there too. They's been
playin' somep'n' they call gin rummy, 'tain't a drink,

suh, it's a game. She sho' am pow'ful fond of keards, M's Ellen is. Yo' go right out an Ah'll bring yo' iced coffee, quick."

"I'll shake off some of this dust first. And, Sam, don't tell them I've arrived. I'd like to surprise them."

"Ah won't tell them, not a word, suh. You'll fin' yo' room all ready, sho' nuff. M's Ellen, she's been expectin' yo'."

It was ready even to a bowl of scraggly crimson chrysanthemums on the table. For a long minute Trent stood looking about him. This room was more like home than any he had occupied since the day so long ago when he had moved in with his uncle. It seemed more like months than a week since he had left it.

What would Jess say when he stepped out through the living-room window? His surprise entrance was intended for her. If Sam announced his arrival she would make her get-away. There could be no doubt of that. He hadn't seen or heard from her since the night in the library when he had kissed her.

Instinctively he put his hand to his cheek. The memory of her repulse still burned there if the flesh did not. He had deserved it, plenty. The fact that he was still seething with fury because of Maury's attempt to kiss her, Claire's hateful accusation that Jess wanted her husband, was no excuse. He should have been doubly on guard against her charm and beauty.

What will she say? The question was in his mind again as he paused a moment before stepping to the garden-piazza from the long window. She wasn't there! Miss Ellen in a gray frock, with a turban of violets on her silvery hair, had been pouring tea. Becky in gingham, pink as a pink bonbon, was teasing Lucky by running to the steps, hissing "Cats-s-s" and pointing, which tactics sent the Airedale pellmell toward the box hedge. Helen Carter in filmy black widened her dark, heavily lashed eyes and crooned "Van, darling," ecstatically when she saw him.

Color burned to his hair as he discovered Philip Maury in a chair tilted back against the brick wall. They hadn't met since the night he had dropped the

owner of River Farm over that same wall. If the eyes
that met his had been knives they would have slashed
him to ribbons. Maury rose muttering something in-
distinguishable. Ellen Marshall broke off a sentence to
exclaim:—

"Vance! You've come! Welcome, my dear, welcome."

Trent pressed his lips to the jeweled blue-veined
hand she extended, an instinctive response to her
affectionate greeting. Becky and the dog flew for
him, the child clung to one hand, Lucky attempted to
scale his leg to lick his face. Maury spoke for the first
time.

"Your favorite son has returned, M's Ellen. I'll be
goin' an' leave the field to him. Still hot on the trail of
the quarry, Major, I presume? I have a little account
to settle with you. But, first, I have a date with Jess;
so long, everyone."

Ellen Marshall's eyes followed him—till he vanished into the living room—came back to Trent. It
had taken all his will power to resist the temptation
to dispose of the cocky man as he had before, but he
managed to smile a wireless "Don't worry" to her.

"Van, give an account of yourself. Where have you
been?" Helen Carter demanded in the proprietary
tone she adopted when speaking to him.

He sat down in the chair Maury had abandoned.
Sam placed a small table at his elbow and hovered
solicitously until he had sugared and creamed the tall
tinkling glass of coffee and lighted his cigarette.

"Anythin' more, suh?"

"That's all, thanks."

"It sho' is fine to hav' a man in de house again,
don't yo's say the same, M's Ellen?"

"Yes, Sam. That will be all."

"Becky, if you lean against Cousin Van's shoulder he
won't be able to drink coffee and smoke," her mother
reminded petulantly.

"She's all right." Trent tamped out his cigarette and
put his left arm about the little girl. "Been a good
child while I was away?"

"Not too bad. What did that punk Maury mean

when he said, 'Still on the trail of the quarry, Major?' What's a quarry, Cousin Van?"

"A place where they get big blocks of stone with which to build. Punk isn't a nice word for a little girl to use, Becky."

"Hmp. Turning the subject, aren't you? I'm not so little that I don't know that Mr. Maury didn't mean you were hunting *stone*. But, I guess I know. It means you're trailing a girl. Claire says Mummy's the woman in your life but by the way she makes goo-goo eyes at you, I bet she thinks she is."

"Becky!" Mrs. Carter's protest was a cross between a self-conscious simper and half-hearted reproof. "I've told you time and again not to repeat what that *silly* Mrs. Maury tells you. I don't see how an attractive man like Phil can stand her."

"I guess he isn't going to stand her long."

"What do you mean, Becky?"

It was a chorus in which the three joined. Ellen Marshall's troubled eyes sought Trent's. He reminded her sternly:—

"Don't repeat things you overhear, Becky."

"I'm not going to, Cousin Van," she glanced slyly from the corners of her eyes, at her mother, "not unless I get those roller skates I want."

Mrs. Carter rose in reproachful dignity.

"You know I never buy your confidences, Becky. We've had a charming afternoon, Miss Ellen. Your gin rummy gets better and better or else mine is getting worse and worse. You're a dear to plan that camping party for Becky and me. Anything I can do to help get ready? I'd love it. I'm thrilled even at the thought of going."

"Thank you, no. Sam and Pink make all preparations. Outing clothes will be all you need. Warm ones, remember. It is getting late for camping. The War Department has leased our mountain on a dollar-a-year contract, Vance. It is to be used as an army bombing and gunnery range. It is late in the season, we may be caught in a snowstorm, but I wanted one more camp outing before the property is turned over to the Government."

When Trent returned from seeing off mother and child in their car Ellen Marshall was sitting looking unseeingly down into the garden, her hands, usually busy with knitting, idle in her lap.

"Anything wrong, Miss Ellen, that I can help about?" he asked tenderly.

"You always help, Vance, just by being yourself. What did that child mean by 'From what I hear I guess he isn't going to stand her long'? 'He' being Phil and 'her' being Claire, I presume. Divorce?"

Better not tell her what he had overheard in the Hunt Club locker room. It was possible that the divorce referred to had not been Maury's, possible but *not* probable.

"Becky is always being mysterious, it's the way she gets what she wants out of her mother, Miss Ellen. I'm sorry to admit that the youngster lets her imagination gnaw its rope at times. You'd think Helen would get wise to her tactics, but, as you could see a few minutes ago, she still falls for them. Her daughter will get the roller skates, pronto. After all, suppose the Maurys are talking divorce? Why should their marital smash-up trouble you?"

"Jessamine and Phil."

"She doesn't love him."

"Your voice isn't convincing, Vance. When she was seventeen they were engaged. You know what happened after that. Claire was appealingly pretty. In spite of huge taxes she is still wealthy. Before you dropped from the sky Phil and Jessamine were often together."

"Jess wouldn't allow herself to love a married man, Miss Ellen."

"Wouldn't she?" He was startled by the sadness of her blue eyes. "That's what she says, but sometimes I wonder. Jessamine is so like what I was at her age—in characteristics, I mean—that often I know what she is going to say before she speaks. I loved a man whom I knew to be utterly unsuitable, who I suspected in my inmost heart—though I kept the suspicion locked in—was unscrupulous. Had he a wife I doubt if that would have stopped me—then. I would have gone with him had not my father horsewhipped him till he ran, with the very whip Sam produced the other night." She shivered and covered her eyes. "That was years and years ago, but I can still see the man I loved cringe under the blows, hear the crack of the lash. That killed a part of my heart, the part that might have loved another."

Trent put his arm about her shoulders.

"Dear Miss Ellen—"

She patted his hand.

"It's gone now, Vance. I've never told that before to anyone. I never will again so long as I live. I wanted you to know why I am anxious about Philip and Jessamine. She's like me. When she loves it will be forever, even if the man proves unworthy."

"I don't agree with you, Miss Ellen, about loving an unworthy man, I mean, she has too much integrity."

"Integrity is such a clean-cut word. I like the sound of it."

"It's even better as a characteristic than as a sound. Where is Jess now?"

"Teaching her class at the old schoolhouse. Didn't Philip say he was going to meet her?"

"He did, but I suspect the announcement was for my benefit. Suppose I shoot along in my roadster just in case she would prefer to ride home?"

"Go, Vance, please. Jessamine is the light of my eyes. I don't let her know it, but she is myself with a bigger, broader, if a more tragic world, in which to work out the pattern of her life. I couldn't bear it if the pattern held heartbreak for her."

"She would be surprised to know how much you care."

The twinkle was back in Ellen Marshall's eyes.

"She's sufficiently spoiled without knowing how I feel. It didn't take you long to realize her integrity, her valiant spirit and lovableness, did it, Vance?" She raised a protesting hand. "A rhetorical question. No answer expected. Only, let me add this, when love comes to you guard it against the winds of the world." She cleared her voice of emotion.

"I am accused of having a see-all, know-all complex; but I hope you have noticed that I have not inquired why Jess and you and Sam were huddling in the hall at midnight like a lot of guilty conspirators, and that I have refrained from asking questions as to the progress you are making in your investigations."

"I have, Miss Ellen, and appreciate your confidence in me. When I get the facts lined up I'll present them as a whole."

"I prefer it that way. I'm too impatient to read a mystery story in installments. Will you be free to join the camping party?"

"This week end on the mountain? I may not be able to go with you but I'll get there before you leave. Now I'll go for Jess."

As the car sped smoothly along the road he thought of Ellen Marshall's confidences, of her fear that Jess still loved Philip Maury. She didn't, he knew she didn't, and yet if the divorce rumor were true she was in danger of being implicated. At the first opportunity he would warn her. "Guard love against the winds of the world." He would know how to guard his love if he won her.

Something ahead brought his thoughts to a crashing standstill. Jess was seated on a stump by the side of the road. Her hands were over her face. Was she crying? Was Maury—responsible? He shot the roadster ahead.

XVI

Jess jumped to her feet and glared down at the laughing man sitting cobbler-fashion in the road. The shock of finding him, as she thought, killed had taken the starch from her knees. They shook like molds of jelly that hadn't fully jelled.

"Johnny Gordon! You frightened me almost to death! I thought you were—"

"Dead? Sure I am. The red chalk on my cheek is a little idea of my own. Realistic touch, what? Sorry I can't stand in the presence of a lady, but I have to stay dead until they find me. It's not orders, but it's my intention to do the act up brown. Always had a yen to be an actor." He lay down again.

"You mean—you're a casualty of the war games?"

"Yeah, verily. Haven't you heard the zoom and whir of planes? I'm a notch on one of their guns. You don't think I'm doing this for fun, do you? The road is no feather bed. If you'll kindly move on it will be to my advantage, as they say in the 'personal' ads. An officer will be along in a minute to check up. If I'm caught talking to you—boy—it might mean court-martial." He placed the cap over his face.

"Johnny, wait just a minute. You owe it to me for the scare you gave me. I've been trying to reach you at Camp. You're always on duty somewhere. Have you heard anything more about the Collins and Peckett deal about—me?"

"You promised you wouldn't ask questions and a promise is a promise, gal. When you thought I'd passed out you liked me a lot, didn't you?" he reproached. "Haven't forgotten that your aunt invited me to join the week-end camping trip in the mountains, have you? It will be a grand chance to go into the matter of your heart attack—or was it conscience?—when you thought I'd passed out and—here comes a car. Get going, gal. Get go ..." The remainder of the sentence was muffled by the cap hastily drawn over his face.

She snatched up her coat and ran, slowed to a walk as the sound of an automobile drew nearer. The strength hadn't returned to her knees and her head felt light. Curious how the ground came up to meet her every few minutes. Something had seemed to crash inside when she recognized Johnny Gordon.

Round a bend in the road a khaki-colored car with two white stars on a red pennant approached slowly. The faces were a blur as the occupants saluted and passed on. She managed to smile and stand erect till they were out of sight, then dropped upon a conve-

nient stump and clutched her head in her hands to
steady it.

Where was her cap? Had she left it beside Johnny?
What difference did it make? After her hospital training she must be a pretty weak sister to collapse at
finding what had looked to be a seriously wounded or
dead soldier. Was the fact that it had been Johnny
Gordon accountable for her present nervous breakdown? Was it possible she loved him and hadn't
known it? No. Situations like that occurred only in
novels. When and if she loved a man there would be
no doubt in her mind or in the mind of the innocent
bystander.

"What happened to you, Angel?"

She looked up into a white, strained face, blinked
unbelieving wet-lashed eyes. She had been so absorbed in self-analysis she hadn't heard the roadster
approach and stop.

"My word, Major. I thought you were still in the
North. I must have had my hands over my ears. I
didn't hear your footsteps or did you drop from a
parachute?"

"Never mind where I came from. Why are you
crying?"

"If you care for intimate details, not only have I
been shedding tears like an able-bodied cloudburst
but the stiffening has entirely disappeared from my
knees, that's why I'm sitting here." She told of stum-
bling on Johnny. "Wouldn't I make a hit in the Field
Service? When I see a person hurt I crumple inside."

"But you don't stay crumpled. Think what a grand
First Aid job you did on my ankle."

"Of course this time the shock came from finding
someone I loved, apparently d-d—"

"He wasn't, so don't say it, Angel." The relief, the
incredible relief, of knowing that it had not been
Maury who had occasioned her tears didn't quite
balance the tightening of his heart occasioned by her
grief for Gordon.

"Stand up." He drew a handkerchief from his pocket
and tenderly wiped her eyes. "That's better. Love
him a lot, don't you?. You told me you did."

"I told you that?" Her eyes, big with surprise between long wet lashes, made him think of fringed gentians. "When?"

"The day we picked up Becky. You said, 'I've gone overboard about someone else' and when I said, 'Johnny Gordon?' you answered, 'Are you by any chance psychic, Major?' What else could I think? It's all right with me. He's a grand guy. How about moving toward home? The maneuvers are over. Where's your hat or didn't you wear one with your uniform?"

"I must have dropped my white cap when I f-found J-Johnny b-back there." She drew a long sobbing breath and indicated the direction by a bend of her head.

"You're still jittery. Sit here while I go for it."

He ignored her protest and started off. Let him go. By the time he returned the silly chills which still played tag through her veins would have quieted. She hadn't seen him since the night he had kissed her. He had spoken to her a few minutes ago as if there had been no passage of arms between them. The result had been a draw. If he could ignore that battle perhaps she'd better. Apparently he believed she loved Johnny. So much the better, in that case he couldn't think she cared for Phil. But he needn't have agreed so heartily that her love for Johnny was all right with him. She must look like a fright. She drew a vanity case from her pocket and repaired damages.

"Cap coming up." Trent held out the white cap with its blue-and-red insignia. "Apparently it wasn't noticed when they checked up on Gordon. I'll put it on for you, your hands are still shaky. You prefer to hold it? Okay. Hop in."

As the roadster slid forward he turned to look at her.

"Got your color back, haven't you, or is it the reflection from that?" He nodded toward the western sky.

As afterglows go, it was a gay one, flaming up in bright pink peaks, turning the road into a rosy ribbon and tipping treetops with reddish gold.

"Gorgeous, isn't it? Thanks for retrieving the cap, Major. I'm as steady now as the cast-iron Confederate at the square. Tomorrow I'll see the humorous angle

of the adventure. I must have looked pretty funny
sitting by the side of the road, head in hands, giving
an imitation of Niobe weeping for her children. You
needn't go out of your way to take me home. Weren't
you headed for the Inn?"

"No. I came to look you up. Miss Ellen said this
was school afternoon. When you didn't get back for
tea she was a little anxious and I volunteered to find
you."

"Have you come back to stay at Karrisbrooke?"

"That's the general idea. Anything wrong with it?"

"Certainly not. Aunt Ellen didn't tell me you were
expected today."

"Careless of her, not to give you a chance to make
another engagement for the evening. Perhaps it isn't
too late now. Stop me if I'm wrong."

It was so exactly what she was thinking that she
had no reply ready. Her thoughts went round and
round with the wheels. The harder she tried to think
of something to say the blanker became her mind.
The silence between them lengthened as did the
shadows in the road.

"That sensational sunset means fair tomorrow." A
thought at last. He threw back his head and laughed.

"Nice going. Now that the ice is broken let's talk.
How did you happen to be on this road? You shouldn't
have come this way while the war game was on."

"I didn't intend to, but Barry Collins came to the
schoolhouse. He had been riding; we couldn't very
well take the path through the fields with a horse
in tow."

"Why did he let you come on alone?"

"The slippery Gus Peckett had trailed him to talk
business. He politely suggested that I move on. I
moved—with alacrity. Any more questions? Or
haven't you mistaken me for a Quiz Kid?"

"Don't get edgy. Have you forgotten you agreed to
work with me?"

"That was before—"

"You needn't say it. I haven't forgotten that I lost
my head and you lost your temper. I was still
seething with fury after disposing of Maury and that

battle of words with his wife, and—as I had remarked earlier in the evening, I'm neither wood nor stone. My part of it won't happen again, I promise. Are we still partners? If we are I have something important to tell you."

"We are as long as you keep that promise. What's happened? Tell me quick."

"There's a rumor that Phil Maury intends to start divorce proceedings against his wife."

"*Phil!* Divorcing Claire! He's lost his mind. What possible ground has he for doing it? She thinks every man she meets is in love with her, but she never even pretends to reciprocate."

"Incompatibility, perhaps. His reason for bringing the action isn't what's interesting me, it's what his wife will do. In her jealous anger she's likely to file a countercharge, may even drag you into the mess. She has a cockeyed notion that you want her husband. Remember?"

"Remember! Am I likely to forget the scene Claire put on the night of Aunt Ellen's ball for the officers? You said 'rumor' that Phil intends to file action for divorce. Does that mean he hasn't started it yet?"

"It might. It's possible that he's doing a lot of tall talking to frighten Claire into laying off him."

"I can't believe it. The Maurys are going on the camp trip this week end. Aunt Ellen planned it to show Mrs. Carter our mountain. She has included Becky, she thinks the child is spoiled and she's fairly aching to get in a little discipline. 'Let me have her a week end and I'll show her mother,' she boasted. It isn't likely that Phil would broadcast his divorce intentions and then come along with Claire, not with Ellen Marshall in the party, she has views about divorce. There's something wrong with that picture."

"I agree with you. Any other men to be included?"

"It wouldn't be Aunt Ellen's party if there weren't. An all-women week end would bore her to extinction."

"Barry Collins going?"

"Yes. He, Johnny Gordon and Jim Lacey—and wife—will protect us women from the Indians. That's a

figure of speech. There aren't any. Occasionally an
escaped convict takes up residence there, but if one
may believe the newspapers, there are none on the
loose at present. Pink and Sam go along as maid and
general factotum and Aunt Ellen, of course, as
chaperone."

"Somehow I can't imagine Miss Ellen on a camping
trip! Can she stand it?"

"Better never let her hear you question her endurance. She takes great care of herself physically and
mentally, lives up to her favorite presciption: 'Ignore
age and you efface age.' "

"And boy, does it work! She was on the garden-
piazza when I arrived. With the excitement of a
winning game of gin rummy still coloring her cheeks
and putting a sparkle in her eyes she looked not a
day over fifty, if that much. How will you get to the
mountain?"

"Motor. Across the river bridge, then up fairly good
roads to the Marshall camp, situated on a ledge from
which one can see the world, figuratively speaking.
There are a half-dozen log cabins, a swimming pool,
rock-lined, at the bend of a waterfall, and a main
cabin for cooking and meals. It will be cold, even in
this mild winter, but the air will be like wine pepped
up with pin-point carbonation."

"You're a high-pressure salesman. I'm sold on the
idea of joining up."

"You can't. Really you can't. There won't be room
for you."

"Don't get panicky. I won't be in your way, I promise. Miss Ellen invited me. Something tells me that
you don't want me in the party."

"Want you and Phil Maury there together! It would
be a nightmare. I haven't forgotten those few hectic
moments the night of the dance if you have."

"Don't worry. We met a few minutes ago and be-
haved like little gentlemen, at least I did. I haven't
forgotten the cause of what you call 'hectic moments.'
A masterpiece of understatement if ever there was
one—I'm going along to camp to make sure that
cause doesn't happen again."

"Terribly sweet of you, Major Trent, but I'm perfectly capable of protecting myself from Phil—if *not* apparently from others."

"That reminder was quite unnecessary, Miss Ramsay. After that you may be sure I'll let romance run its course, even if it results in dragging you into the divorce court."

"Phil won't allow my name to be dragged into the mess, if there is one. He isn't like that. I'll admit he was a terribly spoiled boy, but he has an immense pride in his family, modern as he is, he's always been acutely conscious of his social responsibility. He won't smooch the record with a scandal, and there would be one if Claire fought back. Lots of men break an engagement—it's courageous of them if they are sure they have made a mistake."

"You, defending him. You *must* be afraid of what I'll do to him. Don't worry if you still love him, he's safe from me."

"I *don't* love him, can't you understand? I won't have a row between you two at camp. Goodness! I'd forgotten!"

"Now what, Angel?" His voice expressed intense concern at the panic in her exclamation. The eyes that met his were wide with amazement slightly tinged with apprehension.

"The gipsy. Remember her warning? 'You and one you love are the victims of a plot. Stay away from the mountains.' Perhaps this Maury mix-up was what she prophesied and I thought all the time it might be—" She caught back "Collins' scheme," just in time.

"What did you think it might be?"

"Forget it. I have an imagination which would make my fortune as a writer. Someday when it goes too far it will get its wings clipped. The more I think of it the more sure I am that someone started that divorce rumor to set tongues at the Hunt Club wagging. I'll manage somehow to see Phil tonight and talk with him before it goes any further, and—"

"You won't have to manage. He's waiting for you—I presume it's for you. Can't you see him on the steps?"

She stopped and looked toward the house, its

bricks turned to the color of Burgundy by the light of
the afterglow. Her eyes came back to him.

"Please, *please* don't come in now," she begged.
"Let me out here."

"Anything to oblige a lady."

"Thanks, thanks a lot; and you won't come on the
camping party, will you?"

His eyes widened in mock surprise.

"Not go on the camping party with Helen among
those present? Where did you get that fantastic idea?
Of course I'll go." He stepped from the roadster and
held out his hand. "Hop out. I'll be seeing you—later."

"Where are you going *now?*" She gripped his hand.

"Going?" His eyes were brilliant with laughter.
"Why this exhibition of panic? To the garage. You
won't mind will you, if I promise to enter the house
through the kitchen?" He stepped into the car,
grinned as he saluted with impressive formality.

She watched till the roadster disappeared around a
bend in the drive. No wonder he had laughed at her.
She had made herself ridiculous with her fear that he
would goad Phil Maury into a fight.

"Stay away from the mountains," the gipsy had
warned. "Look out for him."

She could see as plainly as if on a screen the
woman's dirty finger pointing at Trent.

"Hi, there!" Phil Maury shouted.

She shook off the spell of memory and watched the
man approaching. If the gipsy but knew it, Phil was
the person to be warned against Van Trent, not
herself.

XVII

The sun shining between waving tree-branches drew
intricate patterns on Ellen Marshall's gray hair and
matching cardigan as she sat in a rustic chair with

Sam hovering in devoted attendance. The campfire sent forth delectable aromas of roasted chicken, baked potatoes and coffee. Aromas which almost, but not quite, dominated the woodsy fragrance scattered by the trees each time a crisp mountain breeze shook them.

She reminded Jessamine of her childhood impression that the mistress of Karrisbrooke was every inch a queen. A queen, and the rest of us are her subjects, the girl's thoughts ran on as she looked about the circle of men and women seated on cushions around the fire. Curious how the party, as first planned, had dwindled. The divisions engaged in war games had been recalled a week ahead of the date originally scheduled and had taken Johnny Gordon with them. For reasons known only to the hostess, Barry Collins had reneged. At the last moment Mrs. Carter had sent regrets and Becky. Did her deflection account for the fact that "important business" had prevented Vance Trent from coming to the camp?

Nothing had happened to keep the Laceys and the Maurys at home—worse luck, her thoughts trooped on, as Phil looked up from the hot, mealy potato he was opening and met her eyes with a meaning smile in his. The brilliant red of Estelle Lacey's sports outfit beside him was a vivid contrast to his horizon-blue pullover and slacks. Claire sat cross-legged on her green cushion, her white culotte and cardigan as immaculate as if recently removed from tissue-paper wrappings. Her mouth drooped at the corners, her blue eyes gazed unseeingly at the top of a stunted beech, as she pretended to listen to garrulous, beefy Jim Lacey, whose lumberman's-plaid outfit was of blinding brilliance.

"Miss Jess! Miss Jess!"

The startled whisper recalled her attention to the little girl in Brownie uniform seated close beside her. There had been indications, since the arrival at camp in the late afternoon yesterday, that Becky was not entirely sold on life in the wilderness.

"Miss Jess! Miss Jess! What's c-coming across the

fire? A—a—ghost?" The pigtails appropriately tied
with brown ribbon were atremble.

Jess caught the hand gripping her sleeve and held
it in a warm clasp. She laughed.

"A ghost at high noon, silly? It's just a lovely little
cloudmist come to say 'Howdy' to us. There it goes. It
has caught on those stunted trees below. It's off again!
Looks like a wedding veil drifting against the bright
blue sky. Smell the sweet-fern fragrance it left behind? I'll wager it was napping in a clump of that,
before it came nosing-in to find out what we are
doing here."

She looked across the fire as a potato skin landed
on the right shoulder of her cochinelle-pink cardigan.
Phil Maury was grinning at her.

"Quite a bedtime story you made of that cloud,
Jessie. What a *mother* you would make."

Jessamine caught the tightening of his wife's lips,
her furtive glance at her husband. Darn Phil! How
could he be so cruel?

"Bedtime stories are not the entire qualification for
motherhood, Philip," Ellen Marshall reminded in a
voice spiced with annoyance. "There is that little
matter of conduct, of training a child to stand
foursquare to its obligations, till honor, integrity and
keeping the faith become as much a part of him as
his hands and feet."

"My stars, M's Ellen, you sayin' that to Phil? He
doesn't know the meanin' of most of those words." The
shrill protest was unsteady.

"Claire, stop it. To me a sniping husband or wife is
the lowest form of animal life." Ellen Marshall's
reproof brought a surge of color to the woman's face.

"I've had all I intend to take of this so-called conversation." Maury's indignant leap from the cushion
was somewhat hampered by the evident fact that his
feet had gone to sleep. He swore under his breath as
he jumped up and down to restore circulation. Becky
giggled.

"You look awful funny, Mr. Philip, hopping like
corn in a popper."

"Here comes Sam with the dessert," Jessamine announced hurriedly in an attempt to avert the storm gathering in Phil's eyes. He never could stand being laughed at even as a boy, and Becky had become his Number One aversion. "Baked grapefruit done to a turn. Pass it, Phil, while Sam serves the coffee."

Her diversion worked. Maury took the large wooden tray, laden with smaller trays each with its half of golden fruit, from the butler.

"Get busy with the coffee, Sam."

As he stopped in front of Jessamine he exclaimed:— "See that owl on top of the tree, Becky? It's a whopper." As the child turned eagerly he whispered: "The Big Rock at four, Jessie. Important."

Before she could answer he had gone on. From under her lashes she glanced at Claire. Her narrowed eyes were on her husband. Had she overheard his whisper?

It was against camp rules, drawn up and insisted upon by the hostess, for a guest to leave his or her cabin before three o'clock. One needed rest after luncheon in the high altitude, she argued. Without it people got tipsy on the exhilarating air and did crazy things. Impatiently Jess waited in her cabin for the time to pass.

After what seemed hours she glanced at her wrist watch. Three at last. If she started now there would be no danger of running into Phil. He wouldn't leave his cabin for a half-hour, at least. The Big Rock from which the view was breathtakingly grand was only ten minutes' hike to the west along a well-worn trail; she was going east, to the other end of the ledge—the outlook there would be fine and she needed a hard tramp, a chance to think things through, to decide if perhaps it would be wiser to go home till Phil's brainstorm about her blew itself out, as it was bound to in time. Becky was with Pink in the kitchen back of the large cabin taking a lesson in making beaten biscuit; that would keep her happy for a while.

She changed to beige gabardine slacks, stout enough to resist clutching branches and bushes, slipped on a red pullover and matching cardigan. The mountain was posted against trespassers, but the quail season was drawing toward a close and a hunter more enthusiastic than law-minded might be out after birds and send a bullet her way.

She checked up on her pockets: flash, flask and knife. After an instant's hesitation she buckled a belt with holster and revolver round her waist. Silly to take them, but she had been trained by her stepfather, when he took her camping in New England, never to go into the woods without a gun. She might need it to use as a signal for help, if for nothing else, he had told her.

Cautiously she opened the cabin door, reconnoitered. No movement save smoke rising lazily from the cabins to become mere gray stains on the clear blue above. In the camp kitchen the colored woman was singing to the child. The lazy melody drifted through the still air:—

"O mah honey-baby says yo' papa ain'
mad wid yo'."

Becky's voice, thin, sweet, a little uncertain, joined in the refrain:—

"An' ax' um to tell yuh dat I'm startin'
on my journey home."

"I got it right that time, Pink, didn't I?"

Jess smiled in sympathy with the jubilant voice as she stole by the door. She drew a deep breath of the mountain air spicy with fragrance as she entered a trail between stunted trees. It banished the faint doubt of the wisdom of her plan, to make the safari alone. What could happen to her? This zigzag trail must lead somewhere. There were old blazes on the trees beside it. A quail flushed from the brush and darted over her head, the sudden burst of wings set her heart thumping. The bird sliced and bomb-dived through the air till it vanished. She went on humming the refrain of Pink's song.

Had she heard a crack or was it a trick of her nerves? There it was again. The sound as of a twig snapping. Was someone following? Had Phil seen her slip out of her cabin? She stepped softly to the side of the trail and listened. Silence except for the hard pound of her heart and the low, subdued call of a mother partridge rounding up her children for bed.

The trail was narrowing. Looking ahead there appeared to be no trees. There should be a gorgeous view. She poked around to the right. A faint path led into a clump of stunted beeches. "Looks poky," she told herself and cautiously forced her way among undergrowth which clutched at her slacks and red cardigan like dry, tenacious fingers.

"My word!"

Her heart tore up from its roots to drum in her throat, as she peered over a stunted evergreen. A foot in front of her, the side of the mountain dropped sheer and straight as far as she could see. A rock, dislodged by the pressure of her feet, bounded and skipped down the declivity.

She grabbed the tree with both hands. For one delirious moment she was so dizzy she feared she might pitch over, then so petrified with fright she feared she couldn't move. She remembered a screen picture of an air pilot whose hands were frozen to the stick. His eyes had been wide with horror as the ship dove.

With all her strength she rallied her self-control. As plainly as if he were beside her she heard Johnny Gordon say: "Cool and tough would be your line in a crisis, gal." He wouldn't say that if he could see her at this minute, shivering from head to toe as Lucky sometimes shivered in his sleep.

"Take it easy, Angel." It was Van Trent speaking to her this time, memory had reproduced his voice to the least inflection. It steadied her. Her body and mind relaxed though she still clutched the puny tree with tense fingers. Her eyes, which fright had tightly closed, opened. The world, all greens and blues dotted with white farmhouses, became a friendly world, a panorama that spread out its beauty for miles and miles. Fields were patterned in purple shadows and pink-gold sunlight, the river resembled a crimson sash which had been trailed across them.

She looked down again and shivered. One step more and she would have pitched over. "Proving what?" she demanded of herself fiercely. "You didn't take that step. Instead of imagining horrors you'd better thank your stars you kept your head. Let go of that tree, stupid."

At the sound of another loosened rock hitting the ledge as it bounded and skipped to join its fellow, she wrenched free her hands and slowly, cautiously, fearing with each move that she might loosen the rocks under her feet, took three cautious steps back.

"I thought you'd do this. Out-smarted you, didn't I, Jessie?"

Even as she wheeled to face Philip Maury she was nervously aware of the cliff behind her. She shivered as she stepped forward and backed against a small tree beside the trail. No danger of pitching over now. She took courage from the fact that he looked haggard and unhappy. Were he his usual satisfied self she would be afraid of him; "cool and tough" was her line in his present mood. Her laugh was out of nothing except courage.

"Out-smarted me, perhaps, but it wouldn't take a master mind to realize that I hadn't the slightest intention of meeting you at the Big Rock."

"Why not?"

As he approached she stepped quickly into the trail with a fervent inner thanksgiving that her back was now toward camp and not toward the cliff. She rested her hand on the holster at her side. The feel of it filled her with courage and determination to end his persecution now.

"Why should I meet you at the Big Rock, Phil? You bore me to tears with your sentimental patter. This latest gumshoe pursuit makes me wonder if you're getting in trim for an FBI job. I don't even like you. In short, I despise you now that you have become Barry Collins' hired man."

Dark color flooded his face. His eyes widened in surprise.

"When did you learn that he wants to buy my share of the mills? Did he tell you? He swore he'd keep it dark till I put the sale across. I followed you here to talk about it."

She shook her head and closed her lips tight to repress an exclamation that would have betrayed her ignorance of the deal. Her reference had been to the contemptible marriage scheme of Collins and Peckett. Was Collins' offer to buy into the mills his second move to become master of Karrisbrooke? Had his first been his proposal of marriage to Ellen Marshall's niece?

"Thought I came to tell you again that you'll marry me sometime, didn't you?" Maury's strident voice brought her attention back to him. "Thought because your champion was far away—I'm bidin' my time to settle that score with the Major—that I'd seized this chance to make you listen?" His smile was saturnine. "That was my idea when I asked you to meet me, but that can wait, all of it. After lunch Claire put me through a merry little hell about money; we had a hot row. Accordin' to Father's will, I can't sell my share of the mills without M's Ellen's consent. I want you to work on her till she gives it."

"Work on Aunt Ellen! You're crazy. I couldn't influence her. If I could, I wouldn't try."

He caught her hands. Stepped back and pulled her toward him.

"Come on, there must be a grand view from this ledge. We'll sit on the edge of the world and talk it over. You won't desert an old pal in an emergency, you're not that kind." His voice held its familiar wheedle.

She drew back and tried to twist her hands free.

"Phil! Stop! The edge of the world ... I've just escaped it, thank you. I hate high places. They make my spinal cord squizzle. That ledge isn't safe. I was there a few minutes ago. It's crumbly."

"Come on." He stepped back and forcibly drew her with him. "I reckon it will hold till we finish our heart-to-heart. You've got to help me, Jessie; I'm in a spot. I must have money. I—"

She didn't know what happened. She knew only that he released her hands, that instinctively she sprang back as the ground, the very ground on which she had been standing not so long before, moved and took his feet and body with it till only his head with its livid face and terrified eyes and his hands clutching the stunted tree were visible.

"Jess! Jess! Catch me, quick! I'm going down!" he called frantically.

"Hold on tight. I'll help."

The word "help" mobilized brain and muscles for action. She pulled her revolver from the holster and fired two shots into the air.

"That will bring someone, Phil. They'll hear it at camp."

"Jess! Jess! I'm slipping. Hold me! Don't let me go."

"I won't, Phil. I won't. I had to signal first. Grip the tree till I fire again! There! Someone will come. Someone must have heard that second SOS."

She dropped the pistol and flung herself flat—with arms outstretched caught his wrists.

"Hold on—tight—"

Her breathless voice gave out. His weight was pulling her arms from their sockets. If he went he would drag her with him. He wouldn't think of danger to her.

XVIII

This wasn't the first time he had tramped mountain trails in the hunt for Peckett's moonshining still, Vance Trent reflected as he followed a faint path through scrub growth. He had spent hours on the job since the night he had seen the motorboat being unloaded at the old wharf. With no hint of a clue. From the big rock ahead he ought to get a view of the other side of the mountain from the Marshall camp. When he had told Miss Ellen that he would not be able to start with her week-end party, but would join it later, he had had this investigation in mind. He had concealed his car in a wood road with the fervent hope it would not be discovered and destroy the impression when he reached camp that he had just driven from town.

The rock. At last. Boy, what a whopper. Steps had been cut in one side and the top flattened. A place with a view, evidently, he thought as he mounted.

And what a view! Its grandeur took his breath. Mountain tops, like huge, rose-crested purple billows, spread on and on as far as he could see. Fog-seas of violet and gold marked some valleys, silver mists lay in others. No sign of habitation. A wilderness of trees and—

Smoke? He sniffed. Smoke and the smell of something else. He slid down the rock steps to save time, cautiously made his way to the ledge beyond them. Clutched a stunted tree and leaned over.

Nothing visible. Had he imagined the smell of smoke and— He had not. A slight haze rose from a ledge far below. With one hand he clumsily adjusted binoculars, while the other still clutched the life-preserving tree.

Something moved. If he could only focus the thing to bring it nearer . . . It seemed hours before he saw through the strong lenses, distinctly, the figure seated on a cask. He was working at something in his hand. A glint of light. A revolver? The man was a guard. Guarding the moonshining outfit undoubtedly. Now he was standing gazing out over the valley. Now he was looking toward the big rock.

Had the man seen him? Time for a disappearing act before a stone he might loosen with his foot betrayed his presence. He cautiously backed from the undergrowth. Now that he had located the illicit still he would pick up his roadster and appear at the camp. Would Jess be glad to see him? Fool question. Hadn't she said emphatically that he would not be welcome at the week-end party?

"So you expected to meet them here, did you?"

The shrill question derailed Trent's train of thought and stopped his feet at the entrance to the broader trail. Claire Maury faced him. Her eyes smoldered like black coals in a face almost as white as her pullover and slacks. Twigs had caught in her honey-color hair.

She looks mad as Ophelia at her maddest. Whom did she think I expected to meet? He sidetracked the answer which slid into his mind and laughed.

"Well met, Claire. Apparently you know where you are. I don't. The Babes in the Woods have nothing on me. I lost my way."

"Know where I am? I'll say I know. Didn't I hear Phil tell Jess Ramsay to meet him at the Big Rock? There it is behind you. Didn't I see her slip out of her cabin and go in the opposite direction till she was out of sight, to throw dust in my eyes, I presume?"

"Cut it out, Claire, cut it out. They are not here, haven't been here during the last hour, at least. Go back to camp. You'll probably find them toasting marshmallows over a fire. Make it fast. I passed Jim Lacey on my way up the trail; he's out of quail. Shots carry a long way. I'd hate to see a crimson stain ruin that white costume of yours."

He had seen Lacey with a gun, but Lacey had not seen him. He was unprepared for the effect of his suggestion. Her terrified eyes made him realize its gruesomeness.

"Van! You don't really think I'm in danger, do you?" Fright had hoarsened her voice.

"Not if you beat it straight back to camp. I know which way Jim went. I'll follow him and make sure he doesn't shoot. Get going, quck."

She was on her way before he had finished the sentence. She stumbled and slipped along the trail, vanished at a turn. Poor soul, she was eaten up with jealousy. Better give her plenty of time before he followed.

He dropped to the ground, leaned against a stunted tree and lighted a cigarette. Had Jess met Phil by arrangement? It wasn't like her. He had accused her of encouraging Maury in the hope of making her see that danger lurked even in friendship with him. In his heart he knew her to be—

A shot! He laughed. That would send Claire scurrying. Another! He was on his feet. Two, near together. It might be Jim Lac—Again! A signal. Someone was in danger.

He didn't know whether he was on a trail, he knew only that he ran in the direction of the sound of the shots and of a woman's voice calling.

"Here! Here!"

"Coming! Coming!" he shouted. A voice, fainter now, answered:—

"Here! Here!"

It was Jess. Was Maury—Terror lent him seven-league boots. He crashed along a footpath.

"Hurry! Hurry!" a breathless voice pleaded. Then he saw her stretched on the ground gripping two hands. Terrified eyes in a livid face visible above them seemed about to bulge from their sockets.

"Angel!"

"Trent! Trent! Save me!" It was Maury's hoarse voice.

"It's you, Van!" The girl's strangled whisper broke in a sob. "Now, you'll be safe, Phil." His hoarse shout had had all the music of heavenly harps. Her tense mind and muscles relaxed. Van had come.

"You're letting go, Jess! Don't! Don't!" Phil Maury's frantic voice roused her.

"Steady, Maury." Trent spoke directly above her. Two arms reached over her shoulders, a knee came down each side of them, hands gripped Phil's wrists above hers.

"I have him. Let go, Angel. Crawl backward. Fire two shots. Lacey's in the woods. Good! He'll hear that. Slit your slacks with your knife. Make a rope. Hurry! Stop thrashing, Maury, or I'll let you go damn quick. Dig in your toes. *Find* a place, then!"

The cool voice kept on to the accompaniment of the shriek of tearing cloth, and to the gipsy's voice repeating over and over in Jess's memory, "Keep away from the mountains." She shivered as the cold air struck her legs, bare between her flesh-color shorts and beige socks.

"Knot it hard, Angel. Boost yourself, man, for God's sake help. There you are. Phil Maury coming up. Hold it. Hold it!"

She cried out as the struggling man slipped back.

"That won't help, girl." Trent's sharp reprimand steadied her. "Dig in again, fella. Here you come. Rope ready? Okay, tie one end to the stoutest tree you can find behind you, Angel."

Her heart pounded suffocatingly as with the strength of desperation she knotted an end of the cloth rope round a stunted tree.

"Done! Smart girl. Throw the free end till it hits my arm. No! *No!* Don't come! Keep back! Didn't you hear that rock go?" For the first time fear hoarsened Van's voice, fear for her, she knew.

It seemed hours that he maneuvered before he picked up the end of the cloth rope in his teeth. Could he save Phil without losing his own life? If the ground gave way and he went over—It would be the end of the world for her. There was no one like him, no one so understanding, so helpful, so vital, such fun. She loved him. *Loved* him! The realization set her heart aflame, turned her fingers to icicles, the world about her to blinding brilliance.

"Hang on to that tree, Maury, with all your might." The cool voice roused her from the trance of happiness. The lives of two men were hanging on the courage and strength of one, and she had been thinking of herself.

"I've got to use my hands to get this rope under your arms, Maury. Don't struggle! Raise yourself. The tree will hold. It's your one chance. Steady! Stead-y! Once more! I'll have it round you. Boost, man. Boost with your toes again! It's tied! *Don't relax!! Don't* stop helping. Pull on the rope, Jess! Pull like hell. I've got you Maury. Now! Let go the tree. *Let go that tree!* Grab my arms!" He worked his body back against the ground, dragging Maury with him. The veins in his neck stood out like cords.

"Hullo! Hull-o-o!" The shout accompanied the sound of rushing feet.

"Here! Here!" Jess called hoarsely. She pulled mightily, prayed fervently as Trent, flat and taut to the ground, backed slowly and slowly dragged Phil to safety.

"Keep on pulling, Angel. We've got to do it all. He hasn't any fight left in him."

"What the devil—" Lacey panted as he burst into the trail. He dropped his gun and the two birds dangling from one arm.

"Thank God, you've come, Jim. Give Maury a drink from that flask in your pocket and make it fast," Trent ordered. His face contracted as if in unendurable pain as he got slowly to his feet.

"Okay, I'll—Boy, oh boy. Look at Jess, Van! She's fainted. What in thunder is she doing out in panties and socks this cold day? Her legs are purple."

"I—I *haven't* fainted." Jess's heart, which had been shaking her body with its labored thump, slowed down. "Don't look so terrified, Van. I was pulling so—so—hard—that—that when the rope slackened I—I sat down unexpectedly." She laughed hysterically at the same time she felt salt tears on her lips.

"Stop it!" Trent caught her hands and pulled her to her feet. "Stop it." He shook her slightly to emphasize his command.

"I—I—will." She twisted free and knelt beside the man who was sitting up, rubbing the back of his hand across his wet brow. "Ph—Phil, are you all right?"

"Sure, thanks to you and—and Trent." He added the last word as if it had been dragged out of him.

"Is that all you have to say?" She denatured the contempt in her voice. Perhaps a man dragged from the jaws of death couldn't be expected to get hold of himself at once. "We'll leave you. Bring him in to camp, Jim, when he's able to walk. Come on, Van, I'm freezing."

He pulled off his heavy khaki cardigan as he followed her into the trail.

"Tie this so it will cover your knees."

"I won't take it from you."

"Do as you're told and do it quick."

She glanced furtively at his haggard face. The muscles flinched when he moved. His body had been stretched as on a rack. This was not the time to argue. She tied the sleeves of the cardigan about her waist.

They walked Indian file along the narrow trail without speaking. Every pulse in her body was clamoring response to his nearness. When they came to a clearing she said:—

"Providence must have sent you along that trail to save Phil, Van. I couldn't have held him much longer."

"Providence was busy on another line. Claire told me where to find you."

"Claire! Always Claire." She stopped and looked up into his white face. His voice had been harsh with anger. "What did Claire tell you?"

"That you and her husband had planned a rendezvous at the Big Rock, but at first you had gone in the opposite direction to throw dust in her eyes, she presumed."

"And you believed her?"

"Why not? I found you and Maury together, didn't I, if not at the Big Rock? Same old moth-and-candle stuff. My God, I was tempted to let that heel go. Can't keep away from him, can you?"

His contemptuous voice beat her heart to numbness. Why had she thought she loved him? She met his eyes steadily.

"Even though I know you've been through a terrific emotional strain, Major, that you accomplished a miracle when you dragged Phil to safety, I'll never forgive you for that last taunt as long as I live. I hope I *never* see you again. Good-by."

She ran ahead and disappeared around a bend of the trail.

XIX

There were gay white-and-green doilies on the long pine table in the camp dining room. Eight lighted red candles and the roaring flames in the great stone fireplace set flickering shapes dancing on the log walls and across the faces of Ellen Marshall and her guests. Grave faces. Yesterday's near-tragedy had left its mark on their spirits, Jess decided, as she watched them.

It left not only a mark on my spirit but an ache in each individual muscle, she thought. If I feel as if each inch of me had been stretched to the breaking point, how must Van Trent feel who tugged, lifted, fought twice as long as I did?

Hurriedly she brushed the picture of his straining arms and body, his cool, sustaining voice, from her memory before it could take up the matter of their parting clash, which, with the realization that she loved him, had occupied her mind for most of the time since. It seemed years ago that she had cockily declared she wouldn't allow herself to love a man in the service—years ago that Van had warned: "That's thumbing your nose at Fate. Watch out." Not only was she in love with a man in one of the most dangerous arms of the service but with one who was in love with another woman. Her defiance of Fate had certainly packed a boomerang.

She forced her thoughts back to the present and resolutely concentrated on the persons around the table. The smoothness and serenity of Ellen Marshall's face showed what a few days in the mountain wilderness, free from the responsibilities of her life, could do for her. Claire, in a sports suit the tint of her blue eyes, had retired within a protective coloring of sullen silence. Estelle Lacey, an inveterate chatterer,

cheeks as pink as her blouse, was cross-examining
Phil Maury as to his exact emotions as he dangled
from the edge of the cliff. Had his past flashed in
review as happened when drowning?

"Lay off Phil, Estelle." Jim Lacey looked up from
the thick, juicy steak which had heretofore claimed
his entire attention. "You're frightening Becky. The
youngster's eyes are big as fire-balloons."

Jess caught the child's hand under the table and
squeezed it.

"Wish we had some fire-balloons with which to
signal the man in Mars tonight, don't you, Becky?"
she asked and received a faint smile in answer.

"By the way, what became of Trent?" Lacey bab-
bled on. "Haven't seen hide nor hair of him since the
late unpleasantness. Did it do him up?"

"What he did wouldn't hurt anyone." Phil Maury's
voice was ugly. "He hates me. I'll bet if Jess hadn't
been there to watch his grandstand play he would
have let me go. He came in at the final curtain. She
really saved me."

"*Phil!*" Because she couldn't speak in a steady voice
of Van's self-effacing, heroic fight for a man's life, Jess
let his incredible ingratitude go after the involuntary
shocked exclamation.

"Vance returned to Karrisbrooke yesterday, Jim,
immediately after the *slight* service he rendered,"
Ellen Marshall announced. "I received an eye-witness
account of the episode—not from him. You belittle
yourself when you make light of his rescue of you,
Philip. In the face of your reaction it's rather a pity he
didn't let you go. You're hardly worth the risk of a life
as valuable as his." She rose. "We start for home early
in the morning, remember. Come, Becky."

"Miss Ellen, may I stay with Pink and help wash
the dishes? She's—so—so kind of cheerful."

"You may, child. We could all do with a little more
cheer in the atmosphere. Jessamine, come with me. I
need you."

"What can I do to help, Aunt Ellen?" Jess asked as
they walked through the crisp, cold air under a sky

blanketed thickly with stars to the very edge of the faint rose-color horizon.

"Nothing, my dear. You looked as if you had endured as much of the conversation as you could stand without smashing something or someone—preferably someone."

"It hurt intolerably to hear Van's heroic rescue spoken of so lightly. He was magnificent. So cool and in such horrible danger himself. If he hadn't come I couldn't have held Phil. He would have gone over and dragged me with him." She shivered.

"I know, my dear, you poured out the story when you burst into my cabin on your return. I wouldn't have heard of it otherwise. I saw Vance before he left for town. He's coming back tonight. He didn't mention the ledge episode, although I gave him every chance. He was white, and flinched if he moved his arms, as if the muscles had been strained."

"They must have been, unbearably. It was horrible. Why did it happen? I have the feeling that each episode—that's your word, not mine—in which one has a part moves one's life story on. I can't see what possible significance that accident had except to endanger the life of a man who is invaluable to his country and to show Phil up as a little more contemptible than I had thought him."

"Hasn't the 'episode' moved your life's story on, Jessamine?"

The question set her pulse thrumming. Had it? She'd say it had. It had torn her heart wide open. Did Aunt Ellen suspect what had happened to her?

"Try to forget it. Not the nobility of the act, but its terror," Ellen Marshall advised as if no answer were expected to her curt question. "Here we are at my cabin. Look off over the valley. The peace and quiet will soften the sharp edges of the memory of the near-tragic experience."

Side by side niece and aunt stood in the doorway, the red-gold on a level with the silvery hair. Dusk blurred far-off outlines where city lights were pricking a sequin pattern, dimmed the pink afterglow in which a solitary frosty star twinkled like an outsize

gold sequin. Far away a sheep-bell tinkled. A sway-
ing wraith of smoke from the campfire drifted past.

They stood a moment in reverent silence before
they entered the cabin. Jessamine closed the door and
crossed to the fieldstone mantel. Firelight turned her
white jacket and blouse to flamingo, faintly tinted her
pearls as, hands in the pockets of her green slacks,
she watched her aunt poke the smoldering logs.

"This spot is heavenly peaceful. It goes deeper than
the usual Sunday stillness, Aunt Ellen. You were
right, it does ease the ache left by yesterday's terror.
It makes one realize how little one's life counts when
nations across the ocean are being shattered by bru-
tality and hate. Sometimes I wonder if the .tragic
chaos will end before the world is torn to shreds."

"It will, in spite of the Powers of Darkness stalking
up and down the earth it is still God's world. Each
life does count tremendously, my dear. Never doubt
that. Creative work, doing one's job superlatively
well; and for women, the importance of keeping the
home a fortress of love and security for men and
children will count more and more when this country
is drawn into the struggle, as I am sure it will be. The
only time in my long life when I feel old and tired
and licked is when I realize how powerless I am to
help more."

"You powerless, helpless, Aunt Ellen? You're magnificent. Colonel Slade told me at dinner the other
night that the women of the Carolinas had done an
incomparable piece of defense work in building army
morale with their hospitality to the men who were
here for war maneuvers, that you had been the leader
who had set the pace for this county. I'm terribly
proud of you."

"Thank you, my dear."

Ellen Marshall set the poker in its stand and sank
into a deep-cushioned chair. The logs she had stirred
flamed and shot a million sparks up chimney. The
dancing light made grotesque patterns on the chinked
walls, set agleam the lenses of the spectacles on the
open Bible on a bedside table, and turned rustic

furniture, rugs and curtains the shimmering color of a goldfish.

"I'm glad we came here even if the chances were nine to one we'd be caught in a snowstorm, Jessamine. We need to get away from the sordid realities that at times come uncomfortably close to our own lives. Speaking of the sordid, had you heard the rumor that the Maurys are planning to separate?"

"I—I—"

"Don't stammer. Had you or hadn't you? The answer is 'Yes' or 'No.' "

"Yes. I can't believe it will happen. Claire's money keeps River Farm going and if he loves nothing else in the world, Phil Maury loves that home of his."

"Has he mentioned a divorce to you?"

"No. He has hinted at it, but as he is the sort of man who is continually finding fault with his wife I concluded it was the martyr pose."

"I'm sorry you didn't tell me of the rumor. I wish I had heard it before I invited the Maurys for the week end."

"Isn't it unfair to condemn Phil until you're sure that he does intend to start a divorce?"

"He won't. I won't permit it. He's considerably in debt to me. I've been carrying the cotton mills, while he finances that racing-stable, if shoveling money into a hole can be dignified by the word 'finances.' "

Jess remembered the bitterness of Phil's voice when he had said weeks ago: "As if she'd been appointed by the Almighty to run the world." If he had thought that of her then, what would he say if he could hear her latest pronunciamento about his domestic and financial affairs?

"Why are you smiling, Jessamine? It isn't a laughing matter. The man is in love with you—temporarily. He is utterly selfish. He wouldn't consider for a moment that he might drag you into a scandal if he starts a divorce."

"How can he when I snub him at every opportunity? I'm getting so fed-up with this Maury stuff I'm horribly tempted to go home to Mother. Believe it or not, Aunt Ellen, I intend to be like you. Independent of men." If she couldn't marry the man she loved, who had made it plain yesterday that he detested her, she wouldn't marry at all, she told herself.

"I. Independent of men. That's an absurd statement. No woman is independent of men. How long could I carry on without my superintendents at the mills, the plantation managers? I have come nearer leaning on Vance Trent than on anyone in my life. Because I really love him, I presume. Don't get any wrong ideas about spinsterhood. It is a lonely life." A twinkle replaced thoughtfulness in Ellen Marshall's eyes.

"For a girl who intends to be independent of the male of the species you appeared extremely disappointed when Johnny Gordon telephoned he couldn't join the camping party."

"It was not only disappointment. The recall of the army sent here for war maneuvers three days ahead of the scheduled time gave me the shivers, made me sure that something serious was in the offing. Besides, his not coming and Barry Collins' backing out at the last minute made me a sort of fifth wheel on the Lacey-Maury outfit. Lucky I had Becky to play with."

"The arrival of Vance Trent should have eased the fifth-wheel situation."

"He and I don't get on, we just don't talk the same language. Even if we did, he was here only long enough to save Phil's life, then he vanished." Aunt Ellen would never know from that indifferent reply that every pulse in her body leaped into high at the mention of his name.

"You astonish me. I had supposed the Major had seen enough of the world—to be able to talk the language of any woman he met. Light the candles, please."

Jess tipped one long taper after another with flame. A soft glow drove shadows from the corners, brought out the red and pink of the hollyhocks on bedspread and hangings, and gilded the soft gray wool of Ellen Marshall's coat and skirt.

"That's better. Whether you marry or don't I am

not afraid for you, Jessamine. Life is a challenge all the way along. Sometimes it is terrifying, always it is exciting if you decide to be a fighter; and with your Marshall inheritance I can't see you as anything else."

"The Ramsays were not of the Milquetoast tribe, I've been given to understand. Come in," she answered a timid knock at the door.

Becky poked her head into the room.

"It's getting awful big and lonesome up here, Miss Jess." Two tears glistened like six-carat diamonds as they rolled down her cheeks.

A dusky figure loomed behind her. The eyes of the tall Negress were black as her taffeta dress, her teeth were as white as the turban wound round her grizzled head. She pushed past the little girl.

"Time yo' was goin' to bed, M's Ellen." Her voice was rich with tenderness. "Yo' have dat long auto ride home tomorrer, an' yo' never would take no care of yo'self, no how, ef 'twant fer Sam an' me, I reckon."

"Stop scolding, Pink. Jessamine, you'd better turn in early yourself."

"I don't need urging, I'm already dead with sleep. Good night, Aunt Ellen." She pressed her lips to the top of the silvery head. "Come on, Becky."

The child offered her hand and dropped a curtsy.

"Good night and thank you, Miss Ellen. I've had a swell week end."

In front of their cabin the girl and child stopped to look off across the valley. A small arm slipped under Jessamine's and a small voice said:—

"Gee, it's an awful big world, Miss Jess—isn't it?" The break in the whispered question misted Jessamine's eyes.

"But—such a beautiful world, Becky. Suppose we sit on the swinging couch on the porch for a while and watch the stars. We'll bundle up in the robe like this—put your head on my shoulder—comfy?"

"It's s-swell. I love you better than almost anybody I know, Miss Jess."

"Thanks, dear, I love you." By her sandal on the plank floor Jessamine gently swung the couch. "Did you ever see so many stars? I had a funny idea when

I was your age and came here with my mother and
Aunt Ellen, that at night a giant stole out of his castle
on top of the mountain—"

"A *giant!* Is there really a giant, Miss Jess? Is—is
that his voice? Don't you hear it?"

"I hear a radio. Your Cousin Vance has one in his
car. He must have come from town and tuned-in to
hear the latest news. I just imagined that giant, dear,
he was a friendly old soul and I liked him. I pretended that he poked his ten great fingers through the
dark sky that I might get a glimpse of the golden
heaven behind it."

"Were the holes the stars ... Miss ..." The sleepy
voice trailed off to nothing.

Jessamine looked down at the closed eyes and
swung the couch back and forth, listening to the
indistinct radioed voice, wishing that the broadcast
were loud enough for her to hear. Now and then she
caught a few words which, out of their context, had
no meaning, yet sent an unaccountable tingle of excitement along her nerves. The curiously disturbing
voice had stopped. Would Vance tune in again?
Would he speak to her when they met at breakfast?
She had told him she hoped she'd never see him
again. Would he take her at her word?

She looked up with a start as someone stopped in
front of the porch—Philip Maury! Her heart appeared
to have parked in her throat for keeps. This would be
the perfect dramatic moment for Claire to make her
entrance.

"Go back to your cabin, Phil. If you don't, I'll
waken everybody in camp by yelling fire."

"Oh, no you won't, you'll listen. I've got to finish
what I was trying to make you understand yesterday.
Don't call!" He put his hand over her mouth. "Ouch!"
He pulled it away and looked at his wrist. "That brat
bit me."

Becky had emerged from a cocoon of wraps and
stood up.

"I'll bite you again, you—you punk, if you don't let
Miss Jess alone when she tells you to get out. Cousin
Vance—you've come just in time. Mr. Maury—"

Jessamine was on her feet. Did this mean a fight? It couldn't, it couldn't. Not after what Van had done for Phil yesterday.

"*Ssh! Ssh!*" she cautioned. "Don't waken Aunt—"

"What's going on?" Ellen Marshall interrupted as, wrapped in a voluminous lounge-robe, she appeared behind them.

"I was coming to tell you, Miss Ellen." Vance Trent's grave voice sent a little shiver of apprehension along Jessamine's nerves. Even in the dim light she could see the whiteness of his face. "Japan has attacked Pearl Harbor. It looks like war at last."

"It's come," Ellen Marshall said. "Now we know where we stand—united—or we won't stand. I'm going home tonight. I can't stay here—"

"Not *tonight*, Aunt Ellen!" Jessamine protested.

"Miss Ellen, wait until morning," Trent urged.

Philip Maury strolled indolently toward his cabin. Ellen Marshall's eyes followed him, came back to the man beside her. She shook her head.

"No. I can't wait, Vance. It's a desperate moment in world history. I must be at the mills when they open. We are filling defense orders, remember. I haven't felt any too secure about them—now that we are at war, I must be doubly on guard."

XX

The sneak-attack on Pearl Harbor already seemed a hundred years ago. At last she was beginning to emerge from the shock of war declared, Jessamine Ramsay told herself, as she pedaled her bicycle toward the Marshall Cotton Mills. So were the neighbors and the country at large. Humiliating as it was to have been caught napping, the catastrophe had served to unite the citizens of the United States in a gigantic war program.

Not all. Her brows drew together in a puzzled frown. Phil Maury's unhelpful attitude was incomprehensible. His indifference and unbelief that war would come to the country had persisted even after he had been obliged to register in the under-forty-five call to the service.

Since the last night at the mountain camp, she had seen him only at dinners and dances. He had not brought up the subject of the sale of his share of the cotton mills, thank goodness. Apparently he was absorbed in preparation for the Horse Show in aid of the Red Cross to be held tomorrow at the Hunt Club, of which he was president. Would that account for his stiff, remote manner when with her, or did he at last realize that she didn't love him? Was he afraid of what Claire might do or was he carefully preparing the stage for his divorce?

Johnny Gordon had said, the day of Mrs. Carter's tea, which now seemed eons ago, "I hear you've picked three pretty special pals since you came to Karrisbrooke—or they've picked you."

Were he here now he would see by Phil's indifference that the first person he had named was no longer in her stag-line. Van Trent had been summoned to Washington the day after the return from the mountain week-end. She hadn't had a chance to tell him that she hadn't meant that she never wanted to see him again. Not that he cared. Lucky he couldn't know how she held her breath when his name was mentioned, hoping to hear he was coming back. That disposed of the second man on the list. Barry Collins, the third, apparently had lost interest, for which blessing she was devoutly grateful.

She leaned her wheel against a side of the administration building and made a little face of dismay when she saw a saddled horse tied to a hitching-post. It meant that Phil Maury was on the premises.

Glorious day. Crisp and peaceful. It almost eased the incessant aching desire to be with Van, the awareness of gathering war clouds; gave one gay courage, a "God's in His heaven, all's right with the world" feeling.

The sky was a clear blue, one small white cloud was crossing it with a ghostly lack of speed. The smell of stirring earth scented the air. The river sparkled like a restless mass of Oriental sapphires glinting in the sunlight. In a field across the road a man in blue denim overalls was pruning a fruit tree. On a food-shelf outside an office window a robin and a catbird chirped and hopped as they devoured grain. From inside came the steady rumble of machinery. It was unusually mild weather even for North Carolina—a field superintendent had reported that tobacco seeds planted in December were sprouting—while across the water one of the severest winters within the memory of man was impeding and freezing the enemy.

"Here you are, Miss Jess. Miss Ellen was inquiring for you. Watch your step, she's in a devil of a temper."

Barry Collins' voice, which indicated seething irritation, stopped her on the steps. His usually smooth red hair was rumpled as if he had been raking it with his fingers, his gray-green eyes smoldered with anger.

"I just phoned Karrisbrooke at her *order*, to find out if you'd left." The sentence was jerky as if while speaking of one subject another occupied his mind. "Major Trent answered."

"The Major? I thought he was in Washington." Would Collins detect the hint of breathlessness in her voice?

"He said he flew back to keep an appointment. Any idea whether it was military, business, social or romantic? His cousin-in-law, the Carter menace, is still at the Inn. I wondered why she stayed after he left, as I understand that her period of mourning is over."

"It just happens that I am not in the Major's confidence, Mr. Collins," she answered coolly, while in another part of her mind she was thinking, "What could have brought Van here? Me? Silly. Didn't he taunt, 'Can't keep away from him, can you?' Not likely he'd want to see a girl whom he believed to be hypnotized by a married man. Had Aunt Ellen sent for him?"

"I don't know why I'm wasting time on Trent when you haven't yet answered the question I put to you the day we met at the schoolhouse."

"Question?" She had given thanks too soon for his apparent indifference.

"Don't pretend you've forgotten that I asked you to marry me. For it is pretense; I don't believe any girl in the world ever forgot a proposal of marriage."

"Never in the one we knew, perhaps, but things have happened so fast and so tragically since, that it's a different world."

"Okay; we'll admit that the question I asked has been crowded from your memory; I'll repeat it. Will you marry me?"

"Sorry, no can do."

"Don't be flippant." A Collins she never before had seen peered at her between narrowed lids. "I'm getting fed-up with your indifference. I'll take the matter up with your aunt, then you'll say 'Yes'—or *else*—"

She watched him incredulously as he ran down the three steps to the drive. He had *threatened* her. Was his need of money or the assurance that he would marry it making him desperate? Could he by any chance have a hold on Ellen Marshall? It was too fantastic a possibility even to consider, she concluded as she entered the building.

"Miss Ramsay!" The voice came from the telephone room. She stopped on the threshold. The girl at the switchboard pulled out a plug, removed her right earphone.

"Remember you said you'd pinch-hit for Goldie if I needed you?"

"I meant it. What can I do?"

"She phoned she couldn't get here today. She's a whiz at her job but unreliable as a hen crossing the street. I cover up for her a lot. I reckon I shouldn't, but I can't help liking her. She's a live wire and grand company. She keeps me on the giggle, don't wonder guys fall for her. She was stepping out last night, I'll bet. I guess she's got steady-trouble. The fellow she's been going with, he works at the Hunt Club, has been getting madder and madder about the way she took up with the soldiers an' *others*. If you'd take over the board while I have my lunch, it would help a lot."

"I'll be here. At what hour shall I punch the time clock?"

"Twelve sharp. You're super, Miss Ramsay. You don't just do things, you—you—well, I can't express it right, you make a person feel that you're honest-to-God glad to help."

"Glad isn't the word, Lucy, I'm fairly aching to help. Who isn't these days?"

"Who isn't? You'd be surprised if you hung round this joint to find how many are not. You're what I call a snappy dresser. That lime-green pullover and cardigan with the beige culotte—isn't that what the style mags call the divided skirt?—is a little bit of all right."

"Glad you approve. I'll be here when the noon whistle blows."

As she ran up the stairs Lucy's voice echoed through her memory: "She's grand company, no wonder guys fall for her." The words brought with them the prickling sense of uneasiness she felt each time she thought of Goldie's hail to Johnny as the motorcycle passed the shabby car. Should she have spoken to him about it? "Don't be an idiot. Young Mr. Gordon has been around for a number of years," she reminded herself.

She realized the moment she entered the conference room that it was a place of warring factions. Barry Collins had warned her that her aunt was angry. It was an understatement. The air was heavy with the smoke of battle. Philip Maury, in riding clothes, stood at a window staring out. Had he broken the news that he intended to sell his interest in the mills? Ellen Marshall was regarding his brown tweed back with speculative eyes. Was the usually lovely skin of her face slightly gray or was it tinted by the reflection from her print dress?

"Mr. Collins said you wanted me, Aunt Ellen, but this looks like the heart-to-heart between two pluto-crats. I'll go now and return when you and Phil have finished your business discussion." Escape from what she knew to be a fiery session was her one thought.

"Stay, Jessamine. Get your notebook. I want the following conversation taken down word for word.

"I shall not consent to the sale of your share of the mills, Philip. The sale itself would be of minor importance. The real danger is in your indifference to the value of what we can do to help the nation in this crisis. We've just received word to step-up production of bagging fabrics. It would retard work to have a new and strange interest introduced in the conduct of the mills, for whoever came would indubitably have views diametrically opposed to mine."

Philip Maury turned impatiently. His face was white. Anger had fired his brown eyes to burning black.

"I have no intention of selling to a stranger, M's Ellen. Barry Collins wants to buy me out. He's a director, isn't he?"

It wasn't the fact that Collins had been named as the would-be purchaser that caught at Jess's breath, it was the memory of his face and voice as he had threatened, "I'll take the matter up with your aunt. Then you'll say 'Yes'—or *else*—" What had that "or *else*" meant? Could he terrorize Ellen Marshall?

Not so you'd notice it. She swallowed a chuckle as she looked at the woman seated at the head of the conference table. She terrorized? She was unbeatable. Undefeatable.

"So, it is Barry Collins who wants to buy-in, Philip? Why didn't he speak to me about it when he was here a few minutes ago instead of chattering about that horse of yours he intends to exhibit at the Show?"

"He started to talk business and you snubbed him till he was fightin' mad, M's Ellen. He had sense enough to shut up, get out, and let me carry on. He realizes, if you don't, that I'm old enough to dispose of my property *when* and *how* I please."

That was carrying defiance into the enemy camp with brass-band accompaniment.

"Your share of these mills is worth a lot of money,

Philip. It has been in your family a great many years. Where does Collins plan to get the cash to purchase it? Cash is what you need, what you will insist on, isn't it?"

His eyes were those of a trapped animal as he answered her.

"Suppose I do want money? It's a universal want these days, isn't it? I'm registered in the draft. My number may come up any day. I want my affairs settled before I'm called into service. Is that so queer? Barry has money, he's had a corkin' big salary since you hired him. He can put through a deal to borrow the rest needed."

"On what collateral?"

("If Johnny's story is correct *I'm* the collateral," Jess thought.)

"That's the business of the man from whom he borrows it. What difference does it make to you or me where he gets it?"

"The difference is that if Barry Collins couldn't keep up payment of the interest, the owner of the note might decide to step in and take over."

"Would you consent to the sale if Collins assured you that the holder of the note would be a person who could carry on efficiently in case he had to step in?"

"Sorry to dash the hope from your face and voice, but—you misunderstood me. I don't *want* Barry Collins as part owner of these mills, and what is more to the point, I *won't* have him."

"Why in God's name did my father tie me to your apron strings? Give you the power to decide whether I should sell my interest?"

"Keep your voice down, Philip. Shouting at me won't get you anywhere."

"I thought you were sold for fair on Collins." With an effort he reconditioned his voice. "I'm not the only one. There's a general feelin' that he'll get a handsome cut-in when you go. The bettin' is nine to one he'll be handed Karrisbrooke."

"*Go?* What do you mean, 'go'? Die? I've no intention of dying for years and years. In times like these one stiffens and carries on. One doesn't weaken. There is too much to be done here on earth. You ought to know by this time that sentiment has no place in my business life, Philip. From this date, these mills are to run twenty-four hours a day if necessary, seven days a week, and anyone who stands in the way of that schedule, you, Collins or anyone else, will pay dearly."

She leaned a little forward, italicized some of her words by a tap of her forefinger on the polished table.

"Don't you *realize* what this country is up against? Don't you *care* that a U-boat campaign is being waged with success within a few miles, almost within gunshot of our shoes? First the *Allen Jackson* went down in a sea of flames. The *Malay's* rudder was shot away. She *foundered*. Two other ships followed her to the bottom. And *you* stand there and suggest holding up production of what the country needs for defense, while this business is being reorganized. I'm *ashamed* of you."

"Production wouldn't be held up. Collins knows the turn of every wheel. You had him put in the deferred class because he is valuable on your plantation and in these mills which are loaded with defense orders, didn't you? He would step-up production. *Will* you consent to the sale?"

Ellen Marshall was standing. Her icily determined eyes met his, burning with frustration.

"The answer is 'No,' Philip."

His lips parted as if to reply. He shut them hard and crossed the room. At the door he turned.

"I've stood for a lot of interference in my life from you, M's Ellen. I'm through. From this minute I take things into my own hands. There's such a thing as a court of equity, remember, and there's a more drastic weapon I can use first to bring you to terms. Think it over. Good mornin'." The slam of the door shook the windows.

Ellen Marshall's lips tightened in a satirical twist.

"A minute ago I bragged that sentiment had no place in my business life, Jessamine. If it isn't sentiment—affection for his grandfather and for his father—that is preventing me from allowing Philip Maury to dispose of his share of the mills, I don't know what it is. I could have bought him out years ago. God knows, I've been terribly tempted. But his father 'tied him to my apron strings' because he knew he had no business sense. He's proved that, hasn't he, by allowing that stable to plunge him up to his ears in debt? 'Court of equity.' Hmp! I'd like to be cross-examined in court. I'd tell 'em a thing or two."

"Any idea what the 'more drastic weapon' is he threatened to use, Aunt Ellen?"

"No. And I don't believe he knows. Theatrical claptrap. Did you make notes of the conversation—if it can be called conversation, Jessamine?"

"Yes." A little frightened by the whiteness of her aunt's face, her tired voice, she attempted to change her train of thought.

"I have news for you. Barry Collins told me that when he phoned Karrisbrooke to find out if I had started Major Trent answered."

"Vance has come? Now things will straighten out. He gets things done." She drew a deep sigh of relief. Life surged back into her voice. Color crept into her cheeks. She laughed. "I am now giving a demonstration of my independence of man, Jessamine. Type those notes. I'll send a boy up for them."

"I will, Aunt Ellen. I may be late for lunch. I'm to take over the switchboard for Lucy Long for the noon hour."

"Why should you be drafted?"

"I wasn't. I had offered to help Lucy when she needed help, there are more millworkers than switchboard operators available now, remember. Goldie Mellor, who comes on duty at noon, can't get here."

"The girl with hair like corn-silk and eyes big as green emeralds? I hired her. I sized her up as one who would be extraordinarily capable at her job, any job, and who would do anything for money except sell herself. She's too smart for that."

"She's smart, all right. She joined one of my First Aid classes. She asks keen questions but phrases them in such a way that she keeps us laughing. I doubt if underneath she is as hardboiled as she tries to appear. I like her." She resisted the temptation to speak of her concern when the girl had hailed Johnny Gordon. It was his business; if she were to tell, Ellen Marshall might make it hers. Instead she said:—

"Send the boy up in twenty minutes and I'll be ready."

"Just a moment, Jessamine." Ellen Marshall glanced at a pad on the desk. "Estelle Lacey phoned. She wants you to wear your Red Cross Staff Assistant's uniform when you sell bonds at the Horse Show tomorrow. The head of Civilian Defense asks if you will take over air-spotting from ten to twelve mornings. He knows that you are assigned to the Motor Corps, but hopes you will take on the job until someone volunteers. He suggested that from the penthouse of this building you could see to the mouth of the river."

"Of course I'll do it. That fills in the very last unoccupied time I had. I'll report to him tomorrow."

Notes typed and delivered to the messenger, Jess closed her typewriter, crossed the roof and gazed unseeingly down at the river, blue as the sky above it, alive with motorboats making one think of prehistoric water-bugs as they plied back and forth on mill business. The floor under her feet vibrated from the thud of machinery and shook a faint metal accompaniment from the covers of the galvanized iron bins filled with sand stationed every few feet around the edge of the roof.

She relived the scene in the conference room. Set down in black and white, Phil's "there's a more drastic weapon I can use" had an ugly look. That, tied up with Collins' "you'll say 'Yes'—or *else*," had the effect of an icy needle-shower up and down her backbone. The two men were threatening Ellen Marshall.

Phil must have been furious, perhaps a little terrified, to have repeated the gossip about Ellen Marshall's rumored bequest of Karrisbrooke to Barry Collins. Life here certainly was in a tangle at present. Mills running to capacity and Lucy Long intimating that "some round this joint" were not eager to help. She herself, loving and longing for the sound of Van Trent's voice, the laughing tenderness of his eyes. Phil fighting Aunt Ellen, Barry aiding him under cover; Peckett, hovering like a buzzard to pick up whatever bodies fell. Good heavens, what a gruesome thought. Where had it come from this heavenly day? The noon whistle sounded.

As she ran down the stairs to relieve Lucy Long her thoughts raced with her. Aunt Ellen had been so sure that Vance Trent would straighten out the tangle. Could he? It better be soon. Time was marching on in seven-league boots. So was the war. Was he counting on the information he had acquired at the old wharf to checkmate Peckett's activities and, with his, the schemes of Barry Collins? Apparently nothing was being done about it. The oily Gus was still at large. Only yesterday he had rolled his "slinkin' eyes," run his tongue over his lips, and swept off his hat with a flourish as he passed her.

"Here I am, Lucy." She was a bit breathless as she entered the telephone room.

"Gee, you shouldn't have run. I could have waited."

"Run is an understatement. I pelted down the stairs." She slid onto the stool the girl vacated and picked up the earphones.

"Any special instructions?"

"No. Never very busy at noon hour, to hear Goldie tell it. I reckon that's when she signs up for dates. If you want to copy her line, answer, 'Marshall Cotton Mills,' this way, and when a man asks who it is, say, "It's me, Sugar'—they call her Sugar, and I bet you'll get results—and how."

"I'll do my best with the Southern drawl, Lucy. Run along."

The red light. She plugged in. "Marshall Cotton Mills." Her response was a perfect imitation of Lucy Long's version of the glamorous Goldie's. A squeaky inquiry came over the wire:—

"Who is it?"

The voice was disguised. Why? Lucy had intimated that Goldie had soldiers in her stag-line. This was a

time to check up on disguised voices if ever there
were one.

"It's me, Sugar." Her whispered drawl struck her as
being funny. She shut her teeth in her lip to keep
back a chuckle.

"Tomorrow night. Nine sharp."

Somewhere a receiver clicked on its hook.

She stared unseeingly at the switchboard. The situation was no longer humorous. That squeaky "Tomorrow night. Nine sharp" set merry-pranks prickling
along her nerves.

If only she had been quick enough to ask "Where?"
Not so good. The question would have aroused suspicion. The person who had phoned had taken it for
granted she knew. A man who was afraid his voice
might be recognized had made that date with
Goldie. A soldier or one of those "others" to whom
Lucy had referred? Who were the "others"?

"Tomorrow night. Nine sharp."

Suppose that message hadn't referred to a date?
Suppose someone was planning trouble for the mills?

XXI

The morning events of the Horse Show, which had
been held under a brilliant sky and over a pic-
turesque hunting course of panel fences and hurdles,
were over. Luncheon was being served at the Hunt
Club to the accompaniment of the United States
Marines' Song.

> From the halls of Montezuma
> To the shores of Tripoli . . .

blared the local band.

Jessamine hummed the air as she perched on the
broad wall of the terrace in the yellow dress, white

coif and flowing yellow chiffon veil of the Red Cross Staff Assistant's uniform. Horses were being led to the paddocks, their coats shining like satin in the sun, the silks of their riders making a rainbow in motion. Through one of the French windows she caught a glimpse of Ellen Marshall, dressed in gray with a purple feather turban, seated at the long table on a raised platform in the great dining room where judges, exhibitors and officials of the Show were guests. With the tactlessness so often shown by Fate, or committees, she had been placed at the right of Philip Maury, president of the Club.

She was unusually colorless; two lines cut between her dark brows, lines were deeply etched between her nose and lips, yet she was chatting with him as easily as if that stormy session, in the conference room at the mill yesterday, never had taken place. That was Aunt Ellen. She wore neither her loves nor her aversions on her sleeve for the public to peck at; her good manners were inviolable.

"Alone! Nothing to eat? How come?" Vance Trent inquired as he crossed the terrace. One would think from his casual greeting they had parted friends instead of in a bitter quarrel weeks ago. He was wearing jodhpurs and riding boots with his uniform blouse. He had been one of several officers from the Camp who had taken part in the morning events. Remembering what had happened to young Todd on this same course her blood had turned to ice each time his horse had taken a fence.

"My word, you surprised me, bursting from the everywhere into the here like that!" She matched his light voice. If he intended to ignore the past she would. She hoped the exclamation accounted for the color she felt steal to her hair.

"Jim Lacey started for eats for me, soldier, but I can see him through the window waving his arms and doubtless telling his victim, probably an out-of-town man, how it happened that his wonder-horse knocked off the top rail of every fence he went over and came pounding down the stretch without his rider. He was sure of a prize—the prizes are very 1942: Defense

Bonds. I've sold—and I mean sold—those same bonds and stamps till my voice is a squeak and I'm weak from hunger. I ask you, what is a starving girl in comparison with a horse?" She was aware she was chattering, but talking helped drown the sound of her heartbeat, which seemed loud enough for him to hear.

"Sorry I startled you. In future I'll appear and fade out with the deliberation of the Cheshire Cat. This starving girl will be fed at once. You know the summerhouse near the live oak? You ought, it is one of your aunt's benefactions. I'll rustle up luncheon for two and join you there."

"But—"

"Don't argue, *please*. Do you realize I haven't seen you for weeks, that for those same weeks I've lived with that 'I hope I *never* see you again' ringing in my ears? Don't answer, we had both reached the limit of physical endurance that afternoon and weren't entirely responsible. We haven't met since my return to Karrisbrooke yesterday and I have a lot to report—Angel."

The last word did it, sent the blood rioting through her veins. It was heavenly to be friends with him again. She nodded assent and slipped from the wall.

What could he have to tell her that seemed of such importance to him, she wondered as she crossed the velvety green lawn. Thank goodness, Phil Maury was too occupied with his duty as host to know, even if he cared, where she was, and Barry Collins was devoting himself to guests from out of town, two men and two women, typical race followers, who would keep him out of her way for the present.

When she reached the small brick house with its iron-lace-framed porch and red-bud tree beside it, shedding its pods in the light breeze, she knelt on a bench in front of a window and peered into the paneled room complete with fireplace, rose chintz hangings and antique furniture. The decorator had achieved a perfect period effect.

She was looking at a huge electric bulb hung from a tree limb and thinking what an ideal spot the lawn would make for an evening out-of-door performance of a play, when Trent appeared carrying a small folding table and chairs, followed by Caesar, one of the Club boys, in tan livery the exact shade of his skin, with laden tray.

"Howdy, M's Ramsay," he said in answer to her smile and nod.

Trent snapped down the legs of the table and unfolded the chairs on the square of green lawn in front of the house.

"Set the tray here, Caesar. That will be all for the present." As the boy departed Jessamine laughed.

"You certainly get things done your way."

"Why not? Efficiency is my job. Sit here. You Tarheels certainly can cream oysters. Have some of these piping-hot ones. A roll? Light as a feather. This salad looked okay. Avocado, grapefruit, lettuce and cream cheese-balls—all the vitamins—*and* a specialty-of-the-house paprika dressing the waiter recommended." He poured a clear, aromatic, mahogany-colored stream from the silver pot. "Coffee coming up."

"Service in capital letters! Jim Lacey will think I've been kidnaped."

"I took care of that. Told him I was looking after you. Remember I said I had a lot to report?"

"I do. But first, let me tell you what happened yesterday. It may not amount to anything, it may be important."

She told of the phone call while she was at the mill switchboard, of her imitation of Goldie Mellor's voice for the fun of it, the squeaky question.

"Perhaps it wasn't queer, perhaps it was just my war-inflamed imagination which made me suspect subversive meaning behind that 'Tomorrow evening. Nine sharp.'"

"'Tomorrow evening. Nine sharp.' That would be this evening! No clue as to where the girl was expected to be?"

"It was on the tip of my tongue to ask. I caught back the question in time. Goldie was supposed to know. My first impulse was to shadow her from the time she left the mill today. That was out because I had promised to sell Defense Bonds here and be at the ball tonight." Was her suspicion of enough importance to cut those two sharp lines between his brows?

"Why didn't you get in touch with me?"

"I thought of it, then remembered that the girl had many followers and as it was an evening date decided that it was doubtless merely a sentimental rendezvous."

"Considering the fact that *you* got the message, *not* Goldie, your espionage would have been a waste of time. She won't go wherever she was supposed to go. Any other reports to make? We're in this investigation together, remember?"

"I do. You said you had a lot to report and I talked out of turn with my Goldie story."

"Eat the salad while I explain or you will return to your sales-job hungry. First, you may be interested to know that I have been shifted from the Special Assignments Section, the switch is typical of the confusion in war preparations, and am being sent as the head of a parachute division to a so-called Annapolis of the air. There are to be four of them, located East, West, South and Midwest, each one to induct aviation cadets at the rate of 2,500 a month. Officials of the aeronautics board have decided that too little emphasis has been directed toward the lifesavers of the air."

"Sounds like a worth-while appointment."

"It is. There is nothing more important now than training pilots unless it's making planes for them to fly. Flew to the Southern camp to which I've been assigned. Liked it. However, my orders may be changed to 'Destination Unknown' at the ring of a phone."

"I hope n-not!" To cover up the breathless catch in her voice she laughed. "Aunt Ellen will be happy to have you somewhere near to consult. Your fatal charm has worked a miracle. You are the first person to whom I've seen her turn for advice. Has she told you of her recent battle with Phil Maury?"

"Yes, when she and I lunched together yesterday. She didn't mince words in her description of it."

"I wish she would let him sell. The sooner she gets him out of the mills the better for her."

"And for you."

"That comeback was unnecessary, but if you insist on thinking I'm in love with him we'll let it go. Suppose the mills don't produce so much for a month or two? They'd soon get into gear and probably double their output."

"Not with Barry Collins as half-owner. Miss Ellen would be worn to a shred trying to combat his moves. The guy is bad medicine."

"Sure?"

"Sure. I've been North two months—seemed like two years when I thought of the girl I left behind me—all that time wasn't spent on military matters. I discovered that Collins is not—"

"We've been hunting the place over for you, Van!"

Helen Carter, dressed in orchid from hat to shoes, sent her voice ahead as she approached with Doctor MacDonald waddling like an overfed drake beside her.

"If you wanted to avoid notice you should have set the table behind, not in front of the summerhouse, Major. Miss Ramsay's yellow uniform can be seen from the terrace." Her words were tinged with malice.

MacDonald, who had taken on a little more the pouter-pigeon silhouette since his professional visits to Karrisbrooke weeks before, saluted, blinked his funny little eyes and flourished a pudgy hand.

"Ladies and gentlemen, we give you Colonel Vance Trent."

"Colonel!" Helen Carter exclaimed. "Is it true, Vance?"

"The Doc's announcement is a bit premature, Helen. The promotion hasn't been officially confirmed."

"It's in the bag. General Carson is at the Clubhouse looking for you. I told him I'd find you or die in the attempt."

"You won't have to die, Doc. Come, Jess."

"Not yet, Major. Someone ought to guard this commissary department until Caesar arrives. A swarm of kids is likely to descend at any minute. They'd be welcome to the food, but I'm sure the Club needs the dishes. I'll stay."

"I'll send the boy post-haste. I'll see you at the booth. Don't sell all the bonds before I come."

"Hurry, Van. Even if you are a Colonel you can't keep a General waiting," Helen Carter urged petulantly.

Jessamine's eyes followed the three as they walked toward the Clubhouse. The woman, walking between the two men, had linked her arms in theirs. Her orchid hat, on a level with MacDonald's head, reached only to Van Trent's shoulder.

"That seems to be that. Fair Helen, with the face that launched a thousand ships, sure got her man that time. Why be a crab about her, Jess Ramsay? She is beautiful and *not* dumb—decidedly *not* dumb."

Did Van love her? He had said that the time spent in the North had seemed years when he thought of the girl he left behind him. Had he meant Helen Carter? He had changed since the week end at camp. His face was graver, his mouth straighter. Not to be wondered at. War had been declared since then.

She walked back and forth across the soft green turf as she waited and wondered what discovery he had made about Collins. Something that tied the superintendent of the Karrisbrooke plantation up with the old-wharf episode? About time the authorities checked Peckett's moonshining activities. If he were jailed for illegal sales would he drag Collins in with him?

She switched the troubled train of thought, stopped pacing to watch people streaming from the Clubhouse in a fluid rainbow of color, neutralized by the khaki of uniforms, to the music of "Keep 'Em Flying, Uncle Sam," which the band was rendering with patriotic fervor. If one could believe one's eyes, an epidemic of red feathers was sweeping the world of fashion.

Down the terrace steps the crowd went, across the grass toward the gates of the course. Inside, horses

which were to take part in the $1000 Sweepstakes
were being paraded before the grandstand. Thor-
oughbreds, who were to race in the emerald-green
and white of Phil Maury's colors, brought a thunder-
ous burst of applause. She glanced at her watch. An
event would start in fifteen minutes. She should be
back at the booth. Thank goodness here came Caesar
on the run.

"The Major, he tol' me not to bring dessert, jes' to
take the dishes, M's Ramsay, so's you could go," he
explained breathlessly.

"All right, Caesar. I don't want anything more to
eat. Big crowd, isn't it?"

"Yes, M'am. The gran'stan' is packed solid." The
boy's eyes glittered with excitement. His grin exposed
extraordinarily large, white teeth. "An' they're crowdin' in for the bleacher seats. I got a little money on
one of Mr. Maury's hosses, I hope he wins."

"Crowdin'" was right, Jessamine agreed as she
passed the side gate. Gus Peckett was pushing his
way in, gripping the arm of a girl in a white-and-
green sports coat of enormous plaid and a floppy emerald hat which concealed her face. They were coming
toward her. Time to do a disappearing act if she
intended to avoid him, and she did.

She darted ahead of a party of six each one of
whom was talking loudly. Looked back over her
shoulder. Stopped short with the result that two of
the women behind almost fell over her.

"What's the big idea?" one of them snarled and
angrily tipped back the red hat tilted over her nose.

"I'm sorry, I'm terribly sorry," Jess said aloud, while
saying to herself incredulously:—

"It's Goldie Mellor with Gus Peckett. *Goldie*. Did
he phone that message yesterday?"

XXII

She was back in the red-white-and-blue-draped booth
at one side of the grandstand, under the huge sign:—

BUY DEFENSE BONDS
DO YOUR SHARE FOR FREEDOM
FOR
THE SOLDIERS, THE SAILORS,
THE MARINES, THE AVIATORS,
WHO ARE TAKING YOUR PLACE AT THE FRONT

It was difficult to keep her mind on the job of
selling stamps, filling in bonds and accepting checks
and money. It wasn't the strains of "Dixie," being
sentimentally rendered by the band and occasionally
punctuated by "rebel yells," that tugged at her attention, it was the thought, "Goldie Mellor and Gus
Peckett here together! How come?"

A trumpeted fanfare, the thud of hoofs, startled her
back to her surroundings. The first horse was off for
the first gate. The crowd was breathlessly waiting for
the jump. A sound like the soughing of the wind
indicated the relief of thousands that it had been
safely accomplished. The business of selling bonds
was temporarily suspended. She could devote her
attention to the Goldie-Gus angle of the mysterious
phone call. Suppose it had been he? That was out. It
wouldn't have been necessary to date the girl for
tonight if he were bringing her to the races this
afternoon.

She was still puzzling over the problem when the
trumpet announced intermission. People in the grandstand and on the bleachers stood up or walked
around to relax tense muscles and rest strained eyes.

It was a stiff course. Two riders had been carried from the field on stretchers and one horse had gone down never to rise again.

"Great riding, wasn't it, Miss Ramsay?"

The question switched Jess's attention from a riderless horse being led from the field to startled awareness of the man and girl in front of the booth and the scent of cheap perfume.

"The jumping was superb, Mr. Peckett. Good afternoon, Goldie. May I sell you a bond?"

"Howdy, Miss Jess." The girl stopped chewing gum, tipped her head and looked up coquettishly at her companion from under the brim of the enormous emerald-green felt hat which accentuated the yellow of the hair that curled beneath the brim.

"Sure, you can sell me a bond, Miss Jess. Gus is going to buy a twenty-five-dollar baby for me, ain't you, Gussie?"

Startled, inadequately described Peckett's expression.

"I didn't say twenty-five, Sugar, I said I'd buy some stamps."

"Yes, you did, Gus. You promised if I'd come with you instead of with my sweetie, you'd come across. So, lay down the dough, fella." There was a hint of threat beneath the lightness of her voice. Color deepened in her cheeks already rosy with rouge.

"Have it your way, Sugar." Peckett hastily produced a fat roll of greenbacks and peeled off two bills.

"There you are, Miss Ramsay."

"To whom shall I make the bond payable, Mr. Peckett?"

"To me, of course, Sophia-Maria—imagine parents doing a job like that on a kid—Mellor; Goldie's a nickname because of the color of my hair—6 Hillside Road." The promptness and completeness of the girl's information indicated that this was not the first bond which had been purchased for her.

"How are you, Mr. Maury?"

Peckett's smooth greeting brought up Jess's eyes from the bond she was filling in. Phil was glowering at the man who was drawing his tongue across his lips as if pleasureably savoring the situation. The girl nudged his arm.

"Introduce me, Gus," she whispered loudly.

In the split second that Peckett hesitated Jess thought, "That disposes of the possibility that Phil dated her yesterday, that's a relief." Little as she liked or trusted him now, she had been fond of the boy he had been. She would hate to think he was making clandestine evening dates with a girl in his mill.

"Miss Goldie Mellor, meet Mr. Phil Maury. He's president of this society Club outfit, can you beat that?" Peckett's voice bordered on the servile.

"Pleased to meet ya, Mr. Maury." Her glance was arch as she extended fingers tipped with blood-red nails, loaded with cheap rings. "I've heard a lot about you from my steady, the cop who polices the Club grounds all night. He starts his rounds at the brick summerhouse at nine. It can stand watching. It sure makes a swell meeting-place, the hedge that fences in the Club grounds isn't so high there. I ought to know, I've climbed over it times enough to keep a date. He thinks you're an awful smart fella. He's made money on your nags."

That explained the phone call. Goldie's "steady" had asked her to meet him at nine, probably at the summerhouse as he started his patrol of the grounds. No mystery in that. She had been a little previous pouring out the story to Vance Trent, Jess decided.

Color deepened in the girl's face, sparks of anger glinted in the eyes between their heavily mascaraed lashes as Phil Maury ignored the proffered hand.

"Glad of your friend's good opinion, Miss Mellor." His voice was drenched with sarcasm. "The next event on the card will start in five minutes. Better get to your seats, Peckett—I presume they're on the bleachers—or you won't get them."

"Oh, yeah! It just happens they're in the grandstand *and* reserved." The assumption that his seats were on the bleachers had thrown sand into the oil of Peckett's voice. "Say, I've just noticed Goldie is wearing your colors, Maury. Emerald and white. Now what do you know about that? Come on, Sugar."

"Just a minute. Here's your change, Mr. Peckett."
Jess slipped the bond into an envelope. "Don't go
without this, Goldie."

"Bet ya life I won't. I've got five of 'em. When a
soldier guy with dough who I was trying to pep-up—
you'd be surprised how many of 'em had a kinder
sinking what's-it-all-about-feeling—tried to make me
a sort of thank-you present, I'd tell him, 'Nix. Say it
with bonds.' Some of the soldiers here for the war
games were so homesick they just had to spend money on somebody. Why not on me, thinks I. It is kinder
queer I happened to pick on your colors to wear
today, isn't it, Mr. Maury? Next time we meet don't
try that nose-in-the-air act on me; it don't get across.
Come on, Gussie," she cooed, without interrupting the
rhythmic motion of her jaws.

Philip Maury's face was dark with disgust as he
watched the man and girl start toward the grandstand.

"Don't look so confoundedly suspicious, Jessie. Any
woman can wear green and white, can't she? Claire's
wearin' my colors today. I've never seen that gum-
chewer with her bloody nails before and I hope I
never will again. I'll bet she hasn't a brain in her
head."

"She has enough to turn male admiration into Defense Bonds, Philip. She's cheap, but not bad and
there's nothing cheap about her patriotism. I've heard
she's amusing, a fine dancer and 'grand company.'
She gives these 'soldier guys,' as she calls them, an
evening of fun without any emotional entanglement
for either side."

"How do you know so much about her?"

Were his eyes and voice startled, or was she imagining it? He had said he never had seen the girl
before.

"She's an employee at the mill. She was in my First
Aid class and so good at it that she will take on my
cooking class as pupils next week. She's a born teacher. She's honest and loyal."

"Carryin' the torch for her, aren't you? All right
with me. When do you sleep, Jessie? I hear that the

penthouse office has been turned over to Civilian
Defense and that you've added spottin' aircraft to
your other activities. What time is your hitch?"

She mistrusted the hint of intentness in the voice
designed to be light. Was he planning to come to the
roof when she was there? She could block that move.

"Saturdays, from ten to twelve A.M." Neither love
nor hate could pry him from his stables that morning.
Not necessary to tell him that she was on duty every
day at that time till more volunteers came forward.

"Think you'll like it?"

"Yes, but it's a terrifying responsiblity to take on
when one realizes that quick, accurate identification
of hostile aircraft may depend upon a spotter's ability
to recognize the sounds as well as the outlines of
different types of planes. However, I'll learn. Enemy
planes would be likely to follow the river inland from
the sea. On clear days I can see as far as the mouth of
it."

"If those planes ever come. I still think all those
precautions are a lot of hooey."

"They are not. We aren't far from the coast. Our
mills are not the only defense targets worth smashing
in this area."

"Glad you spoke of the mills, it leads right up to
what I want to say to you about M's Ellen."

The rising anger in his voice warned her.

"Again? I told you that day at—at the ledge I
would not interfere in the sale business. So, don't
bring it up. I'm here to sell bonds. Someone is likely
to stop to buy one at any minute."

"No one is thinkin' of bonds, they're hurryin' back
to their seats for the next event. Get this: *make* M's
Ellen let me unload my share of the Marshall Cotton
Mills. I've got to prove within a week that I have a
certain sum of money or that it is forthcomin'."

"You must have lost your mind to think that I or
anyone else can *make* Aunt Ellen consent to do what
she has decided against."

"I'm not so sure." His eyes between narrowed lids
met and held hers. "Tell her that if she doesn't consent I'll start my divorce."

"Really, Phil, you delivered that line with all the venom of a number one screen menace. Aunt Ellen may not want you to dispose of a fortune, but I don't believe your threat of divorcing a perfectly good and—sustaining—wife will send her blood pressure up enough to make her consent to the sale."

His eyes flamed, his lips paled. Instinctively she moved back as he leaned across the counter which separated them.

"I got that crack about livin' on my wife's money all right, Jessie. Tryin' to treat this thing as a joke, aren't you? It isn't, as you'll find out. Ellen Marshall may not care if I divorce my wife, but she may find she's gone in for trouble in a big way when she learns that Claire will drag your name into it."

"Now I *know* you're crazy. Claire wouldn't dare perjure herself like that."

"It wouldn't be perjury, would it, if I told her you had urged me to divorce her, had agreed to marry me as soon as I was free? She would be honestly testifying to what she believed."

"Phil *Mauryl* Is that what you meant yesterday by a more 'drastic weapon'?"

She clasped her hands hard behind her, forced her nerves to steadiness. "Cool and tough, that's you," Johnny had said.

"It is, and a stroke of genius, if you ask me. For one cockeyed minute I thought of settin' fire to the mills—sabotage would have been suspected—for the insurance. Concluded it would take too long to collect, then hit on my present scheme. It's quicker and undoubtedly safer—for me."

"Phil, I can't believe it is you talking."

"I told you I was desperate."

"No one will believe that lie about me."

"There will be plenty in the rumor-clinic who'll whisper behind their hands, 'Have you heard . . .' and spread it, glad of a chance to see the great Ellen Marshall humiliated."

"I still think you're out of your mind. It's a brainstorm."

"A dangerous one for you. I'll give your aunt until noon tomorrow to come across. After that—"

"Oh, Miss Jess!" Breathless, Goldie Mellor appeared at the front of the booth. How long had she been near? Had she heard Phil's fiendish plan? Jess had just time to wonder frantically before the girl announced:—

"Sorry to butt in on what looks like a sizzling heart-to-heart, but I forgot to thank you for pinch-hitting for me at the mill phone yesterday. Ma brought me up to be a perfect lady so I made Gus wait till I came back—"

"I was glad to do it for you, Goldie."

"Sure, I know you were, you're that kind. I had a date with an FBI man. Don't look so tickled, Mr. Maury. 'Tisn't me who's suspected of double-crossing, you bet—me who can sing the 'Star-Spangled Banner' from start to finish without mumbling one word. He was just giving me the third degree about one of the rookies who was here for the war games. He was on the wrong track, the big stiff. There goes the fanfare! Gus will be fit to tie if I don't get back. Thanks again, Miss Jess." She disappeared as quickly as she had come.

"How much did that girl hear of our conversation?" Philip Maury demanded furiously, then he laughed.

"If she spreads it she will be only twenty-four hours ahead of me—if your eloquence fails with Miss Ellen. I must get back to the judges' stand. So long until the ball this evening, Jessie."

Her eyes were wide with unbelief, every nerve in her body was throbbing with anger as she watched him walk away, waving, smiling, calling greetings to acquaintances he passed. Over and over in her mind she was saying, "He *wouldn't* tell Claire that. He *couldn't* be such a beast."

Vance Trent stopped at the booth and glanced over his shoulder at the man crossing in front of the grandstand. His eyes came back to her.

"You're white as the proverbial sheet, Angel. What's Maury been saying to you? Have I got to beat up that heel again?"

"No. *No.*" She clutched his sleeve with rosy-nailed

fingers, achieved an unsteady laugh. "You're a first-class fighting man if ever there was one, aren't you?"

"Just as you say, lady. How about selling me five one-thousand-dollar bonds?" He laid a slip of pink paper on the counter.

She picked up the check, read it. Excitement ousted fright from her eyes.

"Did I really hear 'thousand' preceded by the word 'five' or did I dream it?"

"You heard it. I don't wonder you are surprised. Thousand is the forgotten word in this million-billion era, but it will help."

"Help! It's marvelous! My last sale was a twenty-five-dollar bond. You'll never guess who bought it. Gus Peckett, probably with moonshine profits."

"Peckett here? Alone?"

"No. He had Goldie Mellor with him." How much of Phil's hateful threat had the girl heard? She forced back the terrifying memory. "He bought the bond for her. I told you at lunch that I took her place at the switchboard and that I was all excited about a message, 'Tomorrow night. Nine sharp,' which came through, remember?"

"Every word."

"I felt pretty foolish about my excitement over it when she said today that her 'steady, a cop, polices the Club grounds and starts his rounds at the brick summerhouse at *nine*. Of course, he was dating her to meet him. She lives up to her name, she's a gold-digger, but nothing worse. I like her. Phil—Phil Maury appeared while they were here." Had Van noticed the catch in her voice? "When Peckett introduced them he looked at her as if she were the dirt beneath his feet. It didn't faze her. To return to business—" She nibbled the handle of her pen, inquired:—

"Name, please?"

"Vance Trent. Has its good points as a moniker, what?"

"So good that I wonder it hasn't been snatched up by a girl long before this. 'Mrs. Vance Trent' sure has what it takes. How has a person of your devastating charm managed to escape the bonds of matrimony so long? It's nothing short of a miracle."

The strain was leaving her voice. There was still a hurt little-girl look in her eyes that tightened his throat and made his arms ache to hold her close. He'd play this game for all it was worth till she was back to normal.

"I've escaped by applying efficiency tactics to myself. I won't say it has been easy with glamour girls fairly mobbing me, snipping buttons from my blouses and swamping me with knitted pledges of admiration and devotion, but I've managed to pull through."

"Goon!" she flouted, and laughed her lovely laugh and smiled at him through tears.

Relief took the stiffening from his knees. His foolishness had done the trick. Whatever Maury had said or done to frighten her was sneaking into the background of her mind.

"Here are your bonds, Major. My mistake, Colonel. This sends my sales quota over the top *and* plus."

"Let's celebrate. Drive into town with me for dinner."

"No can do. There's a ball here tonight at which the Show prizes will be awarded. I'm supposed to appear in the receiving line before nine."

The word "nine" tied up suddenly with the phoned message, "Nine sharp." Which linked up with another voice saying: "My steady, the cop, polices the Club grounds all night. He starts his rounds at the brick summerhouse at nine."

Why should those two sentences have flashed into her mind if they meant nothing? One way of finding out.

"Van, do you believe in hunches?"

"Sometimes. Got one?"

"I'm not sure. It may be merely an acute attack of imagination."

"Let me in on it. Perhaps I can figure out which it is. No? You needn't shake your head so violently. I've no intention of putting you through the third degree. Sure you won't celebrate with me?"

"I can't. I'd love it, but I must come to the Club."

"See you at the ball. Here comes a buyer." He turned away, came back.

"I forgot to mention that if ever you want to use my name—it's Vance Trent, in case you've forgotten—with Mrs. in front of it, it's yours, all tied up with white ribbons. I'll be seeing you!"

XXIII

Jessamine thoughtfully regarded her aunt seated across the table in the small dining room at Karris-brooke where the air was fragrant with the scent of pink roses and the burning wax of the tall candles which matched the flowers to a tint. Her gray lace frock had the same silver sheen as her hair. Below a pearl dog-collar hung a massive, diamond pendant. The alexandrite in its center shifted from red to green with every breath she drew. A matching ring sparkled on the third finger of her right hand. She had changed during these last months. In spite of increasing business responsibilities and an aching awareness of the tragedy of the world, she was more mellow, more sympathetically understanding. She had said she loved Vance Trent. Was her affection for him responsible for the change?

His name started his words echoing through the corridors of memory.

"If ever you want to use ... Vance Trent ... with Mrs. in front of it, it's yours ..." Had he meant it? The question tripped up her breath as it had tripped each time she visualized his laughing, challenging eyes with something in their depths she never had seen before.

It had been difficult to carry on conversation at dinner with his words, the sentences "Tomorrow night. Nine sharp" and "I'll give your aunt till noon tomorrow to come across" competing for first place in her thoughts.

"Jessamine, you are looking through me as if a disembodied spirit were drifting behind my chair. If not that, what do you see?"

Ellen Marshall's laugh indicated that at some time in her busy day, she had stopped for rest and spiritual refreshment. The lines that had marked her face at luncheon were lightly etched, not cut deep as they had been then.

"I was seeing you, Aunt Ellen, and thinking that somewhere you had discovered the fabled Fountain of Youth." That was the truth, if not the whole story.

"For that fabulous fountain, substitute a sustaining faith that God's in His heaven; meticulous care of health and body and the self-respect—accent on self-respect—to keep me determined not to be a back number. It's so stupid to permit oneself to be dated, mentally or sartorially. Serve coffee in the library, Sam," she directed, as the butler entered.

"Yas, M's Ellen. Ah'll do it. Major Trent, he come here and changed to dress uniform an' said he wouldn't be here fo' dinner. Ah tole Pink. Did she tell you?"

"Yes."

Sam shook his grizzled head and drew out her chair as she rose.

"The Major, Ah reckon, he's doin' some courtin' of that widow woman at the Inn. Leastwise that's what Pink's boy, George Wash'ton Lewis—he's the son by that first no-account husban' of Pink's—says. You heard that same, M's Ellen?"

"I haven't, but I wouldn't be surprised if it were true, Sam. Mrs. Carter is an attractive woman."

"Ah'll be mighty sorry to see him married to her, M's Ellen, she ain't his kin'; but I reckon she aims to get him. George Wash'ton Lewis says, one day her clo'es is all dark like a blackout, de nex', her dress is like a big pink rose. Yes, marm, Ah reckon she 'bout set to. get him," he repeated despondently.

He picked up a silver tray and followed Ellen Marshall and Jessamine to the library.

"Is that all, M's Ellen?" he inquired after he had served the coffee.

"That's all, Sam, except to tell Zenas to bring the large car round in half an hour. Miss Jessamine is going to the Club."

After he had left the room Jess protested:—

"I don't need Zenas and the large car, Aunt Ellen. I intended to drive myself in the sedan."

"In that costume? The rainbow chiffon skirt, the white velvet top with its jeweled buttons and so-called 'plunge neckline,' are not suitable for a drive-yourself evening, besides the pearls on your neck and in your ears, to say nothing of the diamond setting of your moonstone ring, would be a temptation to a footpad. The roads aren't very safe now. I always draw a breath of relief when I hear you come in. When you're late I'm tempted to start out after you. You'll go in the large car as a niece of mine should."

Resentment at the dictatorial voice sent color to Jess's cheeks. She swallowed an indignant retort and made a deep curtsy.

"Yes, your Majesty. Take a look at the spread of my skirt. Rose, violet, green, yellow, most of the primary colors are there. You were right when you called it a rainbow. Rainbow at night, sailor's delight. Pity the Fleet isn't in to be cheered by it."

"Its charm isn't wasted on me. 'Rainbow at night.' It means to the sailor that the day of storm is behind him, that he may confidently look forward to the favoring winds and sunshine of a fair tomorrow. We're all sailors on our Ship of State. Pray God we see many rainbows at night to help buoy our spirits." Her voice, which had been husky with emotion, cleared.

"Jessamine, what thoughts are lighting your eyes and curving your lips in an ecstatic smile one minute and the next shadowing them like a cloud passing over the sun?"

Should she confide the three sentences that had been working below the surface, keeping her emotions in a state of flux? Not yet.

"For some reason I'm slap-happy tonight—in spots—

Aunt Ellen. Perhaps it's because I made such a spectacular success as bond salesgirl."

"You've a right to be proud of the record. I like your slap-happiness. It's contagious. You may have noticed that I laugh more since you came and, shame upon me, yearn for slacks and lounge pajamas. What greater proof do you need that I have reached my second spring? I hope I can keep you with me, Jessamine? You make my life so well worth living."

"I'll stay as long as you want me, your Majesty, unless Mother or the Government need me." She glanced at the tall clock in the corner. "I promised Estelle Lacey to be at the Club early to help the reception committee make the visitors welcome. Ever so many out-of-town guests who came for the races are staying over for the ball."

Apparently absorbed in dropping a lump of sugar exactly in the center of the blue Sèvres cup, she inquired:—

"Do you think the Major is 'courtin' the widow woman' at the Inn, Aunt Ellen? According to George Wash'ton Lewis her blackout is over, the all clear has sounded for her weeds."

"Vance has never confided to me his intentions, but she proclaims hers shamelessly. When she looks at him she embarrasses me as much as do the long-drawn-out kisses on the screen. I cringe in distaste and stare down at my hands till they are over. You've heard, I presume, that he was engaged to her, that she threw him over for his cousin?"

"I have *not*." The room went into a nose-dive, shot up again. "If I had known, think how many heart-to-hearts he and I might have had—subject: the pangs and pleasures of being jilted!" No one would infer from that gay voice that she had just emerged from a miniature blitz.

"The bitterness of that 'jilted' and your high color, Jessamine, make me fear that there is still some love in your heart for Philip."

"You're wrong. If I sounded bitter it was because reference to my youthful infatuation for him makes me see red. Let's forget it and return to the lady

Carter. She doubtless has based her attack methods on modern warfare. Offensive tactics are the only way to win the war, if one believes the military experts."

"Helen Carter is neither siren nor *femme fatale,* but she's persistent, a liar when it serves her purpose, and out to get her man, who happens to be a rich one."

"Rich! I had an impression that a Major's pay was all Van had after he gave up the efficiency job; that when young he had been dependent on his uncle."

"It was the other way round. His income practically supported the household till the boys were old enough to help. While he was laid-up with a broken ankle, I spent many hours with him when the nurse was off duty. It didn't take me long to discover that he stands four square to his obligations; that honor, integrity and keeping the faith are as natural to him as breathing; that I had found the man to carry on my work if when this war is over he will come to Karrisbrooke."

"Don't you ever make a mistake in your judgment of character?" The question was prompted by the remembrance of Judge Sutcliffe's fear that Ellen Marshall was being fooled by the great-grandson of the man she had loved.

"Not often, my dear, I have been an interested, keen, fairly intelligent observer of the human comedy for a great many years. Sometimes I wish I didn't see right through a person's eyes into his mind. Have you forgotten Philip's threat yesterday of using a more 'drastic weapon' to force my consent to the sale of his interest in the mills? I confess that has me puzzled. I can't figure out what drastic weapon he is planning to use."

Forgotten! If only she could forget his voice as he had warned a few hours ago, "She may reconsider when she knows that Claire will drag your name into it." The threat had been flapping buzzardlike wings above her spirit ever since.

"It is evident that he is desperate for money," Ellen Marshall went on. "I heard today that the attorney of the bank which advises his wife as to her investments is coming to visit at River Farm. He may help him."

"Zenas is at the door, M's Jess." Sam was on the threshold with her black velvet evening coat over his arm. She finished her coffee and rose.

"I'll run along, Aunt Ellen. Anything I can do for you before I go?"

"Turn on the radio for Symphony hour. Sam, after Miss Jessamine leaves come back and set out the card table. I'll play solitaire while I listen. Why are you wearing that old coat instead of the white fox, my dear?"

"The white coat is short. It's a cool evening. My aged knees get cold, also the long coat has a hood which will serve as camouflage in case I am tempted to sit out dances on the terrace or on the porch of that adorable summerhouse you had restored for the Club. It's fun to keep the gossips guessing, 'Who's the man?' "

She hoped she didn't look as silly as she felt while making the explanation. Unless she wanted to be forbidden to go, she wouldn't admit that she intended to make a furtive visit to that same brick summerhouse to find out if her suspicion that Goldie was expected there were true, that the black coat would be less conspicuous than the white.

As she nodded good night something in the eyes that met hers told her she hadn't fooled Ellen Marshall for a minute. Ought she to confide her plan? Of course not. She had nothing with which to back it up but the word "hunch."

She lingered on the threshold to hear the opening of Tchaikovsky's Sixth Symphony. The distant orchestra was playing brilliantly, presenting a fresh, lyrical and tonally charming performance.

The beauty of the music lingered in her consciousness on the drive to the Clubhouse, sent suspicion, dread and the little nagging memory that Van had been engaged to Helen Carter skulking into the shadows like wolves before the glow of a fire.

When she stepped from the powder-room at the Club, Barry Collins, outstandingly handsome and distinguished in evening clothes, was in the hall obviously watching the door.

"Miss Jess, I've been waiting for you." His voice was tense as a violin-string stretched to snapping point. "I want to apologize for speaking as I did yesterday."

"Call that 'speaking'? The courts have a word for it, 'threatening.'"

He put his hand under her elbow as she started toward the ballroom.

"Wait here. There's no one in sight. Please. Please let me explain, Miss Jess."

The man was positively abject. His gray-green eyes were as strained as his voice. Better let him get it out of his system or he'd hold her up like this each time they met.

"All right, but make it fast. I'm expected in the receiving line." She glanced at the tall clock in the corner. It would take at least five minutes to reach the brick summerhouse. Perhaps if she were agreeable to him she could speed-up matters.

"Go on, talk. I'm here."

"Thanks for that smile, Miss Jess. When I met you on the steps I was smarting and aching from Miss Ellen's lashing. Maury, who had promised to back up my proposition to buy his share of the mills, let me down by remaining dumb. Instead of coming across with my proposition I found myself prattling about the horse I had bought. When it was suggested by her that the interview was over, that she and Maury had important business to discuss, I left, so mad I could have shredded raw meat with my teeth."

"That doesn't explain why you should threaten me, Mr. Collins."

"I wasn't threatening. I was just telling you—"

"That Miss Ellen *and* I—would consent to my marriage to you—or *else*—"

"I didn't know what I was saying. I knew only that I wanted you—would take any means to get you—"

In the same hoarse voice Phil had said: "I've got to prove within a week that I have a certain sum of money or that it is forthcomin'." He wanted to sell his share of the mills to get it, this man wanted to marry her for the same purpose.

"You'll never get me that way or any other, Mr.

Collins. That's final. I've forgotten my bag. Please tell Mrs. Lacey that I'll be with her in a moment."

The hall mirror reflected him as he stood looking after her, reflected the prismatic colors of her filmy skirt as she ran past it, reminded her of Ellen Marshall's voice saying: "Rainbow at night ... The favoring winds and sunshine of a fair tomorrow." The thought lifted her spirit on silver wings. Why worry? Phil wouldn't dare carry out his threat. The old clock caught its breath—chimed the three-quarter hour.

In the powder-room, empty at the moment except for the maid, she picked up her bag and slipped on the enveloping black coat.

"You ain't leavin' for home so soon, are you, Miss Ramsay?" inquired the pretty Negress attired in a rose-color uniform which matched the décor of her setting.

"No, Winnie. I'm going to the terrace to—to talk with a person who has volunteered to take over my hitch as a plane-spotter. It's cold outside." Her shiver as she pulled the hood over her hair held a hint of theater.

She left by the side door of the powder-room. Across the terrace. Down steps ... Along the shadow of the row of gigantic live oaks. The excuse she had given the maid for leaving the Clubhouse had been nothing short of an inspiration. The Civilian Defense Committee had been calling loudly for volunteers, nothing more probable than that someone had taken this occasion to offer to help.

Stars thick as a swarm of golden bees. Air clear and cold. Was she on a fool's errand? She had had a hunch that the person with the disguised voice would be waiting for Goldie at the brick summerhouse, that subversive intrigue might be behind the rendezvous. If that were true the girl was an innocent party to it, she was sure. Van had said that *sometimes* he believed in hunches. No one but herself would know if her hunch proved a dud. The summerhouse just ahead. She stole toward it. Her heartbeat went on tiptoe. A distant tower clock solemnly told the hour. Nine. She was on time to the minute.

Someone, something was moving. She held her breath and shrank close to the brick wall. A spark of light! Must be in the middle of the lawn. A cigarette! Gone.

"Coast clear. Okay!"

The same squeaky whisper she had heard yesterday sent icy chills slithering along her nerves. Whose move was it? Hers?

XXIV

It wasn't the first time Helen had maneuvered him into the role of escort, Vance Trent reminded himself impatiently as he drove his open-top roadster toward the Hunt Club with her very near on the seat beside him. When he had substituted as escort for her invalid husband at dinners and parties, it hadn't taken long to discover that she wanted more than companionship.

Her hand was everlastingly out; flowers, something she or the child needed "terribly," for which she didn't dare spend money "now that Hugh is so ill." He had been glad to help, always with the idea that he was making life easier for her husband. After his death he had kept away, mailing checks at Christmas and on birthdays.

He lived over his stunned surprise when she had appeared at Karrisbrooke with Becky; his annoyance when she had announced in a proprietary voice that she intended to stay at the Inn while he was invalided; his seething anger when she had artfully extracted an invitation for dinner that night from Miss Ellen. It had been so characteristic of her.

And as if he had learned nothing from experience he was now driving her to the ball. Served him right for dodging dinner at Karrisbrooke, after Jess had turned down his invitation to dine in town. Even as he asked her he had told himself that he must cut the evening with her short, to be sure he didn't miss his midnight date.

Helen had confidently assumed that he would drive her to the Hunt Club when he spoke to her as she sat on one of the scarlet banquettes in the Inn lounge smoking and chatting with a group of acquaintances. He had protested that he must leave early, he had an appointment, he was sure it would hurry her too much to go with him. When she replied that she was ready to leave that minute, he couldn't humiliate her by turning her down. She had kept him waiting half an hour. He glanced at the roadster clock. Nine-thirty. It was an infernal nuisance having her along. He wanted to be alone with his thoughts, visualize Jess as she had said:—

"Mrs. Vance Trent sure has what it takes." She had declared, once, she would never marry a man in the service. That had been months ago. Did she still mean it? Why not, when you thought of the long separation husband and wife must prepare to face?

"What did you say, Van?" Helen Carter inquired and snuggled closer.

"I didn't speak."

"Heavenly night. Reminds me of those lines from 'Evangeline':—

"Silently one by one, in the infinite
    meadows of heaven,
    Blossomed the lovely stars, the forget-
    me-nots of the angels."

Her dreamy voice sounded an alert. Better smash this mood and smash it quick.

"These particular stars above us didn't appear one by one. Looks more as if a playboy on Olympus had upset a ton or two of golddust on the heavens; they're thick as the freckles on Becky's nose."

"You love Becky, don't you, Trent?"

Now what had he started?

"Sure. She's a grand kid and a mighty bright one."

Becky as a conversational subject was safer ground than poetry.

"Her teachers say she is brilliant—I always led my class—that she ought now to start in the finest school to be had. All very well for them to recommend it, but how can I send her on my small income? Fine schools cost money and taxes are mounting terrifyingly—for a lone woman."

He had established a trust fund to finance the finest education possible for Becky; but it was not wise to let her mother, being what she was, know that at present.

"The small income you're complaining about seems to do you and Becky very well when it comes to living quarters and clothes. The penthouse apartment you swing in New York wouldn't be described as 'shabby' and I've heard it said that Mrs. Hugh Carter is the snappiest dresser at the Inn."

"It's because I'm a good manager, Van." She placed a cigarette between her lips and lifted her face toward him for a light. "Thanks. If I had the income Jess Ramsay has I'd show 'em a thing or two in clothes."

"Has she such a big income? I understand she is paid a salary as secretary to her aunt."

"Pose, my boy, pose. Ever notice her pearls? They're big as outsized peas. Nothing synthetic or 'cultured' about them. Those sensational rings she wears are not costume junk. Someone told me they are family jewels her aunt has had reset for her. Wasn't her mother a Marshall? Hasn't Miss Ellen money to burn? As if that wouldn't keep the wolf from her door she's engaged to that adorable Lieutenant Gordon, whose father is an oil king. Some women have all the luck."

"Remember, she's a liar, doesn't care what she says to gain her ends," he reminded himself to counteract the aching contraction of his heart caused by the assured statement.

"Where'd you pick up that matrimonial tidbit, Helen? I hadn't heard it."

"Johnny Gordon registered at the Inn yesterday.

When I asked, playfully of course, 'How come you're here? Discharged from the army?' he scowled gloomily and said, 'I've come to see my girl.' As everyone at the Inn knew when he was here for the war games that the only girl he looked at—nice one, I mean—was Jessamine Ramsay, that admission of his clinches what you call the 'engagement idea,' doesn't it?"

"What d'you mean by intimating that Gordon was with girls other than 'nice ones'? Did you see him with others?"

"You sound alarmed. He's not your responsibility, is he? I saw him once or twice with a flashy yellow-haired creature. I'll give him credit for a sense of propriety. I might have been the invisible woman by the way he looked through me. He took time out yesterday to date her. On my way home from a tea I passed them walking together. It was almost dark, but the headlights showed up her yellow hair."

Curious that I haven't received the message he promised he'd send if there was a hitch in our plan, Trent's thoughts trooped on to the running accompaniment of a woman's voice. Why didn't he show up at the races if he was broadcasting that his reason for coming to this part of the country was to see Jess? Did she know he saw Goldie? If she did, wouldn't she have mentioned it when at lunch she confided the story of the mysterious phone call?

"Don't you think so, Vance?"

"Think what?"

"That Lieutenant Gordon's division has been ordered into active service?"

"Speaking or speculating about army orders isn't being done, Helen. Here we are at the Club. Lighted from top to bottom. Looks as if the directors were daring our enemies to come and drop a bomb on the house. The world and his wife must have arrived ahead of us. Cars are packed close as sardines. I'll deposit you, then hunt for a space in which to leave this roadster."

"I'll wait for you at the door of the powder-room, Van darling." She laid her hand on his arm. "Isn't it heavenly to be together again with no one between us to—"

"*Don't* wait for me. It will take time to find a parking place in this jam. Hop out. We're holding up traffic. Make it fast," he urged, grateful to the driver behind who was reminding with raucous toots that the roadster was blocking the entrance steps.

He drove around three times before he found a vacant space. Stopped to smoke in the hope that Helen, indignant at his delayed appearance, would pick up another escort. It wouldn't be difficult. Some men liked her type. They could have her. He had disliked her from the moment he had first met her. Had she been telling the truth? Were Johnny Gordon and Jess engaged?

"Major Trent." A colored youth dodged from behind a parked limousine. "I've been follerin' an' follerin' you since you lef' your car."

"Stop and get your breath, Caesar. Now, why have you been trailing me?"

"Jest about an' hour ago, I was parking Mr. Lacey's car for him, he had to hurry into the Clubhouse, when a soldier with his cap pulled down and his coat collar up almost to meet it, yanked my sleeve and whispered:—

"'Boy, do you know Major Trent?' I said 'Suppose I do, then what?' 'This,' he says and flashed five bucks. 'Shoot,' I said; I figured that taking outside money wasn't like a tip from a member, is that right, sir?"

"It sounds okay. What was the message?"

"'Tell Major Trent his orderly reports that the mail got through.' He made me repeat it. Doesn't seem as if that was worth five bucks."

"It isn't. Sure that money was real stuff?"

"Sure, Major Trent. I showed it to the barkeeper. He said it was good, all right."

"Thanks for the message. Must have been another Major's orderly. I'm not expecting mail to 'get through.'"

"I thought p'raps he was batty, he gave me a note for Mr.—"

"Hey, boy! Come help me with this car. Why the

devil—" the angry bellow cut off Caesar's voice before he had a chance to tell the name.

"The mail got through." Trent repeated as he wound his way among cars toward the Clubhouse. "It's a break. Caesar didn't say if he delivered the—"

"Hi, Trent!" Jim Lacey seized his arm as he reached the entrance door. "Don't go in yet. Seen anything of Jess Ramsay?" The redness of his round face accentuated the excited glitter of his small eyes, even his disarranged black tie registered agitation.

"No. Why! What's happened to her?"

"Keep your shirt on, fella. I don't *know* that anything's happened to her. She was to receive with Estelle and the rest of the bunch. No one's seen her. I phoned Karrisbrooke. Sam said she left in the big car before eight-thirty. I reckon I frightened him, he jabbered like a baboon for a second. Never knew Jess to be a minute late for an appointment. That's why I've gone haywire. It's quarter before ten. She should have been here an hour ago."

"Good Lord, I hope Sam didn't pass your message on to Miss Ellen. Zenas may have been held up by tire-trouble. That's out. A car belonging to Ellen Marshall wouldn't be so inefficient as to have tire-trouble. Is Philip Maury here?"

"No. Claire arrived without him, said he would show up later."

Jess missing and Philip Maury coming "later"? "The mail got through." The words clanged through his mind. He crushed down rising panic.

"How about Collins or any one of the dozen lads in her stag-line who may have persuaded her to slip out to the terrace for a heart-to-heart? Check up on them?"

"'Twasn't Barry, I'm sure. He paid his respects to the receiving line, wish you could have seen him bending over the gals' hands. He was dancing when I came out twenty minutes ago to try and locate the Marshall car."

"Have you inquired of the maid in the powder-room?"

"Nope. I haven't spread the alarm. The powder-room has as many air-lane outlets as a broadcasting station. What's the use asking the maid and setting her tongue wagging until we're sure Jess isn't here somewhere?"

"You've got the right idea, Jim. Perhaps she came and left for some reason. I'll take a chance on the powder-room, stop at the door as if I expected to meet her there, while you make the rounds of the terraces. We'll find her."

Without stopping to return greetings he hurried through the hall. He heard Jess's voice as plainly as if she were beside him, saying:—

"Van, do you believe in hunches?"

While at the booth, Maury had said or done something to frighten her. It was evident from the breathlessness of her question that she had had a flash of intuition or what have you—about what? He was up against a stone wall. If he knew to what the "hunch" referred he would know which way to turn.

"Good evening, Major Trent. Looking for someone?"

The maid's soft voice roused him to the fact that he had been standing at the door staring unseeingly into the powder-room.

"Yes, Winnie. I—I was to meet Miss Ramsay here. I'm a little late—"

"You sure are. She got here at quarter to nine. Left her wrap, forgot her beautiful evening bag. I had just found it when back she came and asked for her coat. I said, 'You ain't leaving for home so soon, are you, Miss Ramsay?' and she said, 'No, I'm going to the terrace to talk with a person who has volunteered as a plane-spotter.' Then she pulled the hood over her hair, said something 'bout its being cold and hurried out that side door as if she hadn't a minute to lose."

"Thanks, Winnie. Now I know where to find her."

"She pulled the hood over her hair," the maid had said. That told a story. She didn't want to be recognized when she followed up her hunch. "She got here at quarter to nine." Nine! The hour the girl Goldie was expected to keep a date somewhere. Her "steady" started his evening beat at the brick summerhouse at nine. Had Jess put two and two together and gone there?

The thought shot splinters of ice through his veins. If she had, she might be in danger. This was the night "the mail got through." He dashed into the powder-room, followed by Winnie's excited protest.

"You can't come in here, Major—"

Out the side door. Across the terrace. Down the steps. Running in the shadow of the live oaks. Saying over and over, "She mustn't get caught in that jam, she must *not!*"

XXV

Rigid as a shop-window dummy displaying a hooded black velvet evening coat, Jessamine waited for the squeaky assurance to be repeated. Millions of stars shed a soft glow. The world seemed like a huge room in which a dim nightlight had been left burning for someone who was staying out late. The stillness magnified the few sounds that broke it: the distant, ghostly wail of an automobile siren; the faint rhythm and beat of dance music; the drop of pods; the scatter of seeds from the red-bud tree on the summerhouse roof. Something else she couldn't make out ... She strained her ears. It sounded like—it was—heavy breathing as if a person had been running.

Now what? Should she answer that squeaky "Coast clear. Okay!"—steal from the shadow and then appear startled and embarrassed, intimating that she had expected to meet someone else? If that procedure accomplished nothing more it would reveal the identity of the man who had tried to date Goldie. She fortified herself with the thought, "You're cool and tough, remember," and took a step forward.

"Listen!" The sharp whisper sent her back against the brick wall. That squeaky "Coast clear. Okay!" had not been addressed to her but to the person who had arrived in a hurry.

"You're on time to the minute. Clock just struck nine. Sit on this bench. We can talk and not be seen from the Clubhouse."

Jess remembered the seat on the summerhouse porch under the window on which she had knelt at noon when she had peered into the room. It was just around the corner from where she was standing. If she couldn't see she could hear.

"Suppose my steady, the cop, catches me here with you?"

Goldie! How had she learned that she was expected to be here at nine?

"That cop has been taken care of."

"You mean hurt? Say—"

"Sit *down!* Of course he hasn't been hurt. He's been shifted to duty somewhere else, that's all."

"If you're lying to me—"

"Pipe down. I'm not lying. Do you think we're so dumb we'd *hurt* anybody? We can pull off our stunt without that risk."

If only the man would raise his squeaky voice the merest degree, she would recognize it, or would she? She was taking it for granted that he was either Collins or Peckett. There were other men in the world. Whoever it was must be past-master of intrigue to keep his voice under such perfect control.

"Listen, Goldie. Here's what you are to do."

That "do" had an ominous sound. Was the girl she liked involved in a shady transaction? The man must be whispering instructions close to her ear, for the only sounds audible were her low, breathless answers:—

"Yeah!" "I get it!" and finally, "It's in the bag."

"*Ssch!* Someone's coming. Stay here. Bluff's the line, remember."

The whispered warning was followed by the sound of a door cautiously opened and as stealthily closed. The exit of Goldie's instructor through the summerhouse? How had he obtained entrance to a place that was supposed to be kept securely locked? A Club

member? Was that the explanation? Collins was a
member. Peckett was not.

A light flashed near the red-bud tree. It came from
a large electric hand-torch, not from the bulb she had
noticed hanging from a limb. The dark outline of a
man was visible behind it. The girl stopped in the
middle of the lawn as if suddenly petrified to find
herself revealed in the glare. The huge red-and-white
print of her skirt, the emerald top visible under the
open plaid coat. The yellow hair framing a red and
green kerchief tied under her chin, the scarlet gash of
her mouth, made a blaze of color in the spot of light.

"Here I am, Goldie. Alone? Say, what is this, a
frameup?"

Peckett! His usually slick voice was sharp with suspicion. Evidently the girl had sent for him. "The plot
thickens," Jess told herself. She prickled with excitement. "What shall I do now? If I'm caught what shall
I say? I might back away, with one chance in ten of
not being seen. No. I came to find out what that
phone message meant and I won't give up. There is
something undercover going on, it isn't my imagination." She shrank closer to the brick wall, which for
the moment appeared to be the best friend she had in
the world.

"What d'ya mean by frame-up and where'd you get
that 'Here I am' stuff, as if I'd sent for you, Gus?"

"Didn't you write that if I wanted to find out who
was double-crossing me to be here at nine-fifteen
tonight, Sugar? The note was like your handwriting."

"I take it it wasn't signed. What's the idea cooking
up a phony yarn like that? If you came here to meet a
dame why not say so? It's nothing in my life. And
when you come right down to it, why shouldn't I be
alone, Gussie?" Was Goldie's raised voice designed to
give information to the person who had disappeared
within the house? "Can't a girl step out for the evening without being shadowed? I'll say life in this town
has all the privacy of an enemy plane being tailed by
antiaircraft searchlights."

"If you didn't write telling me to come, why did

you step out, as you call it, here? Only Club members are allowed on these grounds."

"Is that so? How long have you been a member of this swell outfit, smart fella? Perhaps someone phoned me to be here, who knows? Guess I'll stay till—"

"What's the big idea, Peckett?"

Collins! Jess held her breath to listen. Now what? No mistaking that voice, he wasn't trying to disguise it. He was standing in the glare of the electric flash and didn't attempt to avoid it. A break for her that they had all moved into the spotlight. She took a few steps forward. That helped. She could hear and see better. Goldie looked from one man to the other and laughed:—

"Pleased to meet ya at last, *Mister* Collins. Gussie's promised to introduce us, but he keeps forgetting; 'fraid you'll make him jealous, maybe? Perhaps you're the one who phoned me to be here at nine sharp and then wrote him to barge in just to make it harder?" The taunting voice was a challenge.

"*I* phone you! You're crazy. What do you mean by bringing a girl like this on the Club grounds, Peckett? You're none too welcome here yourself. Send her away and be quick."

Goldie stepped toward him. The light played-up her angry eyes, her scarlet mouth.

"And what kind of girl are you thinking I am, Mister Col—" Her sharp voice cracked in a squeak of surprise as the incandescent bulb hanging in the tree glowed, illumined the lawn and cast a spell of amazement over the two men and the girl.

"What's going on here?" Philip Maury demanded as he stepped from the shadow of the trees.

"Say, why the crowd? Is it Visiting Firemen?" Goldie was the first to rally.

"Who turned on that light? Oh, the omnipresent Miss Mellor, perhaps?" The contempt in Maury's voice was like oil on the smoldering coals of the girl's anger. It flamed.

"*I* did not and don't try to high-hat me, Mr. Maury. You don't think I want to advertise being caught in a place like this with a bunch of crooks, or do you?"

"Crooks!" The three men chorused and closed in on her.

"That's what I said. *C r o o k s*—in case you don't know how it's spelled—who are gambling on the chance that Barry Collins will marry his boss's niece. I guess that will hold you for a while. You're all tarred with the same brush, but *Mister* Collins is the mastermind and—"

"Shut up—you—"

"Cut the rough stuff, Barry." Peckett wrenched away the hand gripping the girl's shoulder. "What she says is true. You don't dare deny it with me standing here. It's as good a time for a showdown as any. I'm getting fed-up waiting for you and Maury to pay what you owe me. When you first arrived in this town you told me you'd own Karrisbrooke before you got through, handed me some batty dope about 'getting even' for a wrong done your ancestor, that either you'd marry the girl or you'd have the place and the bulk of the old lady's money when she died—"

"Sorry to disappoint you and spoil sport, gentlemen, but 'the old lady' has no intention of dying."

Four bodies whirled in the direction of the voice, four pairs of eyes threatened to bulge from their sockets. The light played up silvery hair and frock, open sable coat, diamonds on fingers and neck, and Ellen Marshall's faintly smiling mouth as she stood on the steps of the summerhouse with Sam behind her.

Into the stunned silence drifted the faint rattle of gourds, the thump of drums, the blare of horns. "At the Clubhouse they're doing the Conga, snaking round the room, while out here a melodrama is being staged," Jess told herself. "Perhaps this isn't real. Perhaps it's plain nightmare. Perhaps—"

"Miss Ellen, don't believe it." Collins was the first to throw off the spell of surprise. "I do owe Peckett cash, but I've collected money to pay it. I don't know why this cheap girl should lie and say I'm counting on marriage to Miss Jess, to pay debts. I've never spoken to her before."

"You wouldn't have got the chance if you tried to, Barry Collins. I'm kind of choosy about the company

I keep. You've been cheating Miss Ellen and fooling her, while all the time you and Gus Peckett have been double-crossing her with that—"

"I can fight my own battles, Goldie." Amusement tinged Ellen Marshall's voice. "If it will make you feel happier, my dear, I haven't been fooled, though I'll confess that during the few minutes after I snapped on the light I gained much valuable information about my superintendent's matrimonial plans."

Collins strode toward her. As if to meet his belligerent approach she descended one step. Sam, with his arms behind him, followed like a dusky shadow.

"Suppose I do intend to marry your niece, Miss Marshall, with or without your consent? You'll find it to your advantage to give it. If you don't—"

"Keep out of this, Philip." Ellen Marshall's sharp command stopped Maury, who with doubled fists had taken a quick step toward Collins. "You, if anyone, should know that threats do not frighten me. I want to ask the impetuous lover if the girl he intends to marry—intend was the word, wasn't it—has given her consent?"

Collins cleared his throat as if to rid it of the anger choking him.

"That's not your business. The time is past when you can make us all dance to the tune you whistle." He had dropped his usual smoothness and suavity like a cast-off cloak.

"I never have counted whistling as one of my accomplishments, Collins." Ellen Marshall's cool admission was followed by a crisp, "And if I don't give my consent?"

"I resign now. I can count on taking three of the mill superintendents and two of the plantation managers with me. Even you can't carry on after that."

"I accept your resignation, Collins. From this moment you cease being in my employ. That threat of crippling the mills brands you a traitor. I'll check up with the superintendents and managers in the morning. Looks as if we had a flourishing Fifth Column in our midst. Deserting mills that are working on de-

fense orders sounds like treason to me—it may to the
Government."

"You can't f-fire me like this, Miss Ellen." Collins'
veneer of bravado showed signs of cracking. "Suppose
I do want to marry your niece? It isn't a crime, is it? It
hasn't interfered with my work for you, has it? A few
minutes ago you said you hadn't been fooled. Who
made you suspicious of me? Trent? I've known from
the moment he dropped in that parachute that his
coming was planned, that his broken ankle was a
phony. I told Maury that, but we couldn't figure out
why you should import an efficiency engineer when
you think you're *God's* understudy."

"Insolence won't help you, Collins. I gave you a
chance here because—Never mind why. You made
good. You are an expert superintendent, but as I
came to know you better, I trusted you less and less
until my feeling became suspicion. You have bragged
that in time you would be master of Karrisbrooke. I
have heard that before. It's difficult to believe that
even your colossal self-confidence would carry you
that far. Since we took on defense work I have had
too much on my mind to follow every activity of the
plantations and mills."

She came down the steps slowly.

"I advise you and your stooge, Peckett, to leave
here at once."

"*Me!* His stooge. He's—"

"Shut up, Gus. We'll leave when we get ready and
that won't be till I've told Miss Jess—"

"Sam! Give me that!"

"M's Ellen, I reckon I can use it better'n yo'," the
butler protested eagerly.

"Give it to me."

The three men, and the girl watching her, recoiled
as the Negro put a large whip in her hand. The long,
cruel lash curled like a snake on the lawn at her feet.
"Collins, once before this was used on a man who was
a traitor to his employer. Will you leave at once or
must I persuade you?"

"You wouldn't *dare.* I would hale you into court—"

"Hale Miss Ellen into court, *Mister* Collins?" Goldie

Mellor emerged from the trance of shocked silence. "You and Gus Peckett would cut a fine figure with me testifying as to what that motorboat—"

Peckett's arm was around her, Peckett's hand was over her mouth.

"Let the girl go!" The lash curled round his legs.

Ellen Marshall's laugh was grim as he hastily released Goldie and hopped back with a hand on his ankle.

"This *is* useful, Sam. I told you we might need it in case we met footpads or a kidnaper, as I can't shoot. We heard that my niece had not reached the Clubhouse, *gentlemen*. I came to find her. Collins, you and Peckett go—and quickly. Goldie, my car is outside the hedge. Zenas will take you home after he leaves me at the Clubhouse. Take the whip, Sam, we may need it again. Philip, don't stand there gaping, hurry back to the ball. Jessamine may have returned, tell her I'm coming. If she hasn't—"

The break in the usually controlled voice roused Jess from her absorption in the drama being played on that square of lawn. "I've never heard Aunt Ellen's voice break like that before; she's frightened about me," she thought, and took a quick step forward. "I'll call—" A hand came down hard over her mouth, an arm snatched her back, a low, harsh voice warned:—

"Don't speak! Don't move!"

XXVI

She struggled; if only she could make someone hear! She tried to bite the smothering hand. No use. She jerked her head, still in that strangle hold, to look at the lawn. It was lighted only by the stars. A door closed. Shadowy figures were moving between shadowy tree-trunks. They were gone. Had it been a nightmare? Hadn't she really seen—the gripping fingers on her mouth loosened.

"Snooping!" a voice hissed.

Heavy hands on her shoulders whirled her around. She faced a man in a long topcoat. A cap was pulled down to his brows, not low enough, though, to hide a pair of brilliant dark eyes above a turned-up collar. She forgot her aunt's anxiety, forgot everything and everyone but the person at whom she was gazing incredulously.

"Johnny!" she whispered.

He pushed back his cap, stared, opened his mouth wide, as if to shout with laughter, swallowed the guffaw, pulled off his cap, bowed low, said softly, ponderously:—

"Dr. Livingstone, I presume"—then, as if remembering, demanded, "What the devil are you doing here, Jess? Sorry for the rough stuff, but gosh, I was afraid whoever it was listening-in would call out and upset the applecart."

She brushed her hand across her eyes, moved a degree closer and looked up into what was visible of his face between the cap he had replaced and the turned-up collar.

"It is really you. I'm not dreaming. What applecart, Johnny, and what are *you* doing here? I thought you were on the high seas."

"Not yet. I was ordered back to finish a job I had started."

"With Goldie?"

"What do you know about her?" The startled question betrayed him.

"A few moments ago you were whispering to her on the bench outside the summerhouse, weren't you?"

"Suppose I was? She's all right. Look here, you haven't told me yet why you are on the prowl in the Club grounds. Spill it and for Pete's sake, keep your voice low."

Gourds were still rattling, drums were still thumping in the distance while she told him. Beginning with the squeaky phone call she rapidly sketched her reactions to her suspicions up to the present moment.

"So that's how it is. I'll come clean. I phoned Goldie yesterday. I had a hunch it wasn't she who answered. Made a date with her in the afternoon and found she hadn't received my message to be here at nine."

"How would she know you meant *this* summer-house?"

"I've met her here before on this deal. Don't interrupt. It cramps my style. I told her what she was to do, that I would send a note to Peckett—imitating her writing—telling him that if he would come to the summer house *alone* at nine-fifteen tonight he would find out who was double-crossing him; then I sent phony notes to Collins and Maury, presumably from him, with the same cryptic message."

"What a top-notch plot-maker Hollywood lost when you enlisted."

"Go ahead, laugh, but phony as it sounds it worked, didn't it? After I handed the notes to a boy to deliver I came here to check up and make sure Goldie was all set to present our soap-op'ry. When you heard us talking I was going over her lines with her. I thought she had them letter-perfect but at the critical moment she got hot, blew up and let fly the marriage scheme. She was just coming across with the moonshining evidence we were after when Miss Ellen cut in with, 'I can fight my own battles, Goldie.' I could have choked the old lady, if she is your aunt. It won't matter. We wanted to present the sheriff with a complete case, but we've handed him some hot clues and officers are out scouting on the mountain with their dragnet."

"Who is the other party in the 'we' you mention, Johnny?"

"Trent of course. He was fit to tie when you confided at luncheon today how the phone call had backfired. Got in touch with me. I told him I'd already straightened it out with Goldie, but would check up again. If he received a message, 'The mail got through,' he'd know she was on the job. You were in on the Smugglers' Passage stunt; I supposed you knew all this."

"I begin to think I don't know anything."

"Cheerio, you're on the road to knowledge now. I'll tell all. Like to get it off my chest before I leave at dawn. Have a midnight date with the Major. Let's sit down. We may be seen backed up against this brick wall, then my true confession will be lost to the world."

"Comfortable?" he asked when side by side they sat on the bench on the summerhouse porch. "Corking night to spin a yarn. There won't be another like this for me for some time."

His gruff voice tightened her throat. Was he thinking, as she was, that there might never be another? She tucked her hand under his arm, rested her shoulder against his and thought:—

"You dear. Perhaps I do love you more than I know. Perhaps what I thought I felt for Van has been because I missed Johnny." Aloud she prodded:—

"Go on. Tell all from the beginning."

"I can't, because I don't know why the Major was detailed to drop down on Karrisbrooke. Why the gasp? You knew *that* much, didn't you?"

"No. Go on, please." She couldn't explain that into her mind had flashed Phil's statement that they were all puppets being manipulated to serve Ellen Marshall's purpose. Had she planned that chute descent?

"I came into the picture when Trent sniffed moonshine in the air round Karrisbrooke plantation— figuratively not actually—and suspected that Miss Ellen was being doublecrossed. Also, if illegal whisky was being sold, it was of vital interest to the G.H.Q., because of the menace to the men in the Camp. That brought me into it. You had told the Major of my callow FBI yearnings, and when he asked the General to detail me to help, boy, I was tickled."

"Then you had met him before that day at the tea."

"Yes. Fooled you, didn't I?"

"Not entirely, Johnny. I'm not as naïve as I sometimes appear. I suspected you were working together, but the night I found your cigarette case on the floor of his bedroom—"

"What were *you* doing in the Major's bedroom at night, kid?"

She ignored his angry incredulity, told him, and concluded:—

"Now it is your turn to explain the cigarette case."

"Remember the afternoon I called and told you I had met Collins and Peckett? We talked for a few minutes. A sarcastic dig at Trent and his snooping round the mills and plantations one of them got off set me wondering if they suspected that the Major was doing a little sleuthing for Miss Ellen. Smoothy Gus asked for a cigarette. I offered my case. He took it. An officer pal hailed me from a car. I left to speak to him.

"Didn't think of the cigarette case again till I reached Karrisbrooke. Then I remembered it hadn't been returned. Suddenly their dig at Trent fitted in like a piece in a picture-puzzle and gave me a hunch that the case might have been snitched for a purpose and that the Major better be warned pronto. The butler said he wasn't in. I didn't dare leave a note for fear it would be found and our suspicions discovered. Sam saw me walking the hall floor and scowled as if he'd caught me stealing sheep. When Collins went through Trent's desk, hunting for notes or papers which might incriminate him, he dropped the cigarette case. I presume, to pin suspicion on me, but he was in too much of a hurry to know that he left part of the monogram from his shirt sleeve caught in the latch of the window by which he made his exit."

"Where does Goldie Mellor fit into the picture, Johnny?"

"I was told by some of the men in my company that she was a square-shooter and rabid to help the Government. I saw her with Guss Peckett; says I to myself, she may be my meat. Through a mutual soldier-lad acquaintance I met her. After our second ice-cream soda date, I laid my cards on the table, told her we had reason to believe that Peckett and his

side-kick Collins were engaged in the manufacure
and illegal sale of moonshine which might raise hob
with field and millworkers and service men, and
would she help? My irresistible eloquence, added to
the menace to the soldier boys, caught her up in a *pro
bono publico* wave of emotion.

"Would she! She *would.* It developed that she had
an intense admiration for Miss Ellen and you—
'Classy' she called you both—and an equal detesta-
tion for, I quote, 'that snooty Barry Collins.' He had
refused to be introduced to her, giving as an excuse
that he never spoke to a woman employee of the
mills. Not a bad idea when you come right down to
it. That was when she told me of his matrimonial
scheme to acquire you and Karrisbrooke in one scoop.
It seems that Peckett met her to keep a date, fresh
from a few drinks and a set-to with Collins about
money, which had left him boiling mad. He spilled
the plan to Goldie and promptly had an acute attack
of jitters because he had. I guess she's been able to
get anything she wanted out of him since by threatening to tell all."

Jess thought of the Defense Bond and of Peckett's
"Just as you say, Sugar."

"Sounds like blackmail," she said aloud.

"It wasn't, because she had Peckett sized up for
what he is, a heel. She kept him hanging round, sure
he was up to mischief and determined to find out
what it was. She's really a decent sort if only she'd cut
out the gum and those bloody nails. The rookies fell
for her and she was darn nice to them. She'll be mad
as a wet hen when she realizes that she set off the
wrong bomb. I'm not so sure that it was the wrong
one. Miss Ellen got the lowdown on her superinten—"

"Miss Ellen! I forgot her!" Jess sprang to her feet.
"She's looking for me. I knew from her voice that she
was terribly anxious. She won't know where I am. She
may be at the Clubhouse. Come quickly, Johnny." She
ran down the porch steps.

"Just a minute, Jess. We'll say our good-by here." He
caught her in his arms. "I love you. Can't you say
you'll marry me when—or if—I come home?"

She tipped back her head and looked up into his pleading eyes.

"I wish I *could*, Johnny. Honestly, I wish I could—"

"But you can't. Okay, I can take it. Sister, can you spare a kiss—" He didn't wait for an answer.

"Sorry to interrupt but the reception committee is having an acute attack of jitters because you haven't shown up, Miss Ramsay." Trent's voice was as warm as an ice-machine. Remote as the peak of the highest Smoky Mountain.

Johnny Gordon kept his arm about her as he raised his lips from hers. His grin accentuated the whiteness of his face. He saluted with his free hand.

"We'll report at once. Don't be upset about that kiss, Major. Kisses have not yet been clapped on the priority list, sir. It was what is technically known as a sneak-raid. Just saying good-by to my girl. Come on, Jess. After you, sir."

Jess knew from the leaping response of every nerve and pulse in her body to Van Trent's voice that what she felt for him wasn't caused by missing Johnny Gordon. If he had thought she loved Johnny before what must he think after the impassioned scene he had interrupted? Her lips still burned from that kiss.

They walked in single file in the starlight. Trent first, then herself, with Johnny following. By the pool, along the shadow by the live oaks, tips of branches brushed buds against her face. She wanted to cry, she felt so lost as she watched the straight, military figure striding before her, she was so sure now that she loved him, more sure than of anything else in life. Couldn't he feel it when she felt his nearness in every throbbing pulse in her body?

At the foot of the terrace Johnny put his hand on her arm. Would Van wait to go into the house with her? No. He was running up the steps.

"I'm not going in, Jess." Johnny Gordon's voice was husky. "I've said good-by. Hope it didn't make trouble for you. You needn't say it, kid. I knew the minute Trent spoke that it was he, not I, who was the lucky guy."

"He—he doesn't care for me, Johnny."

"Oh, yeah? Remember I told you I hoped someday you'd be eating your heart out for a flapdoodle who didn't know you were in the world? I take it back. I hope you'll get whoever you love."

"I wish I loved you, Johnny!"

"That goes double for me. So long, kid." With a gallant smile and wave of his hand he left her.

Through a blinding mist of tears she watched till his figure was a dim shaow, till the shadow thinned into the night. Why, why had this savage war had to happen? A war which pulled men of all ages, in all countries, up by the roots to fling them, their families, home, businesses, creative talents, into the maelstrom of blood and destruction? ... The waste, the tragic waste of it.

She impatiently dashed her hand across drenched lashes. "Why stand here just thinking? Why not do something about it all? The first thing to do," the practical part of her mind suggested, "is to report to your aunt and relieve her anxiety. Get the nearest thing you have to do out of the way first. If Johnny can go forward to what he knows lies ahead with that gay, 'So long, kid,' the least you can do is to smile and keep up your chin."

The steeple clock chimed. Ten! It had been striking nine as she had reached the summerhouse. She lived over the hour, came to the moment when Van Trent had said "Sorry to interrupt."

The icy voice swept through her memory like a blizzard setting her ashiver from head to feet. Suppose he had seen her in Johnny's arms. Even if you loved one man achingly, it wasn't a crime to let another, practically a brother, kiss you before he left for active service, where, only God and his superior officers knew. Blood burned hotly in her cheeks. There had been nothing brotherly about that kiss, and Johnny's husky voice had betrayed him when he had attempted the light touch:—

"Just saying good-by to my girl—sir."

Had Van's face been etched with haggard lines or had it been her wishful thinking, the hope that it would hurt him terribly to find her in a man's arms, that had made it appear so?

If Sam and gossip were to be believed he was again—perhaps it was still—in love with Helen Carter. If so, why would he care who kissed Jessamine Ramsay? He wouldn't. Then why make a tragedy of her aching heart, wear it on her sleeve, in a world heaped with torn and bleeding hearts? She wouldn't. She reached that decision and the side door of the powder-room at the same instant. "Chin up, gal," she prodded and entered.

Her reflection in the mirrored wall returned her set, stiff smile. "You've got to do better than that," Jess told the looking-glass Jess, as she threw off the black velvet coat and dropped to the rose-colored stool in front of the mirrored shelf.

"Oh, Miss Ramsay!"

She whirled in response to the denatured shriek. The popeyed maid stood in the doorway of the cloak-room with a mink jacket dangling supinely from one coffee-colored hand.

"What's the idea scaring a person to death, Winnie? See a ghost?"

"It's you, Miss Ramsay, sitting there natural as life when folks has gone haywire thinking you was kidnaped."

"Kidnaped! Don't be foolish. You've been seeing too many movies, Winnie." Facing the mirror again she smiled encouragement at the maid's still incredulous face, asked between applications of lipstick:—

"Who—who—is—every—body, Winnie?"

The maid came forward and leaned against the dressing table.

"First, it was Major Trent. He came to the door, said he expected to meet you here. When I told him you'd gone out half an hour before, he stared at me as if he was seeing something terrible, ran through this room and out that side door as if an M.P. was at his heels to nab him."

Van had suspected she had gone to the summer-house. Knowing of the drama to be staged there, had he been frightened for her or for the success of his plan? That last, of course. Had he cared—

"Miss Ramsay, you have given us a scare!" purred a voice she had come to detest.

Jess restrained a primitive urge to twist her fingers in Helen Carter's dark hair and pull. Instead she smiled sweetly at the reflection of the woman in the mimosa yellow frock who had appropriated the stool beside her and was already applying powder.

"Oh, dear, can't I sit out a few dances without causing a panic? One would think it was the first time it had been done at this Club."

"I must say, you're hard-boiled enough about frightening your aunt white."

"Aunt Ellen! Where is she?" Jess was on her feet.

"Van has taken her to her car. He hurried in from goodness knows where a few minutes ago. I heard him tell her he had found you, that you had been with Lieutenant Gordon."

"Van is always *so* thoughtful," she said and hated herself for the edge in her voice. "As Aunt Ellen isn't waiting for me, I'll on with the dance. Coming?"

"No. It has been a dull party. Van and I are going home."

"Dull! With that music?" She hummed accompaniment to the gourds and drums beating out "Deep in the Heart of Texas." "Perhaps I'm nothing but a little play-girl, but I can dance till morning to that tune."

She smiled and nodded to the dark, mirrored eyes watching her narrowly as if they suspected that she was not as casual about facing a barrage of questions in the ballroom as her voice sounded. Lucky Helen Carter couldn't know that every nerve in her body was registering dread as she crossed the threshold.

Her heart gave a frightened leap as from the corner of her eye she discerned a straight, tall figure in dress uniform in the hall beside the door. Van, waiting for the fair Helen, of course. "Van and I are going home," she repeated bitterly to herself, just as Philip Maury started toward her.

"Where have you been, Jess?" he demanded.

She slipped her hand under his arm.

"How adorable of you to be waiting for me, Phil. I'll tell you the story of my young life at supper. I—"

Her voice caught in her throat as she saw Claire Maury in the doorway of the ballroom. Her eyes were brilliant with hate, her mouth tight with determination.

XXVII

Vance Trent in khaki, seated on top of the broad brick wall of the garden-piazza, watched Ellen Marshall's fingers busy with flashing steel needles and dark blue yarn as she sat erect in a straight-back chair. Morning sunshine stealing through the jessamine vine laid a lacy leaf design on the lap of her gray frock, patched the terraces with bright-and-dark-green patterns and put on a bit of high-lighting showmanship for the elms and maples bursting into bloom. Peach blossoms in the orchard beyond the tennis court were like a rosy cloud against the clear turquoise of the sky. A hedge of forsythia gleamed pale gold.

Homes reflect the persons who live in them, he thought. Karrisbrooke is a house with a past, with the patina of generations of gracious living. Aloud he said:—

"Spring has come to North Carolina."

Ellen Marshall nodded assent. Her busy needles clicked an accompaniment to her voice as she said:—

"And with it the awakening of the American people to the task ahead. They've been a long time reaching the realization that private and public self-indulgence and speculation must give place to concerted action to bring about total mobilization of man and business power. It's like being born again to many. We must all do more to help, stand like an invincible army behind our fighting men. I lie awake nights thinking how I can more fully justify my reason for living in the most critical period in the history of civilization."

"You, Miss Ellen! Every hour of your day is packed with helpfulness."

"For one thing, we don't need the whole of this great house," she went on as if following a train of thought. "The maids and garage men are needed in the mills and the service. I shall turn the ballroom and large dining room over to Civil Defense classes. But the revulsion of citizens against softness of living while the men in the service are risking lives, and everything dear to them, for our protection, isn't the subject I asked you to come here to talk about, Vance.

"Jessamine is at the mill penthouse doing what she calls her 'hitch' at air-spotting. We shall be uninterrupted. I determined when you started the efficiency investigation for me that I would ask no questions till you had finished the job, but that theatrical denouement on the summerhouse green last night looked to me like the final curtain. Begin at the beginning, but first come down from that wall and sit here. Voices carry."

He drew a chair beside hers. She dropped her knitting to listen. He began with his suspicion at the tobacco auction that Peckett was a bad egg, that he had a hold on Collins; told of the assistance Johnny Gordon and Goldie Mellor had rendered in his investigations, it had been she who had tipped them off to watch activities at the old wharf.

"That was the night, or rather the early morning, you surprised Jess, Sam and me in the hall, Miss Ellen. I had seen Peckett directing the unloading of casks from a motorboat, one of your mill boats which, if seen anywhere on the river, with whatever cargo, would pass unnoticed. That fitted in with our suspicion of moonshining, but what I couldn't understand was the load of gas drums they piled into the boat until its gunwale was almost under water, enough stuff to run it for a couple of years. That was before we were in the war. I couldn't figure it out. Yesterday when I heard that an enemy sub was loitering offshore I knew."

"Vance! You can't mean—"

"You've guessed it, Miss Ellen. I landed Helen at the Inn after we left the ball last evening, with a speed which must have made her head spin; picked up Johnny Gordon and beat it for the water front. On the way we invested in dungarees, pulled them on over our uniforms, blacked our faces and with battered hats, also purchased at a high price, we were like any other tramps loafing in the shadows. I waited only long enough to see the same boat I had watched load at the old wharf put off to sea, before I contacted the army base by phone. The response was immediate and super-efficient. A couple of armed tankers and two bombers were summoned by radio. They disabled the sub, which couldn't submerge because of needed repairs. It was brought into port with the motorboat, which had kept it supplied with fuel."

"One of the mill boats! Incredible! Collins must have known it was being used. Go on."

"Ticket stubs from a movie theater in this town were found in the pockets of several of the sub crew. The skipper of the mill motorboat not only had provided fuel, but had carried the men craving the bright lights back and forth at ten dollars per passenger. After that episode was nicely washed-up the sheriff and I started for the mountain. We found the still going strong. Peckett had been unable to get through a warning to his men there or at the water front. He had been forcibly detained."

"A motorboat of Ellen Marshall's, supplying fuel to the enemy! Ellen Marshall's mountain supplying moonshine to the corn-whisky-minded! The situation has a humorous angle. You are sure that both were Peckett's enterprises?"

"Yes. If you hadn't appeared on the summerhouse steps at the exact moment you did, we would have had a record of it. A dictaphone was among those present. Goldie Mellor was to accuse the two men. We were sure that each would blacken the other in an attempt to clear himself. Our plan was to secure indisputable evidence of the mastermind behind the moonshining enterprise before we passed it on to you. Theatrical stuff, perhaps, but effective. Johnny Gordon was to be stationed in the wings. We decided that it would be better for him to carry on alone. Had I heard those two heels admit that marriage scheme—"

"Sit down again, Vance. Pacing the piazza may serve to work off your fury but it distracts me. Granted that anger sends poison through the body it had a remedial effect on me last evening. I'll confess that for weeks the immediate future has been shrouded in a heavy fog of doubt. But, when I overheard that matrimonial plan to acquire this estate—and incidentally my niece—when I laid that whip about Peckett's ankles—if only I had known then what you have just told me, I would have put in a few extra licks—anger sent courage, faith in Allied victory, zest for living, surging through me. I was like the Wandering Jew, reborn with youth and the world before me. Go on, before I lay bare more of the rejuvenation of my spirit. Have Peckett and his gang been arrested?"

"Yes. They will be charged with conspiracy to defraud the United States Government of Internal Revenue by aiding and abetting in the operation of an unregistered still and aiding the enemy. That will keep them out of mischief for a while. Collins made his getaway. He'll never return. When he realized that you had overheard his matrimonial plan, consternation blew his iridescent bubble to bits. Even his brag and bluster couldn't put it together again."

"He tried to pull some of the mill directors and plantation managers down with him, Vance, by intimating that he could influence them to leave me. I called a meeting at the mill before it opened this morning. If each one of them is not loyal to me I've lost my knowledge of human nature *and* I haven't. Collins was an excellent superintendent and a helpful director. A romantic determination to revenge what he considered a wrong to his ancestor—he was a traitor too—didn't affect his efficiency. He never shirked his job. As I look back I believe he really loved Jessamine, that he didn't want her solely because of Karrisbrooke."

"It sounds plausible. There are others."

"By the way, has Johnny Gordon gone?"

"Yes, he left at dawn."

"Jessamine told me of his good-by; she said: 'He has been like a brother to me. I couldn't refuse to let him kiss me, could I?' I thought you should know. Now that I am telling all I'll confess that I intimated to her that Helen Carter broke an engagement to you to marry your cousin."

"*You* told her *that?* Helen has been a pain in the neck to me from the moment I first met her. What was the idea?"

"I didn't say you had been. I asked if she had heard. Let's get back to your investigation. I sensed moonshining in the air when I engaged you as an efficiency expert, but I wouldn't prejudice you with my suspicions, I wanted you to have a free hand—and then I moved out of turn by going to the summerhouse."

"Why, of all nights, did you pick that one?"

"It does need explaining. I've told you that Jessamine is the weak spot in my armor. I loved her as a child but felt I mustn't show my great affection for fear of spoiling her. My views have changed with age, real love doesn't spoil—it helps character grow in the right way. After I lost young Todd I wanted her here, asked her to come last year, but she was too tied up in defense classes to leave." She gazed unseeingly at the pink cloud of peach-blossom as if formulating her thoughts.

"Frankly, I schemed. I deliberately inoculated Judge Willie Sutcliffe with the germ of the idea that I was considering making Barry Collins my heir—it seemed incredible he would believe that anyone but my grand-niece would inherit my property, but—he left hurriedly for the North. When Jessamine's mother wrote that the girl was looking thin, that a long visit at Karrisbrooke would be the right change for her, I knew the inoculation had taken."

Vance remembered the serious voice in which Jess

had confided her mother's and Judge Sutcliffe's suspicions. He threw back his head and laughed as he had not laughed in weeks.

"Madam Machiavelli, I salute you."

"It seems funny to you but I'll confess that each day since, when I've said my morning and evening prayers, I've had a guilty sense that the Lord, discounting the good intention behind that idea-germ, was listening with skeptical ear. I was well punished for my deception at first; it looked for a while as if bringing Jessamine here had proved a tragic blunder."

"Because of Maury?"

"Yes. She renewed her friendship and in hurt pride overdid her pleasure at being with him. Claire watched like a cat waiting to spring on an unsuspecting mouse. I was frightened. The young men of the community whom Jessamine would have met socially were at camps serving their country. Philip was under foot here at any hour of the day and Barry Collins at every opportunity, turning on all his charm. I admit he has it. He almost fooled me. Now that I have started confessing I'll make a thorough job of it. After hours of thought I went to General Carson, grandson of an old beau, and asked for—"

"An officer, mentally equipped to observe any irregularities on the plantation or in the mills, must be a bachelor, of good family—emphasis on last requirement—to drop in on Karrisbrooke. Right?"

"Right—to a word."

"You didn't stop to figure what effect that drop-in might have on the life of said bachelor, did you, Miss Ellen? Had you waited a short time longer you wouldn't have needed me to divert your niece's attention from Maury. Johnny Gordon would have filled the bill."

"I'm sorry that your visit here has been such a failure, Vance."

"It hasn't, Miss Ellen. Don't get me wrong. Being here has been the most tremendous experience in my life. I wouldn't part with an hour of it."

"Even with the heartaches? Don't answer. I didn't

mean to pry. I haven't told you how I happened to appear at the summerhouse last evening at what proved to be a crucial moment. Sam burst into the library jabbering:—

"'M's Jess never done got to de Clubhouse, M's Ellen! Do yo' reckon dat chile been kidnaped?'

"Imagination seized the bit in its teeth and bolted. I thought of Jessamine's pearls, of her loveliness, of—why live over my terror? Now I understand the meaning of 'gone haywire.' Zenas had not returned with the car—he confessed this morning that he had succumbed to the lure of a motion picture. I started out with Sam to find her. It was his idea to take along that vicious whip. The second chauffeur drove us in the sedan. I went over every word she had said during and after dinner; remembered that her mood had changed from what she called slap-happiness to gravity; visualized the out-dated black velvet evening cloak and the reason she had given for wearing it. 'I'm taking it in case I'm tempted to sit out a dance on the porch of that adorable summerhouse.' I'll go to the summerhouse first, I decided.

"Jessamine told me the whole story this morning. We decided to put Goldie Mellor in charge of First Aid classes in the ballroom, on a salary, to show my appreciation of her part in the disclosures. What is it, Sam?"

The butler who had been hovering in the doorway stepped forward.

"It's a long distance call for yo' Major, the libr'ry phone, suh."

"It's come," Trent exclaimed and rose.

Ellen Marshall's eyes followed him till he entered the house, came back to the butler.

"Any idea where the call was from, Sam?"

"No, marm. Ah reckon 'tis somepin' 'portant. The Major he look kin' of white, but his eyes, dey was kin' of shinin'. Don't yo' think that same, M's Ellen? There's a young woman aimin' to see yo'. She said tell yo' her name wus Goldie."

"Bring her here, Sam."

Sunlight sifting through the vines patterned the

girl's powder-blue cardigan and skirt with gold tracery as she stopped beside Ellen Marshall's chair. She shook back her mane of yellow hair and twisted a green crocheted beanie between crimson-nailed fingers.

"Perhaps I'm being fresh coming here, Miss Marshall, but I had a hunch I oughter tell you about Miss Jess."

"What's happened to her?"

"Gee, I didn't mean to frighten you white. Nothing's happened to her, yet."

"Sit here, beside me."

Goldie sank into the chair indicated, crossed her knees to display to advantage long beige legs and feet shod in open-toe green sandals.

"And nothing's going to happen if you do something Mr. Maury wants done." Her voice indicated restored aplomb.

"Has Mr. Maury taken you into his confidence, Miss Mellor?"

"Say, don't go high-hat on me, Miss Marshall. There ain't time."

"Go on with your story, Goldie."

"That's more like it. This is what happened at the races yesterday. Gus Peckett bought a bond for me from Miss Jess. We left the booth. I ran back to thank her for taking over the switchboard for me one noon. As I got near I heard Mr. Maury say, I guess in answer to something I hadn't heard, 'Ellen Marshall may not care if I divorce my wife, Jessie, but she may find she's gone in for trouble in a big way when she learns that Claire will drag your name into it.'

"After that I near cracked my eardrums listening. It looked like trouble for Miss Jess and there ain't a girl in one of her classes who, even if she knew she'd never get another for the duration, wouldn't turn over her last bit of lipstick to her if she needed it."

She told of the conversation that followed.

"Mr. Maury talked to Miss Jess fierce as a traffic cop handing out a summons, but he couldn't get her down. Then I stepped up, made my thank-you speech and lit out before he could chuck me out—he looked as if he was gettin' ready to. But the races were spoiled for me. All the time I was thinking: 'Should I have stayed with Miss Jess? She's such a swell kid.' Then I got busy with the showdown at the Club summerhouse and I forgot it. But soon's I went to bed that question 'Hadn't I ought to have stayed?' began to prickle again and I made up my mind to beat it here and tell all before I went on duty at the switchboard. If you're goin' to do what that Maury guy wants, you've got to get it across before noon—or else." She rose.

"Not that I can see you being frightened into doing what you don't want to do, Miss Marshall, but I just had to tell you. I'll be going. My wheel is at the door."

"I shall not be frightened into consent, Goldie. Come to my office at the mill tomorrow before you take over the switchboard. Thank you for coming. Good morning."

Ellen Marshall was standing looking out over the terraces when Vance Trent returned.

"Did I see Goldie Mellor going out the side door or did I dream it?"

"It was she. She came to tell me—"

"M's Philip Maury," Sam announced impressively.

"Where's Jess?" Claire Maury demanded without stopping to greet the woman who was regarding her with hostile eyes or the man whose fingers had clenched as she made her imperious demand. The spots of excitement on her cheeks, red as her sandals, accentuated the snowy whiteness of her coat and slacks.

"Jessamine is at the mill penthouse taking her turn at air-spotting, Claire."

"I thought so, M's Ellen. Phil said he had a business appointment at the mill with *you*, before noon today—and *you* are here. Good-by."

"Claire! Come back!"

Ignoring Ellen Marshall's dictatorial order she dashed into the house. The slam of a door shattered the silence she had left behind her.

"Vance. Stop her. She is mad with jealousy. She
may hurt Jessamine."

"She's mad all right. I knew that by her face last
night when Jess slipped her arm under Phil's in the
Club hall. That niece of yours sure loves to play with
dynamite."

"Don't just stand there and talk. Do something!"
Ellen Marshall's usually cool voice was shaken.

"I'm going after her now—" He stopped on the
threshold and cleared his husky voice. "If I did what
I thought should be done, Jessamine Ramsay would
receive the too-long-delayed spanking of her life, Miss
Marshall."

XXVIII

Jessamine paced the roof of the administration building of the Marshall Cotton Mills. She thought of the
restless night just passed; of her heart, which had
been frozen solid by Van Trent's icy voice, beginning
to thaw and aching unbearably in the process; of
clutching at self-justification because she knew she had
been terribly wrong when she had smiled encouragement at Phil Maury in the Club hall; while all the
time self-contempt slipped in and out of her mind
like an uneasy ghost. Then dawn. Another day. It
would be fair with showers, if those white clouds
were to be believed. Like life, sunlight and shadow.

"Can you tell me if being sorry will do any good,
Lucky?" she asked the Airedale walking sedately beside her. The dog brushed close against her short
beige skirt, looked up and sneezed as if in answer to
her troubled question.

"That means you can't, I presume. Doesn't one ever
learn that after a silly thing has been said or done it
can't be wiped off the slate by regrets or tears?" With
a sharp exclamation she raised her binoculars.

"Only a gull straggling in from the shore that set my pulses hammering, Lucky. I thought it was a plane." She thrust her hands deep into the pockets of her beige jiffy-coat and resumed her watchful pacing.

"Not that I'm thinking of crying, crying wouldn't erase the memory of my imbecile grip of Phil Maury's arm last evening, of my ditto *ditto* coo, 'How adorable of you to be waiting for me, Phil.'" It helped to confess aloud, if only to a dog. "Would you think that after his diabolical threat yesterday I would ever look at him again to say nothing of cooing? My memory snapped a candid camera shot of him as he stood at the booth delivering his ultimatum. It turns me cold to look at it." She shivered and thrust her hands deeper into her pockets.

"I'll bet I'm boring you with this attack of dark and dour blues, Lucky, but you're the only person to whom I can really pour out my heart—you are a person, a grand one. Would you think there was even a sliver of excuse for my super-stupidity if I told you that seeing Van waiting for that cat—"

She dropped to her knees and clutched his ears as he started to run. He yelped and tugged to get away.

"There isn't a cat here, foolish. Becky has been teaching you to chase them, hasn't she? I was referring to the lady—"

"What lady, Jessie?"

She rose hurriedly. Phil Maury was smiling sardonically. He and his smile simultaneously retreated as the terrier growled, dashed toward him and drove him to the railing.

"That will do, Lucky. Charge," Jess commanded.

The dog stretched out in front of her. A growl rumbled in his throat while he kept his dark, button-like eyes on the man in the tan jodhpurs and coat who was ostentatiously cutting the air with a riding-crop.

"You needn't be afraid of him, Phil. He won't bite unless you come near me. Why are you here?"

"To prove that my intuition is on the job. Somethin' in your voice when you said your hitch came on

Saturday made me think that it wasn't the whole story. A few inquiries and I found you are to be on duty every mornin'. So here I am."

"To take over? How thoughtful. There are a billion other things I want to do." She lifted the strap of the binoculars from her shoulder. "Take these and get busy."

"No. My job is cut out for me. I've beat the draft by enlistin'. Did you give M's Ellen my message?"

"The one all mixed up with the sale of your share of the cotton mills and divorce? Too complicated. I knew I wouldn't get it straight. You can tell her so much better than I."

"Decided on the light touch, have you, Jessie? Look here"—the dog growled as he took a forward step—"I'm not going to touch her, confound your hide."

"It's the funniest situation I ever saw." There was no mirth, only malice in Claire Maury's voice as she came out of the penthouse office. "Don't look so stunned, Jess. I'm surprised that M's Ellen doesn't keep a guard at the mill entrance. I walked in, mounted the stairs to the penthouse door, which was unlocked, and here I am. You came that way, didn't you, Philip?"

"I did not. I—"

"Who cares how you came?" Jessamine interrupted impatiently. "If you two people have met here to stage one of your fights I wish you'd get out, quick. I have a job to do."

"It can wait, Miss Ramsay. I didn't come here to see Phil, I came to tell you to keep away from my husband. If you don't and he doesn't make you, he'll go to jail for forging my name to securities—perhaps *you'll* want him after that, I won't."

"Claire!" the girl's shocked and the man's furious voice blended in the exclamation.

"It's true. My attorney will be here next week to check up. I sent for him."

"Next week." That was why Phil must have the money from the sale of the mill or the assurance that it was forthcoming, Jess thought. She waited tensely for him to deny his wife's accusation; he only shrugged.

"I shan't make Jess keep away from me, so I reckon it's jail, my love."

"For heaven's sake, Phil, don't talk like an imbecile. Keep *away* from you! Don't you know, can't you and Claire see that I'm desperately in love with—"

"Lieutenant John Gordon, Jr. Right, Angel?" Vance Trent inquired. "Down, Lucky."

Jessamine incredulously regarded the man who was looking at her with eyes that burned into her heart, while with one hand he held down the dog who had jumped on him in an effort to lick his face.

"I've never met a couple who needed such a heap of a lot of showing as you Maurys." The gravity of Trent's eyes belied the lightness of his voice. "You saw me kissing Jess the night of the dance at Karrisbrooke, Claire; you think it was your husband with her. It wasn't. He, after being told repeatedly to the contrary, toys with the absurd illusion that she loves him. She doesn't. Now, suppose we ring down the final curtain on this comedy and—"

"Not yet." Ellen Marshall emerged from the dusk of the penthouse. A slight shortness of breath indicated that her ascent of the stairs had been hurried. "After you left, Vance, I decided that the Maury family gathering at the penthouse was even more my business than yours, though I had commanded you to do something."

He did it. Does he really think I love Johnny? Jess thought, in the second Ellen Marshall paused. Why not, after seeing that parting between us last night?

"I know now what you meant by the 'drastic action' you threatened if I wouldn't allow you to sell your share of the mill, Philip. Even a Defense Bond booth has ears. Don't bring out that chair, Vance, anyone would think I was an old woman with stiff knees who couldn't stand while she spoke her piece. You might have saved your anger and threats, Philip. Collins couldn't buy you out now if I were willing. He called me on long distance this morning. He was concerned about his salary due, *not* about his treachery. He has left town for good. That word will stand two interpretations."

"Barry! Gone!" A torrent of red swept over Claire Maury's face as four pairs of eyes registering surprise turned toward her.

"The news is a shock to me, too," Philip Maury diverted attention from his wife's confusion, "though he had told me that if his plans here failed, he would leave—not that he thought they would, he was cockily sure of success. You heard what those plans were last evenin', M's Ellen?"

"Yes. I heard—but I had suspected before."

"And let him carry on! Didn't I tell you, Jessie, that M's Ellen was a puppeteer, danglin' the lot of us marionettes from strings which she manipulates to suit her purpose?"

"If she's so smart perhaps she can dangle you out of the jam you're in, Phil." Claire Maury had regained her poise.

Ellen Marshall ignored her malicious laugh.

"Is it a domestic or financial jam, Philip?"

"A little of the first and a devil of a lot of the second, M's Ellen."

"He's right. Forgin' my name to securities will take a *lot* of explainin' in court."

"So, that's what is behind Philip's crying need for cash. Claire, do you ever really think?" Ellen Marshall demanded. "Don't you realize that a moment ago you opened Pandora's Box and let the knowledge of your husband's dishonesty loose on the world? Three persons who might never have known of it, know it now. You never can crowd a spoken word back into the limbo of unknown things."

"Are you upholdin' Phil for cheatin' his wife, M's Ellen?"

"Sniffling won't help, Claire. I am not condoning what Philip has done. He has cheated you. Any more than you have cheated him? You held him back when he wanted to enlist in the service of his country; you shirk the care of your house and allow your servants to waste in a time when waste may mean defeat; you haven't lifted a finger in defense work because you are 'too delicate.' I don't know how an idle, purposeless woman like you can expect to hold a husband in times like these. I'm going to my office. I want you, Philip. We'll see what can be done to get you out of this jam. Because I refuse to consent to the sale of your share of the mills doesn't mean that I won't help you now."

She stopped at the penthouse door.

"Come, Claire. It is your business too. Vance, tell Zenas that I will motor home with you. Wait in your roadster for me. We'll leave Jessamine alone with her dog to finish her so-called hitch."

A smile twitched at her lips and lighted her eyes as she looked first at Philip Maury and then at her niece.

"If one has a reputation for being a puppeteer the least one can do is live up to it, so I'll do some 'danglin'' of the 'marionettes' present. Go ahead of me, all of you, except our plane-spotter. We'll leave her to carry on."

Sam had removed the tea tray. In a short-sleeved white crêpe frock Jessamine stood on the garden-piazza looking toward the deep purple mountains. Her left hand was tucked under her right elbow, her right hand was spread on her bare left arm. The diamonds in the setting of a large yellow-brown topaz on the third finger shot out little sparks of light as she drew a deep breath.

"Heavenly after the shower, isn't it, Aunt Ellen? Hear the birds chattering. The sparkleberry bushes are living up to their name. The sun on the wet leaves makes them glitter like mirrors. I'm getting to be a reliable weather prophet. I smelled rain in the air this morning. Look! A rainbow! Nothing so perfect as a rainbow at dusk. See how the colors melt into the darkening sky. It means a fair tomorrow, doesn't it?" she asked eagerly. Perhaps it would mean that Van and she would be friends again.

"We'll believe it will be a fair tomorrow, Jessamine." Ellen Marshall's voice beside her startled her out of her wistful reflection. "God said, '... I do set my bow in the cloud, and it shall be for a token of a covenant between me and the earth. And it shall come to pass, when I bring a cloud over the earth, that the bow shall be seen in the cloud.' We must keep looking for that Divine promise of clearing in the tragic cloud which is darkening the world today, my dear."

She returned to her chair and picked up her knitting. The Airedale stretched on the floor opened one eye as Jessamine turned. Apparently satisfied that she had no intention of leaving he relapsed once more into slumber.

"A penny for your thoughts," offered Ellen Marshall.

"I was wondering how you could be so serene after that turbulent showdown on the mill roof this morning. How did your heart-to-heart with the Maurys come out?"

"Satisfactorily for Phil and Claire, if expensive for me. As in all probability he will never be faithful to any wife, it will be better for the morale of the community if he sticks legally to his first. Apparently she wants him, why, only the Lord and she know. There will be no more talk of divorce. I had that in black and white before I agreed to redeem the securities which Philip had used as collateral by forging his wife's name to an order to deliver them to him."

"Phil has heaps of faults—as who hasn't—but dishonesty in money doesn't seem like him."

"He had borrowed from Collins, Peckett and from other sources, to keep the racing-stable going. He needed more money. His creditors pressed him—I suspect pressing is too mild a word—to pay what he already owed. The idea of putting up his wife's securities as collateral was conceived in anxiety and born in desperation. Claire suspected what he had done and hinted to him that she had sent for her attorney. He's had a sharp lesson. Old as he is the army may provide a training in self-discipline he never had as a boy. I presume you know that Vance Trent has been promoted?"

Jessamine drew a little sigh of relief. She had been

wondering how she could maneuver the conversation to include him.

"Yes. Doctor MacDonald announced it and Van himself told me he had been assigned to the Southern Annapolis of the Air as head instructor of the parachute division. I hoped he would be here for tea to tell us more about the appointment." If ever there was an understatement it was that word, "hoped."

"He's having tea at the Inn."

"Asking Helen Carter to go South with him, I presume." The voice she had intended to be gaily casual showed a hint of unsteadiness.

"He won't, no matter how much he may want to. He has received other orders. He leaves here in four days. 'Destination Unknown.' It would be like him to think he had no right to marry, because—"

"Aunt *Ellen!* You don't mean—"

"Whatever I mean mustn't be spoken aloud, Jessamine. There he is now, coming across the lawn after putting up his roadster. Karrisbrooke doesn't seem like the same place with no boy to drive a guest's car to the garage. Why don't you run down and meet . . ."

She was off before the sentence was finished, down the emerald green path between the garden parterres where tulips were beginning to show color. Wet steps, more path, more steps—thinking, hoping, doubting. Does he love me? If only I knew. Is Aunt Ellen right? Won't he ask a woman to marry him because he is going into frightful danger? Mustn't think of that, it turns my courage to jelly. "In times like these one stiffens and carries on, one doesn't weaken," Aunt Ellen had said.

Is there any way I can find out if he loves me without downright asking? I could pretend to turn my ankle and faint. Frightened, he might reveal his feelings. Sure-fire, if you believe the novelists. He's waving. . . . The sound as of a cyclone behind her.

"Lucky—be care—"

Too late. The impact of the dog, the slippery step, knocked her off her feet. She crashed to the lawn. For a dazed instant the world started on a merry-go-round.

"Angel! Darling! *Darling*, are you hurt?"

The impassioned voice, the arms holding her close, brought the world out of its spin. She looked up into eyes dark with concern and laughed.

"Authors certainly know their stuff," she said breathlessly. "Thanks, Lucky." She nodded to the Airedale, who with mouth open, tongue hanging, tail wagging, was grinning as if a kneeling officer, holding a girl's shoulders close in his arms, was the funniest sight in a dog's life.

"My dear, what do you mean? Did you strike your head when you fell?" His tender hand was on her hair.

"No, Van. I'm all right. Help me up. Goodness, that grass was wet." She shook out her skirt to avoid his disturbing eyes.

"I watched you come from the terrace like a whirlwind, Angel. Did you think I was Johnny Gordon?"

She shook her head, tried twice before she produced a voice.

"No. Aunt Ellen and I had been talking about you and then, sud-suddenly there you were. Made me think of that first day, only this t-time you came on your feet, not through the air."

"On two sound feet this time." He placed his hands lightly on her shoulders, his grave eyes met and held hers. "Easy does it, Angel, what's behind all this conversation?"

"Aunt Ellen t-told me."

"What?"

"That you were having tea at the Inn and—and I thought you might be asking Helen again to marry you."

"Miss Ellen is a born strategist and a strategist doesn't always stick strictly to the truth. She has confessed. Helen never jilted me because I detested her from the first moment we met, just as I loved, at first sight, the only girl I've ever wanted to marry. Remember I told you I hadn't believed in love at first sight till I came to Karrisbrooke?" He cleared his husky voice. "Come on, let's join Miss Ellen. Something is playing tricks with my throat and my resolution. Perhaps that gorgeous rainbow is sending out electrical radiations."

"Just a minute, Van." She caught his arm, looked up at his face, tight-lipped, square-jawed, met his eyes dark and stern. "It would be like him to think he had no right to ask a girl to marry him because—" Aunt Ellen had broken the sentence.

Suppose she were wrong in thinking he loved her? He had called her "darling" when he had thought she was hurt. Long ago he had said that when he used the word it would be the pledge of a lifetime of devotion. She gathered her courage and plunged.

"I'm about to ask a question, soldier. If it isn't a military secret, please answer, 'Yes' or 'No.' "

"*Don't* ask it. I *can't* tell you anything."

"But I must. Did you mean it when you said that if I wanted to use your name, with Mrs. in front of it, it was mine all tied up with white ribbon?"

"Yes—then."

"Then! Not now? Why have you changed? I'm just the same person—"

"Have you forgotten that you declared you wouldn't marry a man in the service, that it would mean agony of mind?"

"And you said, 'Suppose you fall in love with one?' I have."

"Angel, please—" And then as if the strain were too great to bear, he caught her in his arms.

"I love you! I've loved you since the moment I saw you running toward me, with the sun making a golden halo of your hair. I've dreamed of having you always with me. But, I won't ask you to—marry me—because I'm leaving here in four days. I don't know where I am going, when or how I will come back. I won't submit you to that agony of anxiety."

Head against his shoulder she looked up into his eyes. "I wasn't really grown up when I said that. I was a youngster talking about something of which I knew nothing."

He tipped up her chin. "Pretty old lady now, aren't you?"

His tender amused voice sent soft color to her hair. She ignored his interruption.

"A lot of happiness can be packed into four days, Van. I would have them to remember all my life. If we were married we could fly North to see Mother and the papers would announce, 'After a short wedding trip, Colonel Trent will return to active duty,' so will Mrs. Trent, *very* active duty at Karrisbrooke."

"Don't tempt me, darling."

"You said that word was reserved for just one person. Now I'm sure you love me."

His arms tightened. His strength, the warmth of his body, set every pulse in her beating madly. He kissed her gently.

"Thought I must be noble and give you up," he whispered against her hair. He held her off the merest trifle to demand: "Love me enough to break your heart over my safety? Loving you, wanting you as I do, I am still eager for active service."

"I love you enough to bear—" The rest of the words were choked by tears. She flung her arms about his neck and clung to him.

"Van! Oh, Van, *darling!* You will come back?"

"With my wife waiting? Of course I'll come back. Remember the gipsy? 'You'll be married many, many years, have the same husband all the time and six children.' Her prophecy burned me up then, thought she meant Johnny Gordon, but this is different. If you love me, I'm that husband. Smile. That's better. Let's tell Miss Ellen."

Hand in hand they mounted the path between the terraces. Lucky raced ahead, stopping every few seconds to look back and make sure they were following.

"Do you think for an instant Aunt Ellen doesn't know what has happened? Hasn't known that it would happen from the moment you bailed out above Karrisbrooke?" Jessamine's laugh was unsteady. "You're not listening, Van."

"Yes and no. Wait a minute." He stopped at the top of the steps. "Suppose we hunt up the Town Clerk, now, get a special license and ask your clergyman to come here in the morning? We could start North on those four days of happiness, pronto. How about it, Angel?"

Although he asked a question there was the same decisive undertone in his voice she had noticed the first time she heard it. "Vance has come. ... He gets things done," Aunt Ellen had said.

"*Why* don't you answer? *What* are you thinking?" He caught her hands tight, his usually clear voice was husky, his demanding eyes set her heart thumping like a drum. "You haven't changed your mind?"

"I was thinking," she laughed, freed her hand and slipped it under his arm, "that for an efficiency expert you have the most adorable ideas, Major—my mistake—Colonel. Why are we waiting?"

BRING ROMANCE INTO YOUR LIFE

With these bestsellers from your favorite Bantam authors

Barbara Cartland

Bantam Book Catalog

Here's your up-to-the-minute listing of over 1,400 titles by your favorite authors.

This illustrated, large format catalog gives a description of each title. For your convenience, it is divided into categories in fiction and non-fiction—gothics, science fiction, westerns, mysteries, cookbooks, mysticism and occult, biographies, history, family living, health, psychology, art.

So don't delay—take advantage of this special opportunity to increase your reading pleasure.

Just send us your name and address and 50¢ (to help defray postage and handling costs).